RaShelle Workman

SLEEPING ROSES

#1 in the Dead Roses Series

Also by RaShelle Workman

Exiled
In His Eyes

RaShelle Workman

SLEEPING ROSES

#1 in the Dead Roses Series

Polished Pen Press
Bountiful, Utah

This edition is published by Polished Pen Press in coordination with Literary Underground.

Questions or comments for the author may be addressed via email: rashelleworkman@gmail.com
www.rashelleworkman.com
Twitter: RaShelleWorkman
Facebook: RaShelle Workman Author
Goodreads: RaShelle Workman
Printed in U.S.A.
ISBN: 1468098578
ISBN-13: **978-1468098570**
ASIN: B006NE0H64
Cover Design: Steven Novak NovakIllustration.com
Cover copyright 2009/2011 RaShelle Workman
Typeset by Heather Justesen

DEDICATION

For James, my awesome husband, for his tireless patience and love. For E, K & J—the most amazing children, and my biggest fans.

A dream is fleeting
True love, divine
Your life is your own
It's all in your mind.

PROLOGUE

"My mom's going to kill me. I've got to hurry," she said to Mrs. Archibald as she grabbed her bag and left.

"Bye," she hollered.

"Bye! Don't forget what we've talked about. I need a decision by tomorrow." Mrs. Archibald called after her.

Great, she thought, rushing toward the exit. At the door, she held it open for an old, blind woman. The woman was wearing a plastic rain hat and was hunched over, walking with a cane. Once through, the old woman reached out and touched her face.

"Thank you . . . Oh, dear I'm so sorry. Sweet death." The old woman tenderly removed her hand and did her best to scurry away, muttering something indiscernible under her breath.

"Um, what did you say? Sweet death, what do you mean?" she asked, feeling suddenly frightened. When the old woman didn't answer her, she undid her black umbrella and quickly walked outside into the monsoon-like rain storm. The worst in a century is what the weatherman had said.

Reaching her black BMW, she rapidly got in, heading out of the parking lot. As she turned right onto Bangerter Highway, her car hydroplaned.

"Shit," she cursed, determinedly gaining control. Glancing at the clock on her dash, she noticed it was seven o'clock. She was supposed to be home by now. Vowing to be careful, she gingerly sped up. It was mesmerizing; the squeaking of her windshield wipers and depress rock playing softly on the radio. She was thankful the Highway wasn't congested. In fact, she'd only seen one other car. Through the thick gloominess, she could see the next light coming up. It was green at the moment. Stifling a yawn, she plunged ahead, hoping the light would stay green long enough for her to get through it.

"Crap, just my luck."

Applying her brakes, the car tugged, but continued toward the now red light. Leaning forward, she pushed the brake again, terror constricting her body as she realized she was skimming along the surface of the road. Reacting to her fear, she pressed on the gas pedal trying to swerve out of the water. It only made matters worse. A tire must have caught a patch of drier ground because suddenly her car spun in a large circle.

Once again facing forward, she almost sensed the other car before she saw it. Like the eyes of a monster coming out of the mist, she saw the other cars' headlights heading straight at her. Panic stricken, she realized her foot was still on the gas pedal.

"No!" She screamed, even as she tried to move her foot to the brake.

Time seemed to stand still, her foot seemingly trapped in quick sand. She couldn't move it fast enough. There was no slowing down or changing the path she was on. It was too late. The last words the old, blind woman had said kept repeating themselves over and over in her mind. Sweet death. Sweet death. Sweet death. Like a charging bull, came another realization. Death would not be sweet.

"I don't want to die!"

As the cars collided, all of her senses heightened. She could hear the revving of an engine and the screeching of the other cars' brakes. Surprisingly, her brain registered the man's shirt was blue and the woman driving had black hair and was smoking. Almost in a trance, she watched the red, smoldering ash of the cigarette. What scared her most, though, was she could see the terror in the woman's eyes. The thought came to her that, as soon as she could, she'd tell her she was sorry.

Without preamble came the crunching of metal.

Curious, she thought, there wasn't more noise. A wave of nausea washed over her as she listened disgustedly to the popping of her bones and her flesh tearing. Absently, she wondered why she had no pain. The last thing she heard before everything went black was the sound of her own scream.

3

Sluggishly, she began coming out of the darkness.

Where am I, she wondered anxiously, feeling the heaviness of her body, the grand dullness of her pain. At once, the memory of her car accident paraded through her mind.

I'm not dead, she thought, trying uselessly to move her head or open her eyes, but her body wouldn't respond. She could hear noises all around her. After a few minutes, however, she understood the noises were people talking and they were talking about her.

She attempted to say something, to let them know she was awake, but nothing happened. What was wrong? Through the noise of the voices, one in particular caught her attention.

"I'm sorry to have to inform you the driver of the other car was killed."

"Killed! How," a man gasped.

She thought the man sounded distinctly like her father.

"There was a fire and she was . . ." The other man paused, as if he were unsure he should tell the man.

"She was what," the man demanded, almost hysterical.

"Burned alive," was the grave response.

4

"The passenger in the vehicle, which we've discovered is her brother, as well as the rest of us, had to watch helplessly as it happened."

"No! I've killed her. I've killed her," she tried to scream.

CHAPTER I

"Sophie, darling, take a deep breath, wipe the tears off your face and tell me what's happened," Rina purred in a kind, firm voice.

Sophie woodenly obeyed, picking up her napkin, wiping her face and discreetly blowing her nose. "I'm not sure I want to tell you." The tears wouldn't stop coming. Disgusted with herself, she straightened up, tucked her wavy blond hair behind her ears, glanced at Rina, and then let her gaze fall on her chef salad.

Her favorites as far as salads went with juicy red tomatoes, cooked hard-boiled eggs, and crumbled bacon blending tastefully with the crunchy green lettuce and sweet, crisp carrot slices tossed with chunks of ham and turkey. A fiesta of flavor with every bite, she thought woefully, knowing she wasn't going to enjoy a single bite. "I'm not quite ready to divulge the details of my pathetic life, Rina."

"We've been here for thirty minutes, and twenty have been spent with you crying uncontrollably into your salad! Stop it Sophie!" Rina's caramel eyes betrayed her harsh words, though. They were filled with worry.

Sophie realized now, she should've picked a place with a bit more privacy to talk to Rina about her unraveling life. The Old Salt City Jail restaurant wasn't exactly conducive to revealing her secret hell. She knew people passing by could hear her crying.

Without thinking, she'd asked Rina to meet at her favorite restaurant and one of her favorite places. There were many reasons. Among them, the fond memories she had of coming here with her mom and dad. The restaurant had been around for thirty years, one constant in her life. Before becoming a restaurant, it had been a jail. It was rumored to have held Jesse James once.

The restaurant was divided up into 'jail cells', with long steel bars separating them. Charming chandeliers hung in each 'cell', the bulbs covered in red gingham lamp shades, emitting a warm glow. Shadows danced off the walls as employees and patrons alike walked by. The tables were covered in red and white checked tablecloths, with white cloth napkins encasing the silverware and wrapped in Sheriff's Badge napkin rings.

There were real and fake plants placed abundantly throughout, which made the place feel even more earthy and warm to her. Her mind slipped back to when she was younger. The place had made her feel strangely safe and secure.

Ironic, she thought, realizing she was now, in the Old Salt City *Jail,* going to reveal how trapped her life had become. She was sure her life looked perfect from the outside since she lived in a gorgeous home with a handsome, successful man. In truth, her life was hell. David had been her jailer for two years and she needed to break free of him. Actually, she realized, this was the perfect place to reveal to Rina what David had done and how her husband had kept her captive.

Rina, her best and only friend, was older, kind of like a surrogate mother. They'd met in college and had been friends since, even though Rina treated her like a child. Whatever their relationship, there was a closeness between them deeper than friendship. Rina was there for her and always would be. Sophie wiped her eyes again before continuing, "Of course I want to tell you what happened, but I'm sure I already know what you're going to say."

"Well then, tell me dear. What's going on?"

"It's just . . ." She began, but changed her mind as hostility was springing up inside of her. "Why is it, I wonder, men send roses when they've done something wrong? Is there some secret code book fathers pass on to sons when they reach a certain age? I mean, really, I'd like to know." She was breathing heavily, hardly able to contain her emotions. She wanted to punch something or some*one*.

Patiently Rina uttered, "Hon, you know men are of no interest to me. They have a head, filled with a brain just like you and me, but men choose only to think with their little one—the one that has no brain. Why do you think I've moved onto the better of the two species." It was a statement rather than a question. Smiling genially, she continued, "I don't think you've been crying the last twenty minutes because you've been wondering about flowers." She shrugged knowingly. "Am I wrong?"

Sophie tried to breathe deeply to calm down but knew it wasn't possible at this point. "No, it's about David and I know you don't like David." She choked down a sob before continuing, "I caught him with another woman." Saying the words out loud made it seem more real, she wanted to throw up, her heart torn to shreds like the lettuce leaves in her salad.

"By 'with', you mean he was doing the adultery dance, right?" Rina asked lightly.

"Yes."

"What a predictable ass. What did you do?"

Sophie stared at her, incapable of responding.

"Sophie, come on, it's me. Talk to me."

She knew Rina was starting to get impatient. She opened her mouth to begin the process of sharing her misery, when Rina interjected, "You're right, I don't like him and I didn't want this to happen to you. I hoped it wouldn't."

"Even though you knew it would, right?" Sophie spat out.

"I thought it might, yes," Rina started slowly, "but I'm still sad it's happened because it's you and I love you. You're my dearest friend."

Feeling bad for lashing out, Sophie tried a smile. She knew Rina was there to help her. "I know.

Sorry I got angry. Thanks for coming. I know you're busy."

"I understand. You know you can count on me anytime. Now, are you going to tell me what happened or not?" Rina asked.

"You remember I had my painting class today?" Sophie began.

"Yes."

Speaking clearly, she tumbled ahead. "It let out early, so I drove home. When I got to the house, I saw David's car in the driveway and another car parked behind his. I thought it was strange because, he always parks in the garage and he said he would be at the restaurant all day. Anyway, I parked my car at the curb and went into the house."

She stopped, a gnawing feeling of dread running through her body. It didn't matter how cliché her life seemed right now. It was about to change.

"Sophie? Go on."

"Are you sure you want the play by play of what happened?" Sophie asked, still pondering the feelings within her.

"I'm sure."

Pushing a loose curl behind an ear, she continued, "When I went in the house the first thing I noticed was a woman's purse on the foyer table. My heart began pounding fast and then I heard David's voice coming from upstairs.

Rina nodded encouragingly.

"Hearing his voice, I called out 'David', and was going to go upstairs, until I heard a woman laugh."

"Asshole." Rina exclaimed.

"I couldn't believe it. I was angry and terrified at the same time. Without thinking, I ran up the stairs. I had to know for sure what was going on and I didn't want him to be able to lie to me later. You know?"

"I got it," Rina said understandably.

"The bedroom door was part open. I stayed outside, listening to them talk and his voice was tender and fun, like the David I knew in college . . . and . . ."

"Did you go in and confront him," Rina interrupted.

"Yes, I did. I was thinking, what right does he have to talk to her that way? He hasn't talked to me like that since our honeymoon and I'm his wife!"

"Absolutely," Rina agreed fervently.

"Well, I suddenly had a burst of rage through the sadness and thought, no way, I won't stand for this. I pushed open the bedroom door and yelled, "Stop it! Stop it now!"

"Good for you," Rina cheered, with a smile.

With tears spilling down her cheeks and her hands trembling, she continued in a whisper, "I saw David and the woman in our bed together. I screamed, 'get out, get out of my bed!' *She* hurried and got off, covering herself with the bed sheet and ran into the bathroom. I could tell she was embarrassed."

"She should've been, the bitch. What kind of woman would be so brazen?" Rina asked angrily.

"I don't know." Sophie said softly.

"And, what did *he* do when you came in?" Rina questioned, her voice raised an octave.

"I turned to David, sure he'd be upset or embarrassed but he wasn't. He crossed his arms behind his head and . . ." Sophie stopped, not sure she could tell Rina the sad truth about this man who vowed to love, honor and cherish her. Mumbling, she declared, "He was smiling."

"What," Rina blurted, a look of shock on her face.

She didn't want to say it again, but she cleared her throat and repeated it more calmly. "He was smiling."

"He was *smiling*? I knew he was egotistical but, what a fucking prick!"

Sophie looked pleadingly at her friend. As upset as she was, Rina swearing only made it worse. Profanity never "took" with her and Rina knew it.

Reading her silent plea, Rina retorted, "All right hon, I'll *try* to keep my more colorful insults to myself. Getting back to the jerk, did you walk over and smack the smile right off his good for nothing face?"

"No. I felt broken. I stood there crying like a fool. I guess I was hoping David would say something, come to his senses, apologize, put his pants on, get out of bed, but he didn't. He laid there with a goofy smile on his face. I waited until I couldn't take it anymore. I had to run."

"It's understandable you couldn't take it, sweetie. No one should have to find their spouse in bed with another person," she vented, hostility coursing through every word.

"I still can't believe I found him in our bed with her. Anyway, I drove around aimlessly for a while, unsure of what to do, until I called you." Sophie was exhausted. She wanted to lie down, or hide, or better yet, close her eyes and forget this had ever happened. She knew she couldn't, though. Instead, she sat there, staring once again at her salad. After a few seconds, Rina put a hand over hers, but she still couldn't look at her.

"I'm so, so . . ." Rina started.

Sophie pulled her hand away, irritated by her kindness. She was mad, mad at David for all he'd put her through these past two years, mad at Rina for what she knew Rina would say, and mad at herself for allowing this to happen. Crossing her arms defensive she retorted, unable to look at Rina, "I know I've been blind. I know I should've left him a long time ago, but I was afraid." She looked up at Rina and exclaimed quietly, "I'm still afraid."

"Sophie," Rina started again.

"No. Stop. Stop it! Just listen, please, you've got to understand. He told me he'd kill me if I ever left him. Did I tell you that?"

Rina shook her head no, a flicker of understanding in her eyes.

"He did. A couple of weeks after the incident."

"I remember the incident," Rina uttered.

"Well, because of the incident, and what he said, you can understand I believe him." Looking imploringly into her friends eyes, she added, "Please, say you understand."

Sophie suddenly couldn't take the pain inside anymore. Closing her eyes, she shook her head, trying to wake herself from the horrible nightmare which was her life. Predictably, nothing happened. Defeated, she opened her eyes and stared at her uneaten salad.

Rina scooted her chair closer and wiped away the tears from Sophie's cheeks. Sophie looked up to see an empathetic tenderness which immediately comforted her.

"Sophie dear, it's just awful this has happened. My heart is breaking for you, to see you in such pain. I'll help you get through this. Whatever it takes." Rina leaned closer to her, putting an arm around her. "I know you love David and I know you're afraid of him as well." She paused, pushing a blond strand of hair out of her face before going on. "You're this amazing, beautiful, wonderful person. It'll be all right. Somehow, between the two of us, you'll get through it."

"Thank you for helping me. I hope I can get through it. I really do," Sophie muttered somberly.

"I know it seems hard, but you've got to be strong. You do realize now what a complete ass, um I mean *idiot* David is? Leave him and let's find you some real happiness.

"Strong?" Sophie sighed.

"Yes," Rina continued. "You were strong when your parents died. Look at all you accomplished before you married David. You have your Masters Degree in Art. You've got a teaching certificate. You graduated with honors from both high school and college. Anyone should feel blessed to have you in their life. I know I do. Come on. You can do it."

She nodded her agreement, but had no idea where to begin. The whole idea of moving forward seemed impossible, and too staggering to comprehend.

CHAPTER 2

Lunch lasted a long time. The once friendly waiter became flat out rude by the time they paid their check. He'd kept coming back, asking if they needed anything else. Rina kept saying, "More water", until finally his looks of concern had become glares.

Sophie was ready to leave immediately after she'd told Rina everything but Rina, in her motherly way, had taken over.

"You know, we still have an open position as Art Director slash teacher at Sacred Heart. Why don't I call Dr. Jensen, the Principal and see if we can get you an interview?

"I guess. Do you think I'm qualified?"

"You know you are," Rina responded pragmatically grabbing her cell phone and punching in the number.

"You know what you're talking about," Sophie said, watching Rina amicably talk on the phone.

Rina was the Vice Principal of the most prestigious private high school in Salt Lake City. She had told Sophie earlier in the week they'd been having a tough time trying to fill the position and she wished David would let her work. Rina also said she was perfect for the job. God does work in mysterious ways. *Maybe this job has been waiting for me*, she thought.

"There you go," Rina clucked triumphantly, hanging up. "Dr. Jensen is excited to talk to you. The interview is set for nine-thirty tomorrow morning."

"So soon?"

"Yes, and he asked you to bring your portfolio. Do you want me to go with you to get it in the morning?"

"No, I'll work it out," Sophie mumbled.

"Are you sure?"

"I'm sure." Sophie said firmly, but inside she was hollow. *What am I doing? Is this really what I want? I need time to think.* "I should go. I'm tired, Rina."

"Sure sweetie. You've had a lousy day. Did you want to stay with me tonight?"

"Oh. No. Thanks for the offer, but I'd like to be alone for a while. Clear my head. I'll stay at the Hilton." she replied awkwardly.

"Sure you want to stay there?" Rina asked, looking surprised and a little hurt.

"It's very nice, you know. The one on West Temple."

"Right." Rina sounded reluctant. "At least let me follow you. I want to make sure you get there safely."

"I'd appreciate it," Sophie agreed, glad her friend wasn't fighting her on this.

As Sophie drove to the hotel, she couldn't help thinking about David. She tried to stop, tried to concentrate instead on the beauty around her. Fall was in bloom and the Wasatch Mountains, especially, were a vision, covered in reds, oranges and purples from the maple trees, while the dark green of the pine trees contrasted vividly.

A *painting straight from Heaven*, she thought, remembering when she met David . . .

They'd both attended the University of Utah, and she'd gone hiking in the mountains behind the college at least once a week. She loved being alone but not feeling lonely up there close to nature. She seemed closer to her parents amongst the beautiful trees and the singing birds. She'd even camped in the mountains with some of her friends over spring break several summers ago. It was then she met David. A friend of a friend had brought him along. Sophie thought he was handsome with his thick black hair and tanned skin.

She loved his eyes immediately. They were brown, surrounded with long, dark lashes. He had a quick smile and an ease about him which made her feel comfortable right from the start. He was tall, over six feet, and a little skinny. She was glad he had at least one flaw, it made him seem more approachable. They were introduced and had talked around the campfire until the sun started to come up. They had a lot to talk about. He made her laugh and she needed to feel good.

After their first meeting, they spent the rest of the camping trip together. Rina looked hurt at times, but Sophie knew she couldn't do anything about it. She was attracted to him.

She found out he graduated from some fancy cooking school in New York a couple of years earlier and was in the process of opening his own restaurant in Salt Lake City. He said he was also part owner of a general contracting company, which was flourishing. She'd been excited about the prospect of having a man with his career path set. He seemed to know what he wanted out of life and by the end of the week she could

tell David wanted her in his life as well. He treated her with such respect and made her feel like a queen. She told Rina all of this on the drive down the mountain. She also told Rina she knew she was going to marry him.

"I fell hard for him," Sophie said out loud to herself. She remembered how furious Rina had been, telling her to take her time, to find out more about him. "I wouldn't listen; I should've listened, but no, I was in love."

Sophie checked into the hotel, said good-bye to Rina, and went to her room. It was quaint, but suitable. She didn't need much. *The bed looks comfortable*, she thought, glancing longingly at it, but first she wanted a shower to get some of the days grime off her.

What she'd seen and done today left a mental mark as well as a physical one. She looked in the bathroom mirror, noticing her green eyes were puffy and mascara was streaked down her face.

What a mess, she thought.

More than the physical signs of her horrible day was her reflection showing the ache in her soul. *Why David*, she thought, willing herself not to cry again. The tears came anyway, though. Frustrated with herself, she wiped them away quickly as she undressed.

After checking the temperature of the water, she was about to step into the shower when she remembered she wanted a razor, some shaving cream and a bottle of lotion. Drained, she turned off the water and put on a robe hanging in the closet before calling housekeeping. After putting in her request, she decided to give in to the lure of the big bed and fell wearily onto it.

Although she was tired, sleep wouldn't come. In its place were continued images of when she'd first met David . . .

"I know we've only been dating for a short time, a whirlwind romance," she'd told Rina starry-eyed. Sophie and David were together almost every day.

There were times, looking back, when she wouldn't hear from David. Once it had been a whole week, but he'd always call, apologize profusely and ask her to meet him at their favorite restaurant, his restaurant which he named Sophie's. She was honored. She let some of his questionable qualities slip by because of his lavishness in other ways, like naming the restaurant after her. He also had a special table set aside for the two of them. Sitting grandly atop it would always be two dozen red roses.

He thought they were her favorite because on the night they met, he asked her what her full name was and she told him it was Sophia Rose Barton.

"No one calls me Sophia, though. I like Sophie."

"Sophia is a beautiful name but I'll call you Sophie, if you like." He smiled, caressing her hand with his thumb.

She explained her mother gave her the middle name because of her love for roses. She also explained she almost had been named Ruby Rose because her mother's favorite color was red but luckily her father had talked her mom out of it. Sophia had been his great grandmother's name, which was how her first name was picked . . .

Funny, she thought, as she grabbed a tissue from the box on the nightstand and blew her nose, he just assumed red roses were my favorite flower too. He never asked, but then, I guess I never corrected him either. Rolling over, she pounded the pillow, trying to force the images to go away. Still, they flooded through her . . .

David seemed perfect, well, almost perfect. Once, at the restaurant, she watched David lose his temper with one of his employees and fire her in front of everyone. She was embarrassed by his behavior, confronting him about it later. David waved it aside saying, "Sometimes you have to be rough to get your point across. I have to let everyone know who's the boss. Besides, without me telling them what to do, these people wouldn't have a clue."

She'd accepted his answer because of the gleam in his eyes; not wanting to rock the boat but, oh how she wished she would have understood.

An abrupt knock at her door brought Sophie back to the present. Looking through the peep hole she opened the door to a kindly looking older woman.

"Hello. Here are the items you requested," the small, stocky woman said professionally.

"Thank you." Taking the bag, Sophie closed the door. In the bathroom, she removed her robe. She couldn't help but notice her figure in the large bathroom mirror.

Skin, and bones, she thought, walking over to the shower. She turned it on, checked it for temperature, and stepped in. As she bent to pick up the soap, she noticed her hand was shaking.

"Great," she whimpered, the shaking enveloping her whole body. With nothing else to do, she sat on the tub floor, putting her knees to her chest, trying to calm herself. *How did I allow myself to become like this*, she wondered? *I feel violated; used. Maybe I'm dying*, she thought. *Maybe this is what happens to your body when your heart breaks.*

After a while, the water turned cold. Cautiously, she climbed out. Wrapping herself in one of the big, white hotel towels, she walked over to the bed and lied down. Closing her eyes, she concentrated on going to sleep. It wouldn't come. Instead were more memories of David . . .

They married after nine months together. He proposed after five. It seemed fast, but they were in love and neither of them wanted to wait. She didn't have any close family, and David told her he didn't either. They'd decided on a small ceremony with Rina as her maid of honor and David's business partner as his best man.

Afterward, they took a limousine to the airport, consummating their marriage in the back seat. The experience left her disappointed to say the least. It was soon forgotten when they arrived in Hawaii. Her honeymoon had been anything but disappointing. It was magical, spending their days lying on the white, sandy beaches, eating in fine restaurants and taking in the sights. Nighttime had been filled with dancing, taking moonlit walks and making love.

Sophie rolled over, looking at the clock. It was eight-fifteen. She sat up and dialed the gift shop hoping it was still open.

"Hello?" A woman answered.

"Yes, hello, um, I was wondering if you're still open?" she asked meekly, feeling silly as she said it. Obviously they were still open if they're answering the phone.

"We're open until nine o'clock," the woman answered flatly.

"Great. Thank you." Hanging up, she went into the bathroom where she'd left her clothes, put them on, picked up her pocketbook and went down to the gift shop. After a few minutes, she found what she was looking for.

At the counter, she smiled limply while the woman rang up her sleeping pills.

Once back in her room, she undressed, took two of the pills, climbed into bed and turned on the television. **Law and Order: Special Victims Unit** was on. *How appropriate*, she thought, remembering the day after she and David came back from their honeymoon . . .

The movers were bringing in some of her things. She didn't have much; the hope chest which had been her mother's, her clothes and a couple of lamps. Sophie asked the movers to take the chest upstairs to the master suite. She wanted the chest at the foot of their bed because she wanted to have the treasures within close by, but as the movers were headed up the stairs, David yelled, "No way. It looks trashy and it will not be in our house."

Sophie pleaded, explaining how important it was to her.

He finally relented, saying, "Fine, you can keep it, but only in the basement." Without further discussion, he walked away. She put it down there reluctantly, covering it with an old sheet, hoping at some point he'd change his mind.

He hadn't.

She tried to talk to him about it one other time, but he left her so upset, she knew she'd never bring it up again. From then on, she became a prisoner to David, to the house he owned; to what he wanted.

The next day he sat her down, explaining exactly how trapped she was.

"Sophie," he began, "no wife of mine will have a job. In fact, you won't do anything unless I tell you to do it or say you can. Do you understand?" His voice sounded calm, but she saw the muscles in his jaws tightening as he talked and the ugliness in his eyes.

She nodded, terrified, too shocked to do anything else.

He continued, "You'll keep this house clean. You'll have dinner on the table by five o'clock, even if I'm not here. You'll always look your best. No getting fat. In fact, I've been meaning to tell you, you seem a little hippy now so start losing weight. You can keep your car, but I'll be checking the mileage daily. I want *a list of the things you'll be doing each day. I want the address and phone number of each place you go. I'll be checking up on you. Keep your cell phone with you at all times."* Then his face had become furious, twisted with rage. *"If you aren't where you say you'll be, there will be trouble. I promise you."* He reached over and squeezed her hand with such force, she wanted to cry out, but didn't dare to.

Then he grabbed her face under the chin, pulling it toward him. She had no choice but to look at him.

"Are we clear?"

She nodded again, agony churning her insides. It was clear.

David looked suspiciously at her, but let go of her face, saying softly, *"Listen, Sophie, I know this must seem strange to you, maybe even scary, but it's going to be great. You'll see."* He smiled then. She remembered his mouth seemed distorted, almost too delighted.

"You'll be taken care of. You'll have a place to live, food to eat. You can buy whatever you want, whenever you want. Also, I know you love to paint. Do it. I've turned a room upstairs into an art studio for you." David's face had darkened again, his voice steely, *"Women are always saying they wished they knew what their husbands want from them. Well, I'm doing you a favor and letting you know up front, this is what I want and this it the way it'll be."* He stood suddenly, as if to leave, then turned back to her and said, *"Don't try to leave, either, or you'll regret it. I won't be embarrassed by an ungrateful wife. I*

promise you'll wish you hadn't." His voice changed again, full of elation. "You'll love it. You'll see. I've given you a ring as a token of my promise to take care of you, but I wanted to give you something more. I know how much you love red roses, so I promise there will always be red roses on the foyer table."

He pulled her into his arms, saying into her hair, "It's my special promise to you. You're mine now, Sophie. Mine." He pushed her away, looking intently into her eyes. "You understand, don't you? You're mine." Not waiting for a response, he continued, "Like it or not. Enjoy it or not, this is the way it's going to be." Leaning down, he kissed her lightly on the cheek and walked out, leaving her alone to cry bitterly, unable to believe what had happened.

Of course, she thought immediately about calling Rina, to ask for her help, but she hadn't wanted to hear the I told you so she was sure she get. She was also afraid of what David would do.

Around two o'clock, as promised, two dozen red roses arrived with a note saying,

Sophia Rose, my darling,
You know what to do with these.
I'll love you forever.
David.

She wanted to bash them against the foyer table and run, but realized she had nowhere to go and no money to get her there. Besides, she thought fearfully, he'd find me. Again she'd debated calling Rina, but was too ashamed to tell her.

"What a proud fool I was," she whispered to herself, glancing at the clock. Midnight, usually the time David arrived home from the restaurant.

I wonder what he'll do when he finds out I'm not there, she thought, a pang of fear running through her body. In a way, she was relieved, too, because every night David expected her to be intimate with him in the bedroom. A shiver of disgust ran through her body. Knowing him, he'd probably still expect it, even after what he'd done today. The idea sickened her. He tried to be gentle but it would still, sometimes hurt. She'd come to know, though, it would be over faster if she pretended to enjoy herself. It was difficult, having sex with a man who treated her like property rather than an equal. Emotionally she found it impossible to get in the mood.

For tonight I'm safe, she thought, finally allowing herself to fall asleep.

She dreamt her mom and dad were there, standing over her, telling her tenderly they loved her. They seemed to be protecting her. This was one of her favorite dreams. Peace enfolded her with them there. The last thing she remembered was her mom telling her to wake up because her phone was ringing.

Bewildered, she opened her eyes, answering her ringing cell phone,

"Hello?"

"Sophie, where are you? It's three in the morning."

She sat up nervously, all peace vanishing. It was David. *Why didn't I check my caller ID?*

"Let me come and get you. What happened earlier today was a mistake. I promise to make it up to you if you'll tell me where you are." His voice sounded soft, full of remorse, but she'd heard those words before, fallen for his kind voice before; many times, in fact. She wasn't going to do it this time.

He's so awful, she thought, anger at him forming in her soul. She wanted to shout at the top of her voice, or slam her phone shut, but instead said, as calmly as she could, "David, I'm not coming home tonight. Did you think you could bring a woman into our house, into our bed, and I wouldn't care? What did you expect me to do?"

"Are you at Rina's?" He asked, obviously ignoring her questions.

"No, I'm not. Leave her out of this and leave me alone."

"I'll expect to see you tomorrow. You have an obligation to me, as my wife. You know you're mine and you always will be. One way or the other. Do you hear me," he yelled, before hanging up.

Chapter 3

Sophie cautiously turned off her phone, set it on the bedside table, and laid back down. She knew he'd threatened her; knew if she didn't do what he said, he'd kill her. She couldn't doubt it. Three months ago, she might've wondered if he was serious but 'the incident' had proven to her he was capable of anything.

An obligation to him, she thought, as she slid back under the safety of the covers. He's arrogant and crazy. A bad combination. Her hand absently located the long thin scar on her neck. . .

'The incident', happened almost three months ago. She heard him come in and was waiting patiently in bed, wearing the small, pink nightie she bought earlier in the day. David came into their bedroom, sitting next to her on the bed, a look of pure hatred in his eyes. Instinctively, she moved away from him, which was when she noticed the knife.

"What's wrong?" she asked, terrified.

"Where were you today at three o'clock?"

"Let me check my planner," she responded, her voice quivering.

David threw the planner at her.

He went through my purse, she thought, the trepidation inside her growing. She pretended to look through her planner, even though she knew where she'd been. Looking up, she said, "I was getting my hair done."

With the quickness of a cat, he grabbed her by the neck, pushing the knife into the flesh on her throat. "You're lying," he yelled. "I was there at three-fifteen and they told me you left ten minutes earlier. You'd better try again, and this time the truth or so help me, Sophie, you'll regret it!"

His face was next to hers. She could feel and smell his hot breath. He's been drinking, she thought, tears falling down her cheeks.

This seemed to infuriate him even more, the knife cutting deeper into her neck.

The warmth of her blood trickling down onto her chest, distracting her, she vaguely responded, "You're right. I left the salon early because they were able to get me in ahead of schedule."

"Where did you go then?" he asked, shifting his body a little.

I hope he's uncomfortable, she seethed. Aloud said, "I decided to go to the Southtowne Mall and pick up something to wear for you tonight. I bought this," she declared, trying to look down at herself. "I have the receipt. You can check the time." She held her breath, hoping he'd let her go. "Please, David, I'll go get it."

After a few moments, he slowly took the knife away, shoving her toward the door. "Hurry up. I'm waiting."

Swiftly getting the receipt, she flung it at him, unable to contain her feelings, "There. See?" she screamed.

"Be careful," he growled back, picking up the receipt and looking at it.

What she hadn't told him, and now never would, was her Great Aunt Moira Barton had died several weeks ago. Sophie, being her only living relative, had been the beneficiary of her assets. The lawyer said during their phone conversation it was substantial, requesting they meet. She asked him to meet her in the food court of the Southtowne Mall. Arriving early, she went quickly into a lingerie store, picking out the first thing she saw, before hurrying to meet with him.

The lawyer efficiently went over the paperwork with her, explaining the legalities and how her Great Aunt had come to the decision to give her most of her assets. After she signed everything, he said, "There will still be some legal mumbo jumbo, but I'd say you should receive your first check within the next couple of months."

Her head reeling at the four and a half million dollars she'd inherited, she nodded, unable to believe it.

"Do you have the account number where you'd like us to wire the money, or would you like it mailed to your home address?" The attorney questioned.

"No," she blurted loudly. Lowering her voice, she continued, "I don't want it sent to my home address.

Can I call you with an account number, once I've opened it?"

"Of course, that would be fine. Or I can have your aunt's financial advisor contact you. I'm sure he could open an account in your name, if you'd like." He smiled at her, with a look which said he understood how much her life was going to change because of the money.

"Actually, can I call him?"

"Sure. Fine," he said, fishing through his briefcase, pulling out a card and handing it to her. "You can reach him at the bottom number anytime," he stated, standing.

She stood, too, sticking out her hand. "Thank you for your help, sir. I appreciate you meeting me here and going over everything."

"Just doing my job." He smiled, taking her hand, shaking it warmly. "You know how to reach me if you have anymore questions?"

"Yes, thank you."

Sophie snuggled down deeper under the covers, remembering the feeling of that moment. Was it elation? Joy? A sense of freedom? Maybe all of them together . . .

After David had checked the receipt he looked up, his eyes ravishing her. He actually started to cry, looking from the bloody knife in his hand and back to her. Setting the knife on the table, he fell to his knees.

Blubbering, he said, "Sophie, I thought I'd lost you. I didn't want to hurt you. You know that, right?"

She couldn't say anything; was to scared to. She could only feel shock, with tears stinging her face and her own blood staining her nightie.

Still crying, he stood, coming to her, putting his hands on either side of her shoulders, saying tenderly, "I won't be made a fool of. Understand?"

She nodded, wanting to run, but knowing now wasn't the time. She would wait; make a plan. Watching him take off his shirt, she knew from experience what was coming. Flinching, she closed her eyes while he tried to wipe the blood off of her neck and chest. He stopped, though, when she cried out in pain. It only seemed to increase his desire for her, though, because he threw his shirt on the floor and rushed her.

Kissing her neck, he moaned her name over and over.

Before she could respond, he picked her up and laid her on the bed. She heard him take off the rest of his clothes before straddling her. Kissing her neck again, he took off her nightie.

She wanted to scream, but was quiet, trying to think about her life without him; to think about anything but what he was doing to her.

"Oh, Sophie, my Sophie," he cooed in her ear. "I want us to make a baby. Let's have a son together. It'd be perfect coming from us."

Sophie punched her pillow. *Have a baby with him*, she huffed? Not in this lifetime. Wiping her tears with the sheet, she looked at the clock. It said four twenty-three a.m. She groaned inwardly. I'm not wasting any more time on him.

Sophie slowly opened her eyes. The morning sun blaring in on her face, having poked through the thick drapes. Still a little shaken by her dream, she sat up, looking around. Unsettling, how real it seemed, she contemplated, allowing the dream to replay itself in her mind. Her mom and dad were standing over her, talking calmly, telling her they loved her. It had been comforting, until she realized she was strapped to a hospital bed and couldn't get up. In the corner of the room, seemingly hovering, she'd seen a grayish-black mist with glowing, yellow eyes. It seemed to be calling to her, coming closer to her. She screamed and cried, begging her parents to help, but as hard as they tried, she couldn't move.

"It was a dream," she whispered fervently, lying back down. "I've got to think of something else." Struggling internally to push aside her nightmare, something worse pummeled its way in. Yesterday's ordeal with David.

Overwhelmed with a heavy sadness, she pulled the plain white sheet and flower covered bedspread over her head, not ready to begin her day. Her heart was doing belly flops, the aching pain reminding her, although she'd done the right thing by leaving David, her heart was having second thoughts.

As stupid as it is, I still love him. I'm a glutton for punishment, I guess, or I need serious therapy. "What am I going to do?" she asked herself out loud.

As if on cue, her hotel phone rang. She jumped. The deafening ring cutting through the stillness. At first she didn't want to answer it, afraid it might be David, but she remembered he didn't know where she was.

Gingerly, she answered the phone.

"Hello?"

"Sophie, there you are. I've been trying your cell phone for the last ten minutes."

"Rina?"

"Yes dear, it's me. Who else would it be?"

"Right, well, I turned my cell phone off last night after I talked to David."

"What did he say?" she questioned, her voice sounding worried. "You didn't tell him where you are, did you?"

"Actually, I did," Sophie replied mordantly. "He's sitting here beside me. Would you like to talk to him?" She couldn't help herself. Sometimes Rina's motherly concern frustrated her, and she wanted to be rebellious.

"*What?*"

Sophie laughed a little, unable to maintain her serious tone any longer.

"Ha ha. Point taken."

Glancing at the clock, Sophie noticed it was only seven-thirty in the morning. *She's definitely being motherly.* "You've reached me now, what's up?"

"Oh, right. I called to make sure you weren't having second thoughts about your interview today. You remember the interview is at nine-thirty a.m.?"

"Yes, I remember, and I don't know if you'd call it second thoughts, but it does seem sudden. You know how David feels about me working, and he threatened me again last night. I think he's gone crazy. It might not be a good idea to start all of this now."

"He threatened you? What did he say, the son of a bi-?"

Not ready for Rina's foul mouth this early in the morning, she interrupted, "He said one way or the other, I'm his."

"Is that all? It's a threat, nothing more. He's controlling, and you aren't doing what he wants. He's mad."

"I hope you're right, but it feels wrong." And it did feel wrong. She sensed she'd opened a recurring sore in David. More than his words were the feelings she had when she talked to him last night. Something wasn't right, she knew.

"Come on, Sophie. You're a great painter and I know you'll be a wonderful teacher. I'm sure it's hard. This is a big step for you but now is the time for you to stand up for yourself. Be strong."

Strong. There was that word again, she thought, agitated. "Easy for you to say." She heard Rina sigh. "All right, I'll be there."

"Would you feel better if we called the police? We could tell them about the threat."

"No. No police. I know it may seem weird to you, but part of me still loves him. He's all the family I have left now."

"Not true. You've got me. I'm here for you," Rina said defiantly.

"Thanks, I know." She knew Rina was right. To have anything to do with David now would be foolish. Taking a deep breath, she held it, waiting for Rina to let her go.

"Good. Now, how are you doing?"

Letting out the air, Sophie chortled, "You didn't just ask me that question."

"Yeah, pretend I didn't, dear." Rina laughed back.

"I'll see you later."

"Sounds good. Bye."

Sophie placed the receiver back in the cradle, getting up. She needed a fresh change of clothes and she needed her portfolio, which meant going back to the house. First, though, she decided to take another shower, hoping the warmth of the water would calm her nerves.

As she waited for the water to warm, she studied herself in the mirror. Without realizing it, she was scrutinizing her body, something she'd grown accustomed to doing since being with David. In their relationship, she discovered the smallest thing would set him off, which is why she'd begun a morning ritual of checking her face and body to make sure he would have nothing to get upset at. Once he gave her a fifteen minute

lecture on cleanliness when she woke up one morning with a pimple on her face.

"Yuck," she groaned aloud, "I look like a skeleton."

At five-foot-six and a hundred and five pounds, she did look like a skeleton. Her normal, healthy body weight was one hundred thirty pounds. She liked the curviness of her figure there. Now, after two years of cutting way back, her body was sickly, scrawny.

Except for the ample bosom she'd somehow kept, she thought she had a boy's body. With the loss of twenty-five pounds, all of her curves had disappeared. Her face, although angular, was beautiful. She had fair skin, with big, bright green eyes. Her naturally blond hair was long and layered. It had an untamed waviness to it, which was either a curse or a blessing, depending on the day and the amount of humidity in the air.

She knew she should be happier with her appearance, but she'd never been able to feel comfortable with herself.

Before she married David, Rina was always complementing her . . .

The first time they met, Rina had walked over to Sophie at a party, looked her up and down, and said matter-a-factly, "Oh, I bet you've got lots of friends."

Stunned, Sophie asked, "What do you mean?"

"Well, look at you, you're gorgeous."

Embarrassed, Sophie blurted, "Thanks."

It had been the beginning of an amazing friendship. Secretly, she thought Rina was more beautiful than she was. She was taller by about three inches, and lean. Having

run track in college, it showed on her body. She had long dark brown hair, which she normally kept in a pony tail. It was straight and thick.

Her face, though, was what was most beautiful. It was striking; elegant. She had olive skin, caramel-colored eyes, high cheek bones and a beautiful mouth.

Sophie thought she should have been a model. Guys fell over themselves doing all sorts of wild things to try to get Rina's attention.

Rina rarely dated, though, seemed altogether uninterested in men. And although she wondered, Rina hadn't told her she was gay until two years into their friendship. Rina had come to her apartment crying one night, something she'd never done before or since (the crying), saying someone had broken her heart, but didn't go into more detail. She said in her simple, tactless way, "I've tried men and I've tried women. I prefer women."

At first, Sophie was shocked because Rina had been so blunt, but responded,

"It's about time you finally told me. I've suspected for a while, you know."

Rina had thrown a pillow at her, laughing. As she wiped her tears, she retorted, with an all too familiar gleam in her eyes, "No way. How could you know? I decided for sure tonight."

Sophie hurried and showered, then dressed and drove over to the house she shared with her husband. 422 East 5th Avenue. Salt Lake City, Utah. Although she'd lived in Utah her whole life, this house wasn't her home. She was never comfortable in it. All of the comforts existed, but no warmth.

Perhaps, under different circumstances, she would have loved this house. It was built in 1947, with lots of country charm and a Victorian flare. Made of solid brick, except for the porch, which was wood. It stood two stories, with a full basement. The porch was painted white, and large columns stood on either side of the steps, leading to the front door. The porch also wrapped around the house to the left, where there was another entrance into the kitchen.

One of her first purchases had been a brown wicker furniture set; complete with two chairs, a coffee table and a love seat which doubled as a rocker. She hung pansies, peonies, and climbing ivy all along the porch awning, hoping to feel some happiness in the midst of the black hole of her marriage.

It had helped, a little. She spent many days sitting on the porch, listening to the singing birds, watching while they built nests in the large Maple tree in the front yard.

Go in and get it over with, she thought, knowing she was stalling. She turned off her car and went in. It was eight-thirty a.m. She knew today he should already be gone, but when she entered the front door, she called out his name anyway, just to be safe.

"David?"

When there was no answer, she breathed a sigh of relief, starting toward the stairs. Her eyes drifted to the foyer table, where she noticed a fresh vase of roses sitting on it, but what made her freeze in her tracks was the envelope propped against the vase with her name on it.

"David?" she called out again nervously. After waiting a few seconds, she quickly walked over and picked up the envelope. Tearing it open, she read through it, absently rubbing the scar on her neck.

My Dearest Sophia,

It's regrettable what happened yesterday. It was insensitive of me to bring her into the house. Forgive me. You know I won't let you live without me. You can't. No one will ever love you as much as I do.

Meet me at the restaurant tonight. Nine o'clock sharp! Don't worry about what to wear. I've had something picked up for you. It's hanging on the door to our closet.

Let's put this behind us!
David

Sophie read the note again, before stuffing it into her purse. Brushing a tear from her cheek, she ran upstairs. Going first to the hall closet, she grabbed a suitcase, then walked into their bedroom.

Admittedly, it was a beautiful room, although only on the surface. To her, it seemed cold and lifeless; a dungeon. A place where captor and captive shared space. No love.

Absolutely no fond memories.

Large and spacious, with a high, vaulted ceiling. A large, twinkling chandelier hung from the middle, emitting a romantic glow. The walls were painted soft green, with pictures the decorator had purchased, hanging symmetrically throughout.

The oversized bed was grand and ornate. Carved cherry wood, with a deep cherry finish. The headboard was twice the size of the footboard, delicately carved.

The thick, soft bedding was luscious, when it was made. She noticed, disgustedly, he hadn't bothered to change the white and green striped sheets she'd put on the bed. The same sheets he and *that woman* had been screwing in, when she caught them. The bedding was mainly white, with glimpses of color here and there, on a decorative pillow or sham, or on the sheets.

At the end of the bed was a custom bench. He had it made for her. She knew it was there because he didn't want her mothers' chest to replace it.

There were two night stands, one on either side of the bed. His was cluttered. Stacked with old newspaper clippings he saved because they had talked about him or his restaurant.

There were several different restaurant awards he'd received, books, and a pair of reading glasses, he'd been told he needed, but never used. A small, ceramic, table-lamp sat discreetly on one edge. Horizontally from the lamp, on the other edge, stood an ugly, white alarm clock with big, red numbers.

Hers was the complete opposite. Where his was overflowing, hers was sparse. There sat a lamp, a match to his, a picture of her mom and dad and a small, silver alarm clock.

Directly opposite the bed was a large dresser made of the same wood and finish as the bed, with a plasma TV hanging above it. Perfectly placed on one side, were different sized, blue, green and white oriental vases. On the other side of the dresser, were three Tang horses, also of different sizes.

The wall, opposite the door, was a sitting area, with a large, bay window, covered in plump cushions, two oversized chairs and a small coffee table. The bathroom entrance opened next to the sitting area. The bedroom floor was wood, but mostly covered with a big, Asian inspired rug, the bathroom was all white marble, with green and black accents.

Her vanity was centered between two oversized sinks. A large, jetted bathtub, a walk-in shower and a toilet completed the room. Next to the bathroom lay the entrance to the walk in closet.

Sophie was still unable to believe David left *those* sheets on the bed. It made her sick, literally. Running into the bathroom, she gagged several times, but nothing came up.

Turning on the water, she took a clean washcloth off the vanity.

Wetting it with warm water, she ran it over her face. Looking in the mirror, she whispered determinedly, "Be strong, Sophie."

She brushed her teeth. Took off her clothes. Applied some mascara, blush and lip gloss. When she finished with her makeup, she threw it into her bag, going to the large walk-in closet. There she pulled out a pair of hose and carefully put them on. Next, she put on her gray suit with a light blue camisole.

Feeling a bit dazed, she put on her dark gray pumps, a bracelet and some earrings. Next she grabbed a garment bag, put some clothes and necessities in it and was about to walk out, when she noticed the red dress hanging on the door. The front and back had a deep V-neck line, with red beading, at the thick empire waistline. It was obviously made of silk with a sheer red layer over the top. She had to admit it was beautiful, even while she wondered who'd helped him pick it out.

Probably his assistant, she thought, walking away. Changing her mind, she went back for it. Once it was tucked safely inside the garment bag, she left the room.

She knew she wanted out of this relationship, but didn't want to die in the process. The note in her purse, and the scar on her neck was reminder enough she needed to handle things carefully. *Who knows*, she thought, a flash of hope overcoming her. *Maybe he'll get some help and we can stay together.*

She conceded, at the same moment, she was probably being naive, or even stupid. Deep down, though, she wanted to believe she knew the real David, the one she'd known before they were married, was in there somewhere. It was doubtful, she knew it. She also knew she was frightened. Believing he could change, with help, seemed easier. She wasn't ready to face reality. She'd married a man she hardly knew, and he was a monster. Feeling the need to push aside her thoughts, she focused, instead, on why she'd come.

She entered her art studio. Gingerly, she lifted her portfolio out from behind some canvas David had purchased for her. He wanted her to paint, but she'd never been able to paint in this room. Once, she tried, but no inspiration would come.

Two years, she marveled wistfully, unable to believe she hadn't lifted a brush, except of course, in her paint class. She checked inside, to make sure everything she needed was still there. Once at the door, she glanced back, longingly wishing for things which most likely would never be, imagining how things should have been. With great sorrow, she closed the door, heading toward the stairs.

She noticed the picture right away. She did each time she came to the top of the stairs because it was a picture of her and David, taken at their wedding. They both looked happy. This time, though, she noticed something else about the picture, how innocent she looked. She realized she noticed it this time because her innocence was gone. Walking down the stairs, she couldn't help but think what might have been; what *should* be.

At the bottom, she remembered her mother's hope chest still covered in the basement. Most of her life—no, *all* of her life—was tied to this house, to David. The memories, though most of them not good, were all she had.

"Be strong," she murmured, knowing now wasn't the time to crumble. She needed to get to her interview.

Feeling a burst of courage, she whispered, "I won't let him beat me." Without a backward glance, she left the house.

CHAPTER 4

"Thanks again, Dr. Jensen," she said, standing.

"I appreciate you taking the time to see me." She took Dr. Jensen's outstretched hand, shaking it gratefully.

"You're welcome, Sophia," Dr. Jensen returned.

"Call me Sophie, please," she expressed with a smile. Her interview with Dr. Jensen had gone well. It'd been much easier to get through than she'd imagined.

Dr. Jensen had put her immediately at ease, with his earnest, dark eyes, charming smile, and likable wit. He was of average height, with chocolate skin. His short, black curly hair, had patches of gray throughout. Small, wire-framed glasses sat gracefully on the end of his nose, giving him a distinguished look.

His office matched him, warm, inviting and comfortable. There were two comfortable looking leather chairs opposite his large mahogany desk. Next to one chair, was a small end table. Sitting on it was a fern. Behind the chairs, in the corner, stood a tree of some kind, another fern and some flowering plants. They looked like lilies, but she wasn't sure. There were also several plants sitting, happily, on his windowsill.

He had pictures of his family everywhere including a large one hanging directly behind him. Her eyes had been drawn to the smiling faces of his wife and three boys during the interview. He was open, intelligent, and seemed to love his family.

"Sophie it is then." He leaned over, picking up her portfolio and handed it to her.

"Your work is exceptional. I'm surprised you haven't done more with your talent."

She beamed graciously, appreciating the compliment.

Dr. Jensen continued, "One of my hobbies, aside from a love of plants, is collecting art. I'd buy at least three of these."

Feeling embarrassed by the praise, she reached a hand to her cheek.

Dr. Jensen grinned. "I didn't mean to embarrass you, but seriously, if you're interested, I'd love to talk to you about selling a couple of them."

"Sure, Dr. Jensen. Thank you."

"Thank *you*. It's going to be a privilege having you work here with us. I know I'm excited about it, and I'm sure the students will benefit greatly from you being here." Then he said to Rina, who'd walked into his office near the end of their conversation, "Ms. Sumpter, give her the grand tour, would you?" He looked back at Sophie, "You're in good hands. Enjoy yourself, and we'll meet back later. I'm interested to hear what you think of the place, and especially our Art Department."

"I'll take care of her, Dr. Jensen," Rina chirped.

Sophie and Rina left the office and started down the hall. Rina was talking excitedly.

"His first name is Mark, by the way. He's a great Principal and cares a lot about the students."

"I believe it. What I can't believe is how much he liked my paintings. Do you think he was only trying to be nice?" She was still flabbergasted by his praise of her work.

"Trust me. Dr. Jensen doesn't say anything unless he means it. If he says he likes your work, he really likes your work," Rina stated seriously.

"I've been telling you for years, your work is amazing. Maybe now you'll start believing it."

"I guess," Sophie uttered.

"You're going to love the Art Department. It's amazing. It's just down the hall from the Theater Department."

"Sounds easy to remember." Sophie laughed, feeling excited and a little uneasy about this new experience.

"Don't worry, I'll help you out, and if you have a quick question, I'm sure Phillip Hansen, can answer it for you. Oh, speak of the devil, here he is." To Phillip, she smiled crisply. "Hey, I'd like to introduce you to our new Art Director."

Motioning in Sophie's direction, she continued, "Sophie Berkeley, this is Dr. Phillip Hansen. He's our Theater Director, which means the two of you will probably see a lot of each other."

Smiling shyly, Sophie said, "It's nice to meet you."

"Nice to meet you, too." Phillip smiled back.

"Okay, okay, enough with the formalities. We've a lot to do; let's get a move on," Rina said sarcastically. "Later, Phil . . ." She couldn't finish because her beeper went off.

Sophie noticed Rina was frowning at it.

"What's wrong?" she asked.

"Oh, I'm sure there's a problem with one of the students. It's a 911, which means I'm going to have to cut this short. We might have to finish this later, if you don't mind."

Sophie started to tell her not to worry about it when Phillip interrupted.

"I can show her around if you'd like. This is my free period, so I have some time."

"Phillip, that would be great," Rina said, sounding relieved.

"I'll see you later, Sophie." Noticing the look on her face, she added, "Don't worry, he won't bite." Abruptly, she turned to leave, calling, "Thanks, Phillip."

Sophie was stressed enough coming here, and meeting the Principal of the school, but now taking a tour from a complete stranger, not to mention an incredibly handsome one, it was almost more than she could take. She peeked up at him and noticed a small smile on his face. He'd been watching her, and was obviously amused by something.

"Don't worry," he said, a twinkle in his eyes. "Like Rina said, I don't bite, much."

Sophie hurriedly looked away, bristling.

"Are you ready to have a look around your new department?" Phillip asked.

"Of course," she replied, trying to sound professional, even though she felt like a child.

"It's right over here," he said, walking forward.

She hurried to catch up with him and said, trying to regain her composure,

"You don't need to do this. I can wait until Rina can show me."

"As I told Rina, it's no problem. I'm glad to do it."

"Great," she said, her swirling emotions changing to anger. Not anger exactly, but something weird, and she wasn't sure why. It couldn't be because of him she thought, sneaking another look at him.

Rina had been right, the Art Department was amazing. She'd instantly liked the place, her classroom and the entire private high school. She could understand now why Rina had been trying to get her to work here for such a long time. She'd also had a chance to meet some of the students. The whole atmosphere left her feeling vibrant and alive. Those emotions were followed, though, by apprehension. She realized even if she was able to work things out with David, she'd keep this job. Knowing he didn't want her to work, she wondered what would happen. She knew, but she ignored the thought.

Back in her hotel room, Sophie sat on the edge of the bed wondering what she should do, what she *wanted* to do.

She'd taken another shower, reapplied her makeup and redone her hair. Putting on the red dress, she noticed the time. *Eight forty-five*, she thought, knowing if she was going to see David, she needed to leave now. Panic could only scratch the surface of what she was feeling. It dawned on her these feelings weren't because she was worried about what he would think of her having a job. They were because she didn't want to see him, or speak to him or be near him, ever again.

With David, her life had become routine; habitual even, and she'd accepted it, for whatever reason, but she wasn't going to do it anymore. For the first time in years, she enjoyed her day. She knew she wasn't going to let go of this feeling.

Especially not for David, she thought fiercely.

Picking up her cell phone, she determinedly dialed Rina's number, realizing as she did, she still needed Rina's help; she couldn't do it alone. Rina answered, almost as if she'd expected the call.

"What are you doing tonight?" Sophie asked weakly.

"I'm just getting ready for dinner. Would you like to come over?"

"Absolutely," she answered, her voice gaining strength.

"All right, I'll see you in a few minutes."

"Okay. You realize what a big step this is for me, don't you?"

"I think I do," Rina answered.

"It means I'm leaving David. If I don't go to dinner tonight, he'll know, and he'll be livid." She hesitated again, an abrupt sickness welling inside her.

More than anyone, she understood what David had become, and what he was capable of. She wondered if this was a good idea. Into the phone, she said, "You know, I'm not sure I can do this. I have this feeling David's reaction is going to be awful."

"It may be, but it's still the right thing to do. You've got to. Rina sounded harsh, but it still gave her strength.

"You're right," she conceded, remembering today and recognizing she wanted to have those feelings in her life more often, even if it meant fighting for it. "I'll see you in a few minutes."

"When did you become such a great cook?" Sophie questioned as she leaned back in her chair. She'd forgotten what it was like to be full.

Rina laughed. "I've always been a good cook, dear. You just haven't been able to try it in a while, you know, since you married David, *Chef of the Year*," she answered, quoting a recent newspaper clipping which had detailed the award David won about a month ago.

Sophie laughed, too, trying to push away the uneasy feelings churning inside her.

"Well, thanks. The chicken was incredible. I haven't been this full in a long time."

"You're welcome," Rina said, putting the dishes in the sink.

"Come on, let's leave the dishes and sit in the living room. I've got something for you."

"What is it?" Sophie asked, surprised. Interested, she walked into the living room.

Rina's house was small but comfortable. The furnishings were modern with a twist of warmth, not stark like she'd first imagined it would be. Tasteful was the word. She'd painted the walls a cool shade of gray and although the home was older, she'd updated most of it, including the countertops, which were now a dark gray concrete. The finishes on the cabinetry and in the bathrooms were all sleek and smooth. All of the floors had remained wood, although they'd been changed to a light pine because Rina had said she didn't want concrete on her floors. Most of her furnishings fit the modern style. Simple. Neutral. As if to throw people off, though, she'd purchased a zebra print chaise made out of what looked like real zebra fur. She'd placed it, without discretion,

in the living room where it would be noticed from wherever you sat. She loved it, and figured it was just another one of Rina's pieces of art. There on display for all to see.

"Go ahead and sit down," Rina hollered as she walked into her bedroom. "I'll be right there."

Sophie sat down, looking around the room. She couldn't help marveling at the beautiful sculptures placed perfectly throughout the room.

"When did you get this new one?" Sophie yelled, looking at a sculpture of a woman's torso. *The artists conscious simplicity is incredible,* she thought, impressed. The textures the artist used were stirring, as was the attention to detail. She absently wondered if she'd heard of the sculptor, but doubted it.

When Rina came back into the room, she walked over to Sophie, motioning to the new sculpture.

"I picked the sculpture up a week ago. I found it in a gallery not far from here."

"It's delicate," Sophie admired, graciously. Suddenly she noticed the card in Rina's hand. Confused, she asked, "What's in your hand?"

"It's Sheldon Wodden's business card. I've known a few people who have used him and they've all said he's good."

"Uh-huh," she said, taking the card from Rina's outstretched hand. "What's he good at?"

"Good at his job," Rina returned casually.

She looked at Rina, realizing she'd responded a little too casually. Glancing curiously down at the card, the words on it hit her like a ton of bricks.

"Attorney-at-law," Sophie mumbled, reading the card aloud. "He's a divorce lawyer, Rina."

"Yes, among other things, he's a divorce lawyer."

Flustered, she said, "You're rushing me. I need to do this on my own terms."

"You're right," Rina calmly admitted.

"But when you're ready, I wanted you to have someone who knows what he's doing, that's all."

Sophie watched Rina walk over to the couch and sit down, before patting the cushion next to her, an obvious sign she wanted her to come and sit, too. She wasn't ready though.

Sophie looked at her watch. It was nine-thirty, which meant David had already been waiting thirty minutes. She checked her cell phone and remembered she'd turned it off. She hadn't wanted to listen to the constant ringing she was sure would begin not long after nine o'clock.

"What have I done?" She wondered aloud.

"Come and sit down," Rina said, patting the spot on the couch next to her again.

"You're going to be all right."

Slowly walking to the couch, Sophie sat next to Rina. She looked again at the card, then at Rina. "I don't think it's going to be all right, Rina. I have this feeling I'm in trouble."

Rina took her hand, pulling her body to face her.

"Sophie, I love you," Rina blurted.

"I love you, too, but I don't see how that's going to help in this situation. Did you hear me when I said I think I'm in trouble?" she asked, still thinking about what David might do to her.

"No, that isn't what I mean," Rina uttered, looking flustered. "I'm *in* love with you," she repeated purposely. "I have been for years, probably since the day we met."

Sophie stared at her, not quite sure what to say. Had she heard Rina correctly? Did she say she was in love with me? It didn't make any sense she pondered, bewildered.

When she still didn't say anything, Rina continued, "I've wanted to tell you for a long time. In fact, I was going to tell you the first night we went camping, the night you met David."

Sophie couldn't help continuing to gape at her.

"Obviously, I wasn't able to tell you then so I've been waiting for you," Rina finished slowly.

Sophie pulled back her hand, as though she'd been stung. "You've been waiting for me? What are you talking about?" Sophie knew she sounded insensitive but at the same time couldn't believe

Rina was being serious. Her mouth still open, she waited for Rina to tell her it was a joke, but when she didn't, Sophie continued softly, "Rina, I'm not gay. You know that. I don't understand where this has come from." She stopped, realizing for the second time since their friendship began, that Rina was going to cry.

She wanted to kick herself for her lack of compassion.

"Rina," she said, taking Rina's hand back, "Thank you for loving me." She looked into Rina's eyes, hoping she could see she meant every word. "Your friendship is important to me. I'd be lost without you, and I love you, too. I'm not *in* love with you, though, and I never will be. I'm sorry," Sophie finished, wishing in some ways she could be different. Without a doubt, she knew Rina would always be there for her, would always look out for her. Sexually, though, it wasn't an option.

Shaking Rina's hands, she clamored, "Say something. Blink if you can hear me. Please." Rina's face looked frozen in time, like she'd left her body for another planet. "Rina?" She called again.

She watched the life come back into her best friends' eyes, as she blinked her understanding.

Without warning, Rina started laughing. It was a deep, hearty laugh, the kind which comes after someone has said something hysterical. She couldn't remember Rina laughing this way before, and it was contagious. She knew this was serious, knew Rina was probably trying to avoid the situation, but after a while, she couldn't help herself any longer and started laughing, too.

Several minutes later, they both stopped, the experience leaving her feeling incredibly lifted. Rina reached over and hugged her tightly. Sophie returned it happily.

"Oh, Rina, are you—?" She couldn't finish because Rina interrupted her.

"You don't need to apologize or say anything else. I'm the one who's sorry. Let's forget the last several minutes ever happened. Okay?" Rina reached for the tissue box on the coffee table.

Sophie watched her intently as she wiped her eyes and blew her nose. This was a big moment in their relationship, and she didn't want to ruin it or hurt her dearest friend.

When Rina was finished, Sophie clarified. "Rina, are you sure you don't want to talk about this? I mean, you in love with me, that's a big deal."

"Really, hon, as soon as I said the words, I regretted them."

Sophie pouted a little. "Why?"

"Oh, honey, not because I don't think you're wonderful. You are. It's only, I realized I'm in love with you the way a mother loves her child or a sibling loves her sibling. That's all, dear."

"Are you sure?" Sophie asked earnestly.

"Yes, I'm sure." Then abruptly changing the subject, Rina continued, "Now about the lawyer.

The sooner you call him, the better, I think. He's obviously a busy man and you'll want to get the paperwork started as quickly as possible."

Sophie sat back, unable to believe the quickness with which her friend could switch channels. To appease her friend, though, she said, "Of course, I'll call him in the morning."

Sophie decided to wait until she was back in her hotel room to check her phone messages. She stopped at the grocery store to pick up more sleeping pills, deodorant and a few other items she'd forgotten from the house.

She couldn't help contemplating her evening with Rina.

Although she'd seemed fine, Sophie sensed she wasn't.

Feigning fatigue, she left immediately after their bizarre conversation, sensing Rina wanted to be alone. She hoped Rina was all right. Their relationship was important to her. David was on her mind, as well. Images of what he might be doing kept pecking their way in. By the time she'd arrived at her hotel, her head was pounding. She knew anger could only scratch the surface of what he must be feeling. That alone frightened her.

Once she was inside her room, she placed the grocery items on her bed and turned on her phone. Its irritating beep informed her she had voice messages. She also noticed she had four missed calls. *Not terrible*, she thought, shrugging. Maybe Rina was right. Maybe the situation would be fine.

After listening to the messages, though, she realized her worst fears were correct, and maybe even worse than she'd first expected.

CHAPTER 5

"Hello, hon," Rina offered, knocking on Sophie's classroom door. "Are you ready for your first day as a teacher?"

Trying to look happy Sophie answered, "Yes, I'm as ready as I'm going to be."

"Are you sure? Because you look like you're going to pass out." Rina walked in, sitting across the desk from her.

Sophie had already decided if she was going to break away from David she would need Rina's help. Taking a deep breath she started, "David called me last night; four times. At least I know for sure three calls were from him."

"What about the other phone call, why don't you know for sure?"

Tentatively, Sophie answered, "It was a male voice which sounded a little like David, but the number was unavailable. Honestly, I'm not sure."

"Did he say anything?"

Sophie swallowed nervously, "He shouted, 'You're dead Sophie,' before he hung up." Those words had repeated themselves over and over in her mind all night and again all morning. Saying the words out loud caused the hollow pit in her stomach to fill with fear. Feeling lightheaded, she thought she was going pass out until Rina came to her aid.

"Hang in there, hon," Rina twittered sharply, coming around to the other side of the desk and putting an arm on hers. "You're going to be . . ."

"Don't say it again, okay? I'm *not* going to be fine. David doesn't just say things, he means them. He's going to kill me, I know it." She glared up at Rina, daring her to disagree.

"Sweetie, first take a drink." Rina picked up a bottle of water from her desk and handed it to her.

Gratefully, she drank it all.

Pulling over a chair, Rina sat next to her. "Now, listen to me. David is a scary man, in more ways than one. I know. I get it," Rina agreed, putting a hand up to stave off the interruption on Sophie's lips. "I have to tell you, I think he's only trying to frighten you. More importantly, are you sure the last phone call was from him? I mean, really, hon, what if it was just a prank call which coincidentally came on the same night you stood David up?"

Sophie wasn't convinced, and to make matters worse, she could tell Rina wasn't either. She knew Rina was worried too. "I know you're trying to be supportive but, and I think you'll agree, you have no idea what he's going to do, do you?"

"No, I don't, but it takes a sick person to actually kill someone. Do you think he's fucked up enough to kill you?"

"I hope not, but then I had no idea he'd be an abusive, controlling husband either." A breakdown was imminent, growing inside like an uncontrolled tumor. She knew it would reveal itself soon, and couldn't help wondering when.

I've got to be strong, she told herself desperately. The words 'be strong' having become her ritual mantra she tried to focus on them. Seeing Rina at a loss for words didn't help her feel better either.

"Look, I wouldn't have thought he would stick a knife to my neck, but he's been getting progressively worse these last several months. I'm petrified."

"Sweetie," Rina began.

Sophie interrupted, "You have no idea what it's like to wake up every morning, knowing your entire day will be scrutinized, knowing one wrong move will send David into a fit of rage. He yells, throws things and has even forced me to do things . . . I can't go on. Some things are better left unsaid."

"You're right," Rina consoled tenderly. "I had no idea it was that awful between you two. Honestly, I tried not to think about it. I was afraid I'd try to kill the bastard if I knew too much."

"I need you to at least pretend you understand how hard this is for me, getting a job and leaving David like this. A part of me wants to take my money and run, far away. It would be easier, I think," Sophie said. She didn't want her inner hysteria to appear but there it was. She'd spoken aloud what she'd been thinking since the phone calls last night. She wanted to run.

"Honey, I don't think it would be easier to run. You'd always be wondering where he was or if he'd found you. This way, you're facing him head on."

"I appreciate your support. You know I rely on you for good advice and under different circumstances I'd accept your words without question. This time though, my gut is telling me to run, and run far. Rina, you're the only person holding here and, no offense, but I wonder if that's enough.

"Excuse me. I didn't realize you were in here Rina." Phillip faltered, stepping into the classroom. Turning around, he started to leave. "I'll come back later."

"Phillip, it's kind of you to check on Sophie her first day of class. I knew I could count on you to help out the new teacher," Rina stated coyly, winking at Sophie.

Sophie stifled a laugh. In spite of her fear and uneasiness, Rina could still make her smile.

Phillip looked from Rina to Sophie, a smirk on his face. "You know me, Mr. Helpful."

"I'll be sure to put a gold star in your file under Assists fellow faculty."

"Great. I'll expect to see it at my next review." He flashed a quick, genuine smile and left.

"See you, Phillip." Rina laughed before turning back to Sophie, her demeanor serious again.

Sophie was stunned at Rina's quick mood changes. She wondered if Rina shouldn't have been an actress instead of a Vice Principal.

"He's a great guy, that one. It's too bad about his life. He's going through kind of a rough time, too."

"Oh?" Sophie mumbled, interested in hearing more, but not sure she had the stamina.

"You're going to make it through this, sweetie. Trust me. Now, why don't you call your lawyer? You have just enough time before your students arrive." Rina glanced at the clock on the wall. "There are still a few problems I need to get handled this morning. I'll see you later." Rina stood and walked over to the door. Before leaving, she said, "Let's meet for lunch. I want to know how your first day is going and find out if we have any Picasso's or Monet's among us."

Sophie gave a brief smile of affirmation. There was another matter she wanted to talk to Rina about. "Rina?"

Poking her head back in, Rina answered, "Yes, dear?"

"About last night, what you and I talked about? Are we good?"

Rina smirked like she couldn't believe she'd bothered to bring it up. "Whatever happened last night is forgotten," she said and was gone.

Sophie shrugged hoping Rina meant it. She seemed like she did. I guess that's one less worry. Sighing, she pulled Mr. Wodden's card out of her bag and dialed his number.

"I'd like to speak with Mr. Wodden please." Sophie noticed tiny beads of perspiration building at her hairline and on her forehead.

"May I tell him who's calling?" the woman on the other end asked.

"This is Mrs. Berkeley."

"One moment please," the woman responded, putting her on hold.

After several minutes on hold, however, her resolve was all but gone and she was about to hang up when a gruff voice came on the line,

"This is Mr. Wodden. How may I help you?"

Startled, Sophie answered, "Yes, um, a friend of mine gave me your card. She said you handle divorces and I guess I need one."

She heard the gruff voice chuckle, a low baritone, before he returned, "If you're only guessing you need a divorce, perhaps you should call back when you're sure."

She didn't quite know what to say.

"Are you there, Mrs. Berkeley?"

"Yes," she replied flatly.

"Was that a yes, you need a divorce, or yes, you're still on the line?"

"Both," she said automatically, then regained some composure and repeated more firmly, "Yes, I want a divorce. Can you help me?"

"Of course I can, Mrs. Berkeley. Why don't you come over to my office at five o'clock tonight and we'll get started."

"So soon?

"I had a last minute appointment cancellation. They're going to give it another go, which leaves me time to see you."

"Okay, I can be there at five."

"Good. Five o'clock then. I'll let my secretary give you directions. Hold on Mrs. Berkeley until she picks up."

The secretary came back on the line and gave directions.

Sophie hung up in a hurry. Her stomach was churning. Barely making it into the bathroom, she ran into the first stall and threw up. After splashing water on her face, she arrived back in her classroom just as the bell rang.

Time for class, she thought, still feeling queasy.

Mr. Wodden's office was small but cozy. At the moment, Sophie was sitting on a soft, camel-colored leather chair flipping magazine pages.

The receptionist said, "He'll be another few minutes."

The waiting room looked like a personal library with books from floor to ceiling. There were a couple of coffee tables, some side tables with lamps on them and a ceiling fan swirling above. The sofas and chairs were all different colors yet somehow matched the room perfectly. Comfortable, safe.

The intercom buzzed at the secretary's desk.

Sophie watched the heavyset, jolly- looking, older woman with white, curly hair talk into the receiver, hang up, pull out a file, then stand and look directly at her.

"Mr. Wodden will see you now," she said, removing her oval, silver, reading glasses and setting them on the desk. "Follow me, please."

Sophie stood and followed the woman, spellbound by her bouncy curls.

"Here you go." She smiled, opening the door, gesturing to walk in ahead of her. Swiftly the woman followed handing a file to the man sitting behind a huge desk, his back to her.

"Have a seat, Mrs. Berkeley," he insisted deeply, not turning around to face her.

"I'll be done in a moment."

Sophie anxiously looked around his office but there wasn't much to see except a few certificates hanging at different angles on the walls. The ceiling lights were blaring down on her reminding Sophie of what an interrogation area might be like. She noticed the vast contrast between his personal office space and the reception area. Where his office was cold, the reception area was full of warmth.

Mr. Wodden swung around, a bright smile on his face.

Blinding, she thought. *His teeth are really white.* She sensed she would like him, though.

"Mrs. Berkeley." he started, sticking out his slender hand, "It's nice to meet you." His bright brown eyes shimmered with kindness.

She was surprised by his appearance. Because of his gruff voice, she expected a tall, bigger man, and he was exactly the opposite. He looked like he was only about five foot four and didn't look like he weighed more than one hundred fifty pounds. The huge difference between what she thought he'd look like and what he was reminded her of the wizard from *The Wizard of Oz*. Although his face looked young, he had salt and pepper hair and a thick mustache which swallowed his top lip.

She noticed he was waiting patiently, with his hand outstretched, so Sophie put her hand in his and he shook it vigorously.

"It's nice to meet you, too," she said in a small voice.

"Have a seat," he offered, taking his.

Sitting, she waited for him to lead the way, "The first thing I need to know is if this divorce has been agreed upon by both you and your husband."

"No, it hasn't, and I don't think my husband is going to take it very well either," she rushed. *I've got to calm down*, she vowed, taking a deep breath. She waited while he wrote something down.

He made a guttural noise before he continued, "Do you feel you're in danger?"

She watched him closely, wondering how much to tell him. Making her decision, she lied, "No, I don't," and hoped she sounded convincing.

Immediately Mr. Wodden put down his pen and clasped his hands together as though waiting for her to elaborate.

Floundering nervously, Sophie picked at a nonexistent piece of lint from her pants.

"Mrs. Berkeley," he questioned, after a few seconds.

"I can handle him." Sophie responded firmly.

He waited another brief moment before picking up the papers in front of him and eyeing her speculatively asked, "Would you like me to have the divorce papers delivered to your husband for you? It wouldn't be a problem. It's quite normal, actually."

"Thank you but no, I want to give them to him. He needs to know I'm serious about this." As timid as she was about everything going on in her life right now, she believed he deserved her to be up front with him about what she was doing.

"If you're sure," he conceded, visibly doubtful. You'll need to check your reason for the divorce and sign at the bottom."

She took the papers, checked the box next to *Irreconcilable Differences*, signed them quickly and handed them back to him. She tried to smile courageously.

Checking over the papers, he grunted. "Good."

She could tell he wanted to say more but was plainly keeping his opinions to himself out of professional courtesy.

"We're almost done. Let me make a copy of this," he stated. He turned his back on her, apparently making a copy. When he turned back around, he handed her what looked like the original. "You're done, Mrs. Berkeley."

"Is that it? There isn't more to it?"

"Actually, it's the beginning. He needs to sign those. Then we need to discuss how you're going to divide your possessions, bank accounts and such."

"He can have it all. It's all his anyway. I don't want any of it." Sitting back in her chair, she crossed her legs certainly. She didn't want anything more to do with him.

"You say that now but perhaps in a day or two you'll change your mind. If something happens, feel free to call me." He placed his copies back in the folder his secretary had brought in before he continued.

"Now, concerning the money, the fee to process and file your divorce papers is three hundred dollars."

Sophie nodded she understood.

He continued, "If, for some reason, we have to go to court to divide assets or contest a dispute, the fees will increase."

"Sure, Mr. Wodden. Makes sense." She hoped David never found out about the inheritance money her aunt left her. *It might get ridiculous-ugly then*, she thought.

As if reading her mind, he sat back down. "I'm going to ask this bluntly, Mrs. Berkeley. Is there anything of *yours* he might want? It goes both ways, you know." His deep baritone voice seemed to shake her core.

Perhaps it wasn't smart, leaving out that she didn't need his money, because she had plenty of her own. How could she explain everything to him, though, without going into immense detail? To her, it made perfect sense. She didn't want to tell anyone else about the money. Her life with David had taught her to share as little as possible. This money was her secret treasure. Something of hers he couldn't touch, squander or use for his own selfish means. And, if it came to it, the money was her way of escaping David. Nervously, she uttered, "Besides me, no." She glanced at her pants, hoping he wouldn't notice her voice had changed a little.

Mr. Wodden didn't seem convinced. "Care to elaborate?"

She laughed uncomfortably, "No, not now anyway. He owns his own restaurant. He's part owner of a contracting company. He's well off, which is all I'm going to say." She tried to sound firm.

"Fine. Get back to me in a week, week and a half and let me know what's going on." He stood and stuck out his hand again. "Good-bye for now, Mrs. Berkeley."

She took his hand, saying, "Good-bye Mr. Wodden, and thank you for your time."

She gave the old receptionist a check from her personal account before she left.

Out in the fresh air, she happily repeated her 'be strong' mantra.

Maybe I can do this, she thought.

CHAPTER 6

Sophie nervously glanced into her rearview mirror again, and saw the same white car from the hotel was still there. She decided to see if she could lose it by quickly changing lanes, and speeding up. She looked back, breathing a sigh of relief. The white car hadn't changed lanes and was quite a ways back. We must have been heading in the same direction.

Seeing the sign for her exit, she crossed three lanes of traffic just barely making it to the exit ramp. Checking her rearview mirror, she became terrified to see the white car behind her again.

"It could still be a coincidence. Stay calm," she said out loud.

At the light she took a right then a left heading for the school at the end of the street. She drove as quickly as she could through the residential neighborhood with students everywhere.

The car was still following her.

Okay, she thought, *now is the time to panic.*

She turned left into her reserved parking space reaching for her cell phone with the other hand. Twisting around, she faced the man in the white car as he drove by. She stared at him, trying to see clearly what he looked like. His hair was brown and he had a dark colored jacket on.

He was looking at her as well, grinning wickedly, and then he looked away, increasing his speed as he continued down the street. He took a left and was gone.

Definitely no coincidence, she thought. He was following me; the question, though, is why? It wasn't David, so who was it?

"Is everything all right?"

Sophie jumped, letting out a loud scream. She turned around and saw a man's face at her window.

"Don't," he yelled.

"Phillip, is that you?" She hit the end button on her cell phone and rolled down her window.

"Sorry. I didn't recognize you for a second."

Phillip, clearly embarrassed, grinned sheepishly. "Are you okay?"

"Yes, I'm fine," she replied anxiously, getting out of her car.

Phillip stepped onto the sidewalk. He stood there waiting for her.

Oh this is great, she thought, mortified. He's going to think I'm nuts. She locked her car and stepped onto the sidewalk next to him. Casually looking around, trying to calm her nerves, she noticed the car next to hers. It was white.

"Is this your car? Did you just get here," she questioned, incredulously. *Was he the one who was following her*, she wondered?

"Yes, it's my car and no, I didn't just get here. I've been here a while. I saw you pull in."

"If you've been here a while, what were you doing? Why didn't you go inside?"

Phillip smirked a little. "Well, if you must know, I was listening to a book on CD. Didn't you see me?" He had a bewildered look on his face.

"No, I was . . ." she trailed off, because she noticed his jacket. It was dark—dark blue to be exact. Still surveying him, she also realized his hair was the same color as the man in the car who had been following her. Frightened anger welled up inside of her.

"How dare you follow me," she yelled.

Perturbed, he responded, "I *didn't* follow you. I've been right here a while, probably thirty minutes or more." He started to walk away but must have thought better of it, because he turned back around. "Why would you think I was following you?"

Scared and confused, she knew she was being irrational. "A white car followed me here. The man inside had the same color hair as you, the same color jacket, only maybe not as . . . oh, I don't know," she cried, to upset to care what he thought. Finding a semblance of control although her voice shaking, she muttered, "Sorry. When I saw your car I got upset. I'm sure you can tell I'm still upset. I shouldn't have accused you, though. Again, I apologize."

Phillip walked back over to her. His eyes softened and he seemed like he was going to comfort her. Instead he kindly stated, "Sophie, I'm telling you, it wasn't me. You pulled in next to me. I noticed you sitting there, clutching your cell phone, and thought you might need some help." Dejectedly, he walked backward, toward the school entrance. "I'll see you inside." Turning on his heels, he quickly walked away.

Sophie was eating lunch in the teacher's lounge, trying to avoid eye contact with anyone. She was sure Phillip had told everyone what a nut she was and couldn't blame him, but no one seemed to be acting strange toward her.

Two teachers had come in, said hello to her and then sat at another table. The room had four round tables spaced randomly throughout. Two moderately sized windows, a refrigerator, a microwave and several countertops, to be used for getting a meal ready. There was a large rectangular table under the windows with a paper cutter sitting studiously atop it as well as several different colors of construction paper.

Trying to act normal, she mournfully put another bite of salad in her mouth as Rina walked in.

Catching her attention, Rina sat next to her and asked, "Salad again. Do you have more bad news for me?"

Sophie swallowed. "Well, I accused Phillip of following me to school this morning. Is that bad news?"

Slumping a little, Rina questioned, "Why would you accuse him of following you?"

Blandly, she told her what happened.

"Do you think David is having you followed?"

"It's possible," she answered wearily.

"Did you use a credit card to pay for your room?"

"You know I did. You were with me." Then it occurred to her where Rina was going with her questions.

"Do you think he found me through my credit card?"

"Of course. With all the technology out there, definitely."

Alarmed, Sophie asked, "What should I do?"

"I think you should switch hotels, or come and stay with me."

"I'm not staying with you, Rina. I don't want him to hurt you."

"Come on, hon, he's not going to hurt me. I'd beat his cheating, ah, butt to a pulp."

She let out a slight giggle at Rina's clever blustering. Shaking her head determinedly, she went on, "Maybe I should call the police."

"A good idea, dear. For now, though, let's change the subject and talk shop. How are your classes going this morning?"

She breathed a sigh of relief. She didn't want to talk about David anymore and knew Rina was trying to help take her mind off her problems.

"They're good. A little rocky, but better than yesterday and the day before. I'm getting the hang of it. I like teaching," she said, while thinking to herself, *if my first few days are any indication of the way teaching is going to be, I've found my niche. I've enjoyed myself more in the past three days than I have in the past two years!*

"Hello? You there?"

"Yeah. I was thinking," she responded sheepishly.

"Well, don't hurt yourself, hon," Rina laughed jokingly before continuing, "I've got to run. We'll talk more later. Okay?"

"Sure. See you."

It was the end of the day. Contentedly, Sophie was relaxing at her desk. She wasn't ready to go back out into the world yet. She was at peace here, as though in a bubble, protected from her problems.

Since high school, she'd wanted to be a teacher. Now she was one, the reality was far better than she expected. She enjoyed planning the lessons and thinking of ways to inspire her students to love art the way she did.

She had to admire her classroom. It was large. On one side were desks for the students and on the other side were twenty-five casels, all standing, regally awaiting the next masterpiece to be painted. Her desk was in the middle of the two sections, with a large chalkboard covering the entire wall behind it and a plethora of paints, brushes, chalk, pencils and all manner of art supplies bulging out of honey-glazed oak cupboards on the opposite wall. Windows covered the other two walls, allowing natural light to illuminate the room.

Putting away some paperwork, she prepared to leave. She picked up her purse and walked over to the door, realizing sadly, she had to pop her own bubble. She knew she couldn't stay in dream land forever. Turning out the light, she closed the door.

She'd already determined she wanted to find another way to get to her car. The school was huge and confusing. Most of the walls were covered with lockers, although above them they were painted off-white. There were lights spaced intermittently throughout where the walls met the ceiling.

The floor was a white glazed marble with flecks of black, gold and red. Only the white signs with a listing of classroom numbers and department information helped a person know where they were. It wasn't that the school couldn't afford more but they chose to spend their money on the students and their needs. This made it difficult to find her way around hence, her need to take a different route to her car.

Turning to her left, she walked to the end of the hall, and took a right. Near the end, she was surprised to discover the theater. In no rush to get back to her hotel room, she decided to have a look inside.

She was impressed.

No expense had been spared in here. It was magnificent, probably seating five hundred or more. The chairs were thick and covered in a dark burgundy material. Wood railing deliberately placed in large rectangles covered all of the walls. The wood was ornately carved and stained in dark-mahogany, as was the ceiling.

She was shocked to see hanging from the center of the ceiling was a large glass chandelier. She couldn't help but draw in her breath at the beauty of it all. It was without question, breathtaking.

Along the front three rows of seats were students watching several other students on stage. They were trying to learn a song. Intrigued, she sat down to listen. Surprised at how comfortable the chairs were, she leaned back, allowing herself to take in the whole scene better. One of the students suddenly jumped up to make a comment. She recognized the voice, but couldn't place which student he was. An instant later, she realized he wasn't a student at all.

It was Phillip, Theater Director and snubbed rescuer.

Admittedly, she had a physical attraction for him. Her life might be in a wreck right now, but she wasn't blind. He was ruggedly handsome, with thick, brown hair and hazel eyes, lined with long, dark lashes. His nose was slightly crooked, which looked perfect on his face. He had full lips surrounded by dark facial stubble.

Over six feet tall, he was about the same height as David. The similarities, however, ended there. Where David was thin, Phillip was muscular. He wasn't big like a bodybuilder, she reasoned. He looked more like he led an active lifestyle.

At the moment, he wasn't wearing the jacket he'd had on earlier today. Instead he had on a long-sleeve button up shirt. He'd rolled the sleeves up to his thick biceps and his shirt had been untucked.

Amused, she watched him run his fingers through his hair. *He's beautiful*, she admired.

Scooting down in her seat, she let her head rest against the back of it. Comfortable, she enjoyed watching him as well as his students. She wondered what it would be like to spend time with him. Scolding herself, she tried to think of something else. The last man she'd been this drawn to turned out to be a lunatic.

I've got to be careful. Plainly, I can't trust myself.

Wallowing in her self-pity, she closed her eyes and fell asleep.

"You look peaceful, lying there. You must not have a care in the world."

Sophie heard him talking, but his face was shrouded in darkness.

"Don't worry, Sophie darling, I'm going to make you pay! I'm going to make you suffer, like she suffered!"

Alarmed, she opened her eyes and sat up. Looking around, she tried to find him. She knew the voice had sounded like David. She didn't see him, though. Everything seemed normal.

I must've been dreaming. *Relax*, she told herself.

Placing her bag over her shoulder, she stood to go. On stage, only two students remained. She could hear what they were saying, and laughed inwardly. *It sounds like they're doing a romantic scene*, she thought, mortified. She could hear some of the students in the seats below laughing.

Smiling, she picked up her books. Stepping into the aisle, she smacked hard into something.

"Ouch," she cried, her books tumbling to the floor.

"What in the . . ." she demanded, looking up.

Startled by the realization she'd smacked into someone instead of something, she whispered, "Oh, it's you." Embarrassed by thoughts of her encounter with him earlier, and what she'd been thinking about him before she fell asleep, a blush started to color her face.

Grateful for the darkness, she quickly bent down to pick up her books.

"Damn. Sorry," Philip said seriously, bending down with her to help with her books. He was so close she could feel his breath on her cheek.

Trying to keep her voice from quivering, she returned, "It's no problem. I should've been watching where I was going." Standing, she tried to squeeze past him, but he stood as well, blocking her escape.

"Well, I've got to go," she said, trying once again to get past him. He had a mischievous look on his face and a gigantic grin. He was making her nervous.

"Would you mind helping me with something first," he asked, putting a hand on one of her arms.

"Uh, help you with what?" she returned nervously.

"I need you to help me show these students how to do this scene."

"No way, I couldn't. Trust me, you don't want my help," she rushed, laughing uncomfortably, trying to get past him again.

Walking past her, Phillip purposefully headed down toward the stage. For a split second, she thought she was going to make her getaway.

She was wrong.

Phillip turned back toward her and hollered loudly, "Come on, Mrs. Berkeley. I need your help, but more importantly, these students need your help. Don't let them down."

All of the students heard him, and turned in the direction of his voice. When they noticed he was looking toward the back of the theater, they followed his gaze. All eyes were on her.

"What do you all think? Should Mrs. Berkeley help me show you all how to do this scene?" Phillip continued, hopping up onto the stage. He stuck one hand out, as if reaching toward her and put his other hand over his heart.

"Please, Mrs. Berkeley. *I* need you," he chortled dramatically.

Oh, he's good, she thought. But not good enough.

"No thanks, Dr. Hansen. I'm sure you can find someone else to help you."

"Mrs. Berkeley, you'd be doing us all a big favor, and," he paused before saying the last sentence slowly, deliberately, "I believe you owe me one."

She turned around and looked at him, trying to read into his words. She knew he was talking about what she'd done this morning, but didn't know if he was seeking revenge or if he only wanted her help and needed an innocent favor. Her decision was made for her though, because the students all started chanting, "Berkeley! Berkeley! Berkeley!"

"Fine," she whispered fiercely, as she walked toward the stage.

Phillip joined in with the students, clapping heartily, then strutted over to a set of stairs leading up to the stage and stuck out his hand.

She ignored it, walking coldly past him, toward the middle of the stage. *He's definitely getting me back for earlier today*, she thought angrily. Turning toward him, she smiled sweetly. "Where do you want me?"

Phillip walked over to her, all business now, and said, "You'll need to get rid of these." Prying the books out of her hands, he slipped the bag off her shoulder, setting them on a sofa situated on the stage. He walked back over to her, taking her by the shoulders and moving her over a little, the all too familiar smirk on his face the whole time.

Turning his back to her, he faced the students which were still on stage, talking to them.

"This is a romantic moment. Jesse and Josephine have proclaimed their feelings for each other. They can't deny them anymore. They don't want to." He started walking back toward her while he continued, "They're done talking. This is about how they're feeling." Phillip's words were full of emotion, passion.

She could understand why he was the Theater Director.

All of a sudden, he turned around and grabbed her, pulling her tightly against his chest. She stood there, her heart pounding rapidly, unsure of what to do. His finger gently lifted her chin, giving her no choice, but to stare at his face. She tried to avoid his eyes, but couldn't resist the warmth in them.

Without realizing it, she wrapped her arms around his waist and parted her lips, her body waiting for the kiss she knew was coming. In the back of her mind, a tiny voice whispered she should turn and run, but she didn't want to listen. Her body responded to the fire she sensed coming from him. In the moment, she decided she could stay here, with him, forever.

She forgot she was on a stage, forgot the students watching them. All she could think about was Phillip, and how amazing his arms were. She drew in her breath as he leaned down, his lips parting as well. She raised her mouth to meet his, closing her eyes.

And then he released her.

Gently pulling her arms from his waist, he cleared his throat. Their eyes locked for a brief moment before he turned away, once again talking to the students on stage.

"Body language can say volumes more than words can. You've just got to feel it, to mean it." He glanced back at her, then walked over to the students and continued talking.

She stood there dazed a moment, full realization of what she'd almost done swallowing her whole. She looked over at Phillip, then down at the students, feeling her face getting redder by the second.

One of the female students yelled, "Whoa, Mrs. Berkeley. That was hawt!"

Finally responding to the voice inside her head, she grabbed her books and her bag. A sob in her throat, she ran off the stage and out of the theater. Just outside the doors, she leaned against a wall to catch her breath. Embarrassed and angry, she decided she was tired of being made a fool of.

Vowing to change, she walked resolutely to her car.

"No," Sophie groaned softly, looking at the clock. It was six-thirty a.m. "Time to get up," she moaned, but it was the last thing she wanted to do like doing. She rolled over, away from the glare of the clock, willing herself to go back to sleep. It didn't work. Instead, images of her embarrassing encounter with Phillip popped into her head.

There's a great reason to get up, she thought irritably, pulling the covers back and swinging her legs over the edge of the bed. She stood quickly, but immediately had to sit down again, a sudden wave of nausea washing over her.

"Great," she whispered, hurrying into the bathroom, stubbing her toe on the edge of a wall as she turned the corner. "Ouch!" She wasn't used to her new hotel room.

She'd switched last night, paying cash from her personal account for the week. She hoped this would keep whomever David had hired to follow her away for a while. The voice in the back of her brain was back, telling her she was being naïve again.

I can't help it, she thought, her head hanging directly over the toilet bowl. I want him to get over it. I want to be free. Her stomach seemed better for the moment. Wiping her mouth with toilet paper, she threw it disgustedly into the bowl and flushed. Standing, she realized she needed to pee. Once she was done, she walked over to the sink to wash her hands. Staring at her pallid complexion in the mirror, she wondered what could be wrong with her. She didn't puke.

Having no answer, she pushed it aside as a mild case of food poisoning, and walked over to turn on the shower. Walking back to the sink, she pulled her toothbrush and toothpaste out of a bag and scrubbed her teeth.

CHAPTER 7

The next several days went by smoothly. Sophie was exhilarated by teaching, her students, the research, and her painting. She'd missed spending time in a studio. She also realized how much she'd missed spending time with other people, without worrying what David would think, or if he'd be mad or trying to keep track of every second of her day.

David was still in the back of her mind like a sore festering but she tried not to think about him. Instead she relished every moment, unsure of how long it would last. Her only problem had been the stomach virus she had.

At first she'd thought it was food poisoning but it had been going on for too long. It was strange, though, because other than feeling a lot more tired and the occasional need to vomit, she didn't feel sick.

She'd vocalized this to Rina after she'd thrown up once while Rina had been in the bathroom with her. Rina had said it was probably stress-related and she needed to see a doctor. Finally she conceded and made an appointment. It was for the following Tuesday afternoon.

Done, she thought, putting the last paper she had to grade in a file and locked it.

"Are you about finished?" Rina asked teasingly.

"Oh, you startled me," Sophie exclaimed.

"Crap," Rina quipped, leaning against the door, with a smile dancing on her mouth.

"Listen, some of the other faculty are getting together tonight for dinner and drinks, maybe even some dancing. You interested, dear?"

"Oh, wow, you know, it sounds like fun, but with this stomach virus, or whatever it is, I don't feel up to it," she answered. She could tell Rina was disappointed by the look on her face. "Honestly, I don't think my queasy stomach could handle the smells of a restaurant, let alone the smoke at a club."

Rina looked ready to interrupt. Hurrying on, she continued, "Thanks for asking. Some other time, okay?" She walked over to Rina, who'd put a hand on her hip, frustration oozing from every pore and put a hand on her shoulder. "You go. I know you could use it. Have fun, and try to stay out of trouble," she finished, smiling.

"Are you sure?" she asked, a flicker of relief passing over her face.

"Absolutely," Sophie said seriously. "I'll be mad if you don't go."

"Great," Rina said, beaming at Sophie's encouragement. They started walking together, presumably in the direction of their cars when Rina stopped, turned to her and said, "Speaking of mad, when are you going to give you-know-who the you-know-what you've had in your bag for the past several days?"

She knew exactly what she was talking about and responded, "I was thinking I'd call him tonight and see if I could set up a time to meet him."

"You know he's not going to be happy when he sees you've brought him divorce papers. Do you want me to go with you," she questioned, moving again.

Following Rina's cue, she caught up to her quickly and said firmly, "No. I want to do this one on my own. I'm trying to be strong."

Rina stopped again. "You know I'm all for your standing on your own but, in this case, I think some support might be good."

"Rina, I'm surprised at you," she said, shocked. "I would've thought you'd be proud of me, doing this on my own."

"Oh, honey, I *am* proud of you." Rina shrugged as she started walking again.

"It's only, I want you to be safe and . . ." Rina paused not finishing her sentence.

"You think I'll chicken out. Right?" She couldn't help but smile, even if she was starting to feel upset. "Trust me, I'm going to give them to him and I going to do it alone. I want to show him I can make it without him."

"Great, sweetie. Just be careful, though," Rina responded, wrapping her arm around Sophie's waist. "Now, I've got one more thing to talk to you about."

She gave her a blank look. Sophie had no clue what Rina was going to say.

"Come on. I can't believe you never told me you liked to act." Rina laughed.

Realization sprang over her, followed by an immediate gush of blood pummeling her head. She stammered, "Wh-What have you heard? Nothing happened."

"That's not the way I hear it. I've been hearing rumors of romance and hot almost-kissing action floating through the halls."

Sophie didn't say anything. Her heart pounded loudly in her ears, making it difficult to hear. *The nerve of him*, she thought, irritated.

"Is it true you've already fallen for another man? Our handsome Dr. Phillip Hansen maybe?"

Feeling hostile, she said, "He's the only thing I don't like about this place. You realize he's torturing me, don't you? You know, because I accused him of following me a while ago."

"Torturing is a strong word," Rina said, then lowering her voice, she choked out, "What has he done? I mean other than almost making out with you?" Rina doubled over with laughter.

"You think this is funny? He hasn't said a word to me since that afternoon. Whenever our paths cross, he smiles this goofy smile and winks at me." Unable to resist Rina's contagious laughter, Sophie started laughing, too. "It isn't funny. I'd like to smack him." Sophie giggled, trying to regain her composure.

"You're right, Sophie, dear. I'm sorry," Rina said, wiping tears off her face.

"Uh-huh, I can tell."

They'd reached Rina's car. Watching her get in, she said good-bye, then turned toward her car. She'd taken three steps when she felt a hand on her shoulder. Her heart leapt into her throat, as she stopped and spun around. It was only Phillip.

"Hello," she said crisply.

"Are you going tonight," he asked.

She shook her head no, knowing he was talking about the dinner and dancing plans. Turning around, she started to walk away. Phillip placed a hand on her arm. Angry, she whipped back around, and shouted, "Stop touching me!" Spinning back around, she hurried toward her car. He must think I'm a loon. She could imagine how strange she must seem.

When she was almost to her car she heard him say, "What did I do?" She figured it was a rhetorical question since she'd told him what he did. He'd touched her.

Then she heard him say, "Sorry."

Sophie climbed into her car and drove away. Glancing once in her rearview mirror but was unable to see him. "Yeah, he thinks I'm nuts," she muttered, knowing he was probably right and feeling a strange pang of sadness. It hurt a little to know he probably wouldn't ever touch her or talk to her again.

Once back in her hotel room, she called David. She didn't think about it, just dialed.

"Sophie, how nice of you to call," he cooed sardonically.

"Hello, David. How are you," she responded nervously, unable to think of anything else to say.

"Great. Just wondering where you are and if I'm ever going to have my wife back."

Not wanting to go there, she said, "I wanted to get together, to . . . you know, talk."

"Sure. Absolutely," he drawled. "I'll be here at the house waiting for you at one o'clock tomorrow afternoon."

"Fine. I'll see you then." She quickly closed her cell phone and threw it on the bed. She was uneasy and knew it was because David had sounded entirely too calm, too casual.

Experience had taught her it was the calm before the storm.

Sophie closed the door and turned around, listening for any sound. The house was quiet. She wondered if David was home; her watch said five after one. She glanced over at the foyer table and noticed sitting on top were the perfect yet, to her, repulsive red roses.

Feeling nervous to go in, although it was still technically her house, she stood there and glanced into the rooms she could see from where she stood. The house looked clean. She couldn't help but wonder who had cleaned it, but decided she didn't care."

"David," she finally called loudly.

He appeared from around a corner in the dining room.

"Hello, Sophie. Long time no see," he said, venom oozing from his lips as he leaned against one of the beige painted entry walls.

"David," she yelped, instinctively wrapping one hand around her throat.

"What you got there," he asked, pointing at the papers she clutched in her other hand.

She intuitively realized she'd made a terrible mistake coming to see him alone. His eyes gave him away. His demeanor was calm, but she saw the fury in his eyes.

"Oh, these. Nothing important. You know what? I just remembered . . ." She paused, trying to think of something to say. "Um, I need to go." Quickly, she turned and opened the door wanting to get out of there as soon as possible. She heard him come up behind her, reach above her and push the door closed, then watched him reach down and lock it.

"No, Sophie. Stay and show me what you came to show me," he said softly.

She knew she was trapped, and reacted as any trapped animal would. She turned to face him, uncontrollable rage welling up inside her. She slammed the divorce papers into his chest.

"These are divorce papers," she yelled, bravely glaring into his eyes. "You need to sign them and mail them to the address—" She stopped because David grabbed her by the back of the hair and pulled down hard. "Ouch! Let go of my hair! You're hurting me," she cried and then screamed. She grabbed his hands, trying to force him to let go.

He stood there, staring hard at her, a steely, malicious look on his face. She could tell he enjoyed watching her struggle.

Still feeling some rage in her, she tried to knee him in the groin, but he anticipated it and turned his body, her knee landing in his thigh. This only seemed to infuriate him further because he pulled down harder on her hair. The pain shot through her like a bolt of lightning, sending her body instantly to the floor. He followed her down, straddling her.

Speaking slowing, but with his voice full of malice, he asked, "Did you honestly believe you could come into my house and give me divorce papers?" He stuck one knee on her chest, pressing down hard. She could barely breathe.

Frantically, she tried to push him off her. "Please, David. Stop. Please." She whispered, barely able to get the words out.

He looked down at her saying fiercely, "You ungrateful, stupid bitch. You'll be more than begging when I get through with you." He quickly got off her, but before she could catch her breath, he grabbed her by the back of her hair again, whipping her around, as he began dragging her up the stairs.

"No, David! Don't." She tried to use her legs to climb the stairs because they were rubbing into her back. Her head pulsed with pain from where he still had a hold of her hair. She literally thought her hair would rip out at any minute. At the top of the stairs, she had momentary relief.

She screamed once again, "Let me go. You're hurting me."

"I'm hurting you. I'm hurting you," he spat. He was breathing hard, but continued as he dragged her into the bedroom. "Do you know what you've done to me? The embarrassment you've caused?" He stopped talking a moment, roughly picking her up before depositing her, like a rag doll, onto the bed.

She looked into his eyes and saw the wild furor there. There was no talking to him. He was too far gone. He straddled her once again, then with one hand grabbed both of hers and held them above her head. She tried to squirm, but he slapped her hard across the face.

"Hold still or I'll finish what I started." As he said this, he looked over at the bedside table. She followed his eyes, seeing the filet knife sitting on it.

"No," she cried, terrified.

"You're my wife. You're supposed to do what I say, when I say it. I want a baby and we're going to make one right now." To prove his point, he ripped open her blouse.

"No! No! We're through," she screamed, understanding what he was going to do.

"Don't tell me no," he yelled again, slapping her face harder this time. Reaching under her, he undid her bra.

He still had both of her hands above her head.

Desperately, she tried lifting her body to move him off, but her movement only excited him. She could tell by the bulge growing on her stomach. She was disgusted and afraid, but amid her fear, she had a moment of lucidity. She stopped moving and closed her eyes, letting the tears flow, hoping he was so aroused he'd only be happy with the sudden change in her.

"Better," he said, obviously pleased. He moved to one side and put his hand up her skirt. "Doesn't it feel good?" He cooed.

Sophie bit her lip, trying not to yell.

"Now, will you be a good girl while I get my pants off?"

She kept her eyes shut tightly, unable to speak.

"Sophie," he barked. "I'm going to let go of your hands. Why don't you take off your panties while I take off my pants?"

She still didn't move. Without warning, he smacked her again in the face.

"Open your eyes, Sophie! *Now!*"

She did as he said, knowing there wasn't anything else she could do.

He let go of her hands, then climbed off the bed and started undoing his pants.

"Take them off," he yelled. She silently obeyed.

"Now lie back down."

Sophie did as commanded, staring at him acceptably, while coyly lifting her hands above her head. She could tell he relished his pretend power over her. She watched him get completely naked, and slowly climb back on the bed. He lifted her already somewhat raised skirt and started to position himself to enter her. She gingerly glanced over at the bedside table, making sure he wasn't watching her face.

There, next to the knife she saw what she was looking for. During her moment of lucidity, she'd remembered he kept his precious restaurant award there and she knew it was made of solid granite.

I won't touch the knife, even if killing him would be exactly what he deserves, but the restaurant award will work, she thought bravely. She looked back at him and saw his head was down.

He was moaning. "You want it; you know you do."

Swiftly, she grabbed the granite award, and with both hands smashed it down on his head with all of the force she could muster.

He shrieked in agony and grabbed his head before going silent. Adrenaline was pumping through her veins and with the strength of a lion; she shoved him off her with such force he rolled off the bed and onto the floor. Without a second thought, she jumped up, ran down the stairs, unlocked the door and ran out of the house, hoping she'd never step foot inside his house again.

Once inside her hotel room, she locked the door.

Hefting one of the chairs, she placed it in front of the door. Still not feeling completely safe, she put the other chair in front of her door as well. Quickly undressing, she threw her clothes in the trash can, revolted by the touch and smell of them. She wanted to burn them, but knew it wasn't possible. Instead she turned on the shower and climbed in, letting the hot water pour over her body. She was frightened, but at the same time, invigorated. She'd rescued herself from an awful situation.

On her own!

She wondered briefly, if she should call Rina and tell her what happened but decided not to. Telling Rina would cause her to rush over in an effort to comfort her. She didn't want the comfort now.

"What should I do?" she whispered. Nothing came to mind. She knew she could call the police, but she'd seen enough television to know there wasn't a whole lot they could do for her. He hadn't killed her, after all, and she was still his wife. She knew the bruises on her face would help, but not enough to hold him for long. She finished her shower, still unsure about what to do. One thing was for sure. She was exhausted. Pulling on a pair of pajamas, she climbed into bed and stayed there until Monday morning.

CHAPTER 8

Sophie didn't like going to the doctor. She reasoned half the time they had no idea what they were talking about, and the other half, when they did know, it was never good news. At the moment, she was sitting on an exam table, waiting for the doctor to come back and talk to her.

The room was formal, equipped with an examination table, a computer, some cabinets, a sink and magazines. The walls were a pale yellow. No framed pictures hung from the walls, but someone had taped a few posters on them instead. A cute, cuddly kitten, hanging from a tree branch with a caption underneath, which read, **Hang in there!**, and others along the same inspirational line. She read them, trying to distract herself.

They weren't doing the trick.

Dr. Johnson had asked a bunch of questions she thought were unnecessary, including why she had a bruise on her cheek, although she knew he was just doing his job. Then he'd asked her to go to the lab and have her blood drawn, which she'd done. Dr. Johnson had told her he wanted to check her white cell count and a few other things, but hadn't told her what.

What could it be, she thought. She worried she might know, prayed she was wrong. *Please be wrong,* she was thinking, as Dr. Johnson knocked before coming in.

"Well, I've got your blood work back," he said with a smile.

"And," she asked, trying to urge him along.

"And you don't have a stomach virus or anything else wrong with you."

"I don't. Then why am I throwing up? Why do I feel nauseated?"

"Well," he said, still smiling, "You're pregnant. About five or six weeks along, I'd say."

"What? No," she blurted, too shocked to say more.

"You had no idea? Wasn't this planned?"

"No, well, I mean, my husband and I had been trying." She was physically incapable to elaborate, all of her newly found courage disappearing. Without realizing it, she crumpled into a ball on the examination table and began sobbing uncontrollably. Her heart ached with the pain of hating the man she loved.

Dr. Johnson rushed over to her and said, "Mrs. Berkeley - Sophie, it'll be all right. If you don't want this baby, we've caught the pregnancy in time; there are alternatives."

His words only made her feel worse.

"Sophie, why don't you go home and talk to your husband about it. I'll have my nurse give you some information. You can call me when you've made a decision. Sophie?"

She heard him talking to her but it didn't register.

"Doctor, what's wrong? Is she going to be all right," the nurse questioned professionally.

He uttered something inaudible to the nurse. Then Sophie heard the door close.

The nurse came to her. "It's going to be all right, Mrs. Berkeley. Dr. Johnson went to get you something to help you relax. We'll call your husband. You're in no condition to drive. The doc may need to admit you. Don't worry. He'll take care of you."

The nurse's words resonated deep within Sophie's brain. *Dr. Johnson was going to call David!*

"No," she cried, sitting up. Rapidly, she wiped her tears with her sleeve. "I'm fine," she lied. "There's no need to call my husband. I don't want him to know about the pregnancy yet." Then more earnestly she urged, "Please, tell Dr. Johnson right now not to call him. I mean it! David cannot know." She hopped off the exam table, grabbed her purse and opened the door to leave. "Tell Dr. Johnson I'll call him in a few days with my decision, and make sure he doesn't call David."

The petite, bleached-blond nurse was obviously flabbergasted, unsure of what to do. Finally she muttered, "But the doctor was going to bring you something to calm you down."

"Yes, I know, but I'm fine now. See?" She gave the blond nurse a big smile. "Now, tell him not to call David and I'll be in touch. Okay? Thank you so much," she finished, closing the door, not waiting for a response.

"Why have you been avoiding me? You haven't returned my calls; you practically run when you see me in the halls. I've been patient because I figured you needed some space, but enough is enough. I'm your best friend. Spill it."

Sophie grimaced inwardly at Rina's tirade, waiting for her to sit across the desk from her. "Hello to you, too, Rina," she stated lightly, lifting her head. "Fine, I'll spill it."

Rina looked at her with a confused expression, before beginning a concerned interrogation.

"What happened to your face? Why is it bruised? Did David do this? Why didn't you tell me about it? What happened?" But, before Sophie could say anything, she questioned, "Is this why you've been acting weird lately?"

"Weird, huh? Yes, it's been because of what David did to my face," she answered, pointing to the menacing bruise on her cheek. "There's another reason as well."

Rina's head seemed to expand with anger. Sophie could almost hear the words before she said them. "Fucking, insane lunatic. Why can't that asshole pick on someone his own size?"

She listened patiently, even though she never enjoyed Rina's mouth. In this case, she wholeheartedly agreed.

Relenting, Rina murmured, "I'm listening, sweetie."

"The first thing is, I took David the divorce papers on Saturday."

"Yeah, and apparently I was right. He didn't take it well, did he?" she retorted, touching her face tenderly.

"No, he didn't. But, believe me when I say, I think he may have come out worse in the situation than me." She was surprised she sounded so confident. When she thought of what he'd done, and had tried to do, a knot of fear bound-up her insides. Pushing the thought aside, she sat up a little straighter reminding herself she'd escaped, she'd hurt him too, and he hadn't been able to finish what he started.

"What do you mean? You didn't kill him, did you?"

"No, I didn't kill him, but I did smash his precious 'Restaurant of the Year' award down on his head."

"Do you know for sure? You didn't kill him?" Rina quipped, obviously concerned.

"Yes, I know. He's called my cell phone a few times since then and left messages."

"I'm disappointed he's still alive, but I'm glad you didn't kill him." Rina breathed a sigh of relief.

"Well at the time I didn't care one way or the other, but I'm glad he's not dead, too."

"Why didn't you care at the time? What did he do?"

She looked down, glancing at Rina out of the corner of her eye. She'd decided she wasn't going to tell Rina, but now realized, she should.

"Sophie, what happened?"

"He slapped me a few times, obviously, and he. . ." She looked over at her classroom doorway to make sure no one else was around. "He tried to rape me." She could see Rina had something to say, but wanted to explain away what he'd done to her. "I mean, I know he's still my husband, which means I guess rape isn't the right word, but he wanted to force me to have sex with him."

"Sophie, dear, you just repeated the exact definition of rape." Rina touched her bruised face again and said, "Shit Sophie, I want to kill him. Is there anything I can do? You said he tried. Did he hurt you? I mean, other than there?" She questioned, motioning toward her bruised face.

"No, not really," Sophie whispered, a tear trickling down her face. She brushed it aside, sitting up taller, and added, "Actually, I'm fine. I didn't let him do it. I stopped him."

"Oh, I'm glad, sweetie. I'm proud of you, you know. I knew you had it in you." Rina reached over and embraced Sophie.

She let Rina hold her for a long time, enjoying the safety of her friend's closeness. After a few minutes, she gently pushed away. "Thanks for being here for me. I know I'm a mess. If you can handle it, there's one more thing I'd like to tell you."

"Okay." Rina looked guilty.

"What's the matter?"

"There's something I need to tell you, too."

"Sure. Go ahead. Your turn." She wondered what was wrong. Rina looking guilty was a rarity.

"Well, David's left me several, colorful messages as well. Sixteen to be exact." Rina stopped, looking at her imploringly.

"What is it, Rina? What did he say to you?"

"Oh, honey, it doesn't matter what *he* said, it's what *I* did in response."

"What?"

"Sophie, I hate to say this but I called him back and, after a few colorful words of my own, let it slip you were going to give him divorce papers."

"Oh . . ." She now understood more fully why he'd been out of control when she went over. It explained, a lot.

"Can you forgive me," Rina asked, her face ashen.

"Of course. I know you didn't mean to do anything to hurt me, right?" She could tell Rina was beating herself up inside enough for both of them. Rina made an honest mistake, let her temper get the best of her. "What's done is done."

"Right."

"All is forgiven Rina. Really. Anything else," she asked, tenderly.

"No. What else did you need to tell me?" Rina eyed her friend. "You *did* kill him, didn't you?"

"No," She said in mock severity, knowing her friend was trying to lighten the mood a little. "I'm pregnant." She let the words spill out effortlessly.

After an uncomfortable minute, realization dawned on Rina.

"That's why you've been throwing up," she said, obviously shocked.

Sophie nodded, thinking, apparently the thought hadn't crossed Rina's mind either.

"Yes. My doctor thinks I'm five or six weeks along."

"Well, at least you've found out in time. When are you going to terminate it?"

Sophie noticed she'd gone right to abortion as the solution. It was something she'd been seriously considering. "I know it seems like the obvious answer, but I've thought a lot about it and it's not for me. I don't want to have an abortion. I want to keep this baby." She could tell Rina was shocked. Sophie had known she would, which was the main reason she'd been avoiding her. She wanted to seriously consider her choices on her own.

She knew she could afford to keep it, but more importantly, she knew she wanted to, wanted to give this baby the love, time and attention it would require, the same attention she'd received as a child, and up until her parents died. The prospect excited her more than she probably ever could express.

"Sophie, maybe you don't realize what you're saying. A baby. *His* baby. Why would you want to keep it?"

"I know. At first I thought it was a crazy idea, too, but the fact is, I've loved him, and when this baby was conceived, it was done willingly and happily."

"Come on, really? I mean you've told me a lot about your relationship. How happy was it," she stated in matter of fact tone. "Are you sure you're being honest with yourself?"

"Okay, you're right," Sophie conceded. "Maybe not completely willingly or happily, but I have loved him, and this baby came from there." She looked at Rina pleadingly, then said, "Please know I've thought a lot about this and I need your support."

"I adore you and I'll support you dear. You know I will," Rina answered slowly.

"Thank you. I'd hoped you'd come around. One other thing, though, I want to keep it a secret for now. I've got a lot going on and I'm not ready to share this with anybody else."

"I agree. I think keeping it quiet would be for the best."

Sophie reached out and lovingly grabbed her friends' hand. "You're my dearest friend. You know that, don't you?"

Rina smiled as she stood and said, "Sweetie, I'm your only friend."

Sophie watched Rina walk to the door. She knew Rina was right. She was her only friend, but she called after Rina, "I wouldn't have it any other way."

Rina turned, giving her a wink, then said before she left, "Thanks. I'll talk to you later, dear."

"Bye," she returned.

Alone, in her hotel room, she pulled out her planner.

Time to get organized, she thought, dialing the first of several numbers on her to-do list.

"Hello, I'd like to speak to Mr. Wodden please."

"Sure, may I tell him who is calling?"

"Yes, this is Mrs. Berkeley."

"Fine, Mrs. Berkeley, one moment please."

Sophie waited on hold until a deep, male voice answered. "Mrs. Berkeley. How can I help you?" Mr. Wodden asked.

"Mr. Wodden, I gave my husband the divorce papers, but I don't think he'll sign them." She paused, hoping he'd tell her what to do.

"I was afraid something like this might happen, but listen, it's not a problem. I'll have my assistant mail him a copy of the papers by certified mail. This way we'll have documentation he's received them."

"Okay, great. I was wondering, what if he never signs the papers? Do I have to stay married to him," she asked nervously.

"Good question and the answer is no. Here in Utah, we can file separate paperwork and then, if within six months he still hasn't signed the papers and he hasn't formally contested anything, the state will officially consider you divorced."

"That's a relief. Is there something else I need to sign then?"

"No, the rest of the paperwork is up to me and my office. There will, however, be a few additional fees. I can have my office bill them to you, if you'd like."

"Sounds good. I appreciate your help. I'll need to give your secretary my hotel address."

"It's no problem. I'll transfer you back to Mrs. Morgan. She'll get the information from you. Did you have any other questions or concerns?"

"No. Mr. Wodden, thank you."

"You're welcome. One moment while I transfer you."

She hung up after giving Mrs. Morgan her address, then quickly dialed Dr. Johnson's office. When the woman answered, she asked to speak with him. The woman informed her Dr. Johnson was extremely busy right now and could she take a message.

"Would you tell him it's Sophie Berkeley and it's important?"

"Oh, Mrs. Berkeley. Hang on a moment. Let me see if I can get him for you," the woman responded.

Seconds later, Dr. Johnson answered. "This is Dr. Johnson."

"Yes, this is Mrs. Berkeley. I wanted to thank you for your help the other day and apologize for any inconvenience I may have caused."

"No, no problem. Is everything okay? Have you made any decisions yet?"

"Yes, I'm going to keep the baby."

He seemed to breathe a sigh of relief, as he said, "What a great idea, Mrs. Berkeley. Would you like me to recommend an OB-GYN?"

"Thank you. A recommendation would be appreciated."

She called the OB-GYN he'd recommended and made an appointment. Then she called the last number on her list, Eva Simms, a real estate agent. She told the agent what kind of a house she wanted, her price range and location. Eva promised to call back in a few days with something to show her.

Sophie was finished and sat back to enjoy a moment of contentment. It was six o'clock. She called a local delivery place and enjoyed eating in while watching a movie. She was asleep by eight thirty.

"Let's make this quick as possible. I don't want anything to go wrong."

"Yes, doctor."

"I'm going to make the incision. My number fifteen blade, please." After a moments pause, he continued, "Thank you Nurse Sumpter. Here we go. I need suction, please. All right, let's open her up. We need to get the baby out pronto."

Sophie sat up with a start, beads of sweat covering her forehead and tears soaked her face.

The dream seemed so real, she thought putting a hand over her abdomen to make sure it hadn't been cut open.

"Baby, what are you doing to me?" she whispered, before her morning sickness took over and she had to run to the bathroom.

After flushing the toilet, she brushed her teeth, and took a shower. When she was done, she got dressed and then graded some papers.

Around four o'clock, Rina called. "Hello, prego. What you doing?"

"Watching a movie. You?"

"I'm calling to tell you you're going out with me tonight."

"Rina, I don't know. I'm still not in the mood and I worry about the smoke."

"Don't worry. We're going to a nonsmoking club tonight. You'd better get in the mood, because I'm picking you up at eight o'clock. We'll have some dinner before meeting some friends at the club by ten."

"Will you take no for an answer?"

"No way! Oh, and wear something nice. We're dressing up. C'mon, it's Saturday!"

"Who are these *friends*?"

"You'll find out when we get there. I'll see you in a few hours. Bye."

Sophie hung up the phone, still grinning. *It could be fun.* Opening the closet, she pulled out the red dress, the one David bought her.

"No reason it should go to waste and it would serve him right if I wear it to a party and have fun," she murmured, defiantly.

They ate at The Melting pot. Set in the bottom corner of a huge, old building; it was cozy. Rina had made reservations so they were immediately taken to their table.

The table had two burners sitting on top. She was excited, having never eaten here before. Rina explained the menu and way this restaurant, which was fondue, worked.

First, you had to pick the cheese mixture you wanted, then you chose the meat's you wanted and finally, the chocolate mixture you wanted.

Sophie and Rina placed their order and then talked and talked. The waitress came by occasionally to melt the cheese, warm the oil and chicken broth for their meat and then melt and mix the chocolate.

The food was great, the atmosphere amazing. Sophie didn't say much, letting Rina do most of the talking. She realized, lately all of their conversations had been about her.

Obviously, Rina would have a lot to chat about. It was good listening to Rina talk about her life drama. By the time they reached the club, Sophie realized she hadn't thought about her problems once in several hours.

The club was incredible. It was on the fifteenth floor of the Red Lion Hotel. Vast could barely describe it. There were several dance floors, on two different levels. Along the walls were tables and chairs placed in a way which allowed you to talk to friends while looking at the amazing views of the city. If the city lights weren't of interest, one could watch the throngs of people on the dance floors, pulsing to the beat of the music, all seemingly enjoying themselves, drinking, laughing, dancing, kissing.

Several people came over to talk to Rina. She graciously introduced Sophie to all of them. She was having a lot of fun. Sophie thought about the last few years of her life.

She realized she had forgotten there was this big world, with lots of people in it.

By midnight, though, Sophie was drained.

"Would you stop looking at your watch," Rina said, as she sipped on her cocktail.

"I know. It's just I'm worn out," Sophie complained.

"Stop whining and take a look around. There are a lot of gorgeous men in this place, most of whom have looked your way at least once. Try to enjoy yourself and you might meet someone amazing tonight."

"Rina."

"Oh look, there's Phillip." She waved him over.

"No, don't," Sophie scoffed, trying to grab Rina's hands.

As Phillip arrived, Rina said, "I see some friends I need to go talk to. I'll see you both in a while."

"See you, Rina," Phillip said, running his hands through his hair, sitting down. He looked at Sophie. "Hello. You look nice."

"Phillip." She uttered coolly.

"That's it," he said harshly, although he was smiling. "What have I done exactly to deserve this revulsion from you?"

She could only stare. She was speechless. She wasn't sure if it was his close proximity or his incredible smile, but she couldn't say a word.

He wasn't backing down and continued, "As I recall, you're the one who accused me of following you. You're the one who walked out of the theater without saying a word. You're the one who yelled at me the last time I tried to talk to you. Am I wrong?"

Still, she couldn't speak. She was transfixed, watching the way his mouth moved, the way he was leaning back on his chair. She wanted to slap herself to stop her foolishness, but instead sat there helplessly.

Phillip started laughing. "I've been trying to be cool, give you your space because I was hoping you'd realize I'm a good guy." Taking a sip of his drink, he asked, a confused look on his face, "Are you all right?"

"Um, yes. I'm fine, no thanks to you," she said, snapping out of it.

"No thanks to me? Sophie, what did I do?"

"Are you kidding me? At least once a week, I walk into my classroom with hearts drawn on my chalkboard and the students making kissing noises when my back is turned to them. It's incredibly humiliating."

"It wasn't my intention," he said, still chuckling, then took another drink.

"I'm sure I'll get over it." She laughed as well, realizing it didn't really bother her. Taking a drink of her water, she glanced at him again. He was looking at her inquisitively. Her stomach had butterflies doing the Hokey Pokey inside. She couldn't understand how he could cause these feelings in her. He was handsome, but she'd known lots of handsome guys, including David, and none of them had ever made her feel this way. She sighed inwardly, looking down.

I liked it better when I was mad at him, she thought crossly.

"That's quite a ring on your finger. How long have you been married?"

"Huh," she said. He pointed a finger at her wedding ring, and understood what he meant.

"Oh, two years," she replied, putting her hands in her lap.

"I was married for seven," he began, while he stirred his drink. "My divorce became final about a month ago." He stopped a moment to gulp the rest of his drink before he went on, "She was having an affair. Told me she was in love with him and he was going to leave his wife soon. She left me for him."

She was staring at him again and couldn't help it. She didn't know any man who would open up and share like him.

He's probably drunk, she thought. He must have realized she was in shock because he laughed.

"Hey I know, I pass along too much information. At least that's what my sisters tell me."

She laughed, too. "Yes, it's a lot of information, but its okay."

"Yeah? All right, what else would you like to know?"

His eyes were twinkling with pleasure.

"I'm getting divorced," she blurted, then blushed, embarrassed she'd told someone other than Rina. It was weird but good, she had to admit.

"You are?" he questioned, looking surprised.

She nodded, unsure of what else to say.

This is crazy, she thought, anger at David welling up inside of her again. He'd affected her in many ways. She was incapable of having a normal conversation with another human being, well other than Rina.

"What's wrong with me?" She felt her face heat up.

"Nothing," he returned quickly.

"Marriage is hard. Honestly, I miss having my wife around. She's a pilot based here in Utah which is why I moved out here, but. . ." He shrugged, then finished, "Regrettably, by the time I got out here, it was too late."

Sophie realized she wanted to talk to him, wanted to tell him about it; at least a little bit of it. *It's nice to have someone else to talk too*, she thought. "I never should've married my husband. I saw the signs, but I ignored them."

"It happens. Don't be too hard on yourself, though. It's easy to overlook problems when you're in love. I know."

"You think?" She wondered, a splash of relief reviving her. "I feel like I should've realized what kind of man he was. I feel somehow what's happening is my fault." She couldn't believe she was saying these things to him. It was gratifying. He was easy to talk to.

"No, trust me. It takes two people for a marriage to fail. I thought it was my fault, too, at first. I figured I must have somehow pushed her into the arms of the other man. Finally, though, I realized it was her choice to go after the Restaurant Man."

"Restaurant Man?" she questioned, intrigued.

"Yeah, it's what I call him because she won't tell me his name. I guess he's the owner of some fancy restaurant here in Salt Lake."

A creepy, eerie sensation crawled down her spine. The hairs on the back of her neck prickled. "Shut the faculty door!"

He burst out laughing. "I like it."

She laughed, too. "But you don't know his name?"

"No, only he's here in Salt Lake. She's afraid I'd go to his restaurant and cause a scene, and she's probably right."

"You don't know the name of the restaurant either?" she questioned, feeling faint.

"No. Why do you ask?"

She tried to brush the question aside, but he asked again, "Tell me why you want to know. Something's wrong, I can tell."

"It's nothing, really, my husband owns a restaurant here in Salt Lake," she finally said.

"You're kidding me." He sat back, staring at her in amazement. "What are the chances?" He took a long drink, the ice smacked against his lips.

"It's just . . ." She wished he knew the name of the restaurant or at least the guy's name. It seemed like too much of a coincidence.

"What?" he questioned, encouraging her to continue.

"It would be weird if your wife and my husband were having an affair."

"Weird would be an understatement," he responded flatly, finishing his drink. She noticed he was looking at her curiously and wondered if she'd said something wrong. Maybe she'd been too personal, but she forgot her worries a moment later because he changed the subject.

"Have you ever been to New York?"

"No, I haven't. Do you miss it?"

"I do miss some things about it. The people. The energy. Being able to walk to work. Those kinds of things."

"Oh." She nodded, interested.

Nodding back, he continued, "What I don't miss is the heat and the humidity. Did you know on a hot day with a hundred percent humidity, you can be walking down the street and actually *feel* the asphalt give under your feet?"

"No. You're kidding," she answered, laughing a little. The hairs on the back of her neck had settled down and she was once again enjoying his company.

"It's true. It softens up to such a degree you literally sink in a few inches in some spots."

"Wow, I can't even imagine. How can people want to go out when it's so hot?"

"I don't know; I guess you just get used to it. Plus, there are so many great things, they make up for the heat. The city feels alive, like it has its own soul. It's really amazing!"

"You make it sound like it is. I've always wanted to go, but haven't had the chance."

They continued talking for a long time. She had to admit she was enjoying herself. He was interesting and fun. She decided she wouldn't tell Rina, though, because she knew she'd gloat.

At around one-thirty Phillip said he had to go and asked if she'd like a ride home.

"I'm not sure," she replied, a little hesitantly, looking for Rina. She got Rina's attention and put a finger to her watch, tapping it as a sign she wanted to go. Rina shook her head no.

She sighed and said to Phillip, "Sure, thank you."

As he pulled into the hotel, he asked, "This is home, huh?"

"For now. I'm still in the process of finding my own place."

"Seems kind of expensive on a teacher's salary."

"I'll manage," Sophie intoned, getting out of the car. Closing the door, she bent down. Phillip rolled down the window, allowing her to lean in. "Thanks for the ride," she said lightly.

"Sure. See you at school."

CHAPTER 9

"It looked like you had a lot of fun Saturday night," Rina beamed, sitting next to Sophie.

"I had fun, yes. Was that your plan all along, to get Phillip to come over? You wanted to ditch me for your more fascinating friends, right?"

"Well, I had to do something, hon," Rina returned just as sarcastically. "You've been boring me to tears lately."

"I know." she retorted sincerely, letting her head fall to her chest.

"I'm kidding, sweetie. The truth is, I wanted you to have fun. I've been out with Phillip a few times and knew he was harmless and great to be around. He's fun, right?"

"He is. I had a good time talking to him." Sophie raised her head, knowing they were both joking around. She enjoyed the banter between them. They both did.

"Did he tell you he's only recently divorced his wife, Cynthia?"

"He told me he'd recently gone through a divorce, but I didn't catch her name."

"Kind of sad. I can tell she hurt him. But he's gorgeous, don't you think?"

"He's not bad." Sophie smirked.

"Not bad? Are you kidding? Plus, he can carry on a conversation. He's one of the few men I actually enjoy talking to."

Laughing nervously, Sophie said, "Yes, he's a talker. I just figured he was talkative because he had a few drinks in him."

"Uh-huh, sure, whatever you need to tell yourself, sweetie." Then Rina leaned down and put a hand on her arm as she continued, "You can't fool me, you know." She cleared her throat. "And I don't think Phillip drinks. In fact, someone told me he's a recovering alcoholic. Personally, I think he's one of those few men in the world who aren't afraid to share their feelings."

"Well, it was nice talking to him. He seems like a good person. You want to know something peculiar, though?"

"What?"

"His wife was having an affair with a guy who owns a restaurant." Rina stepped back, obviously stunned.

"Don't you think it's a little weird?" Sophie asked.

"Very weird. Did he say what the guy's name is?" Rina asked, frowning.

"No. He said he didn't know. Said she wouldn't tell him."

"Hmm, interesting. Maybe you two are meant for each other."

"What? How do you figure?"

"Seems like fate, don't you think?"

"Look, Rina, I know what you're trying to do, but it's not going to work. I'm married, remember?"

"Technically, yes, but don't you want to know what it's like to have a relationship with a good man?"

"I would, someday, and I appreciate you looking out for me. Don't push this, though. Please. I'm not ready."

"We'll see," Rina retorted smartly.

"I've got to go to class. I'll talk to you later," Sophie said.

"See you, mama!"

She glared at Rina before casually looking around the room. No one seemed to have noticed anything about the comment. She caught the eye of another teacher, gave her an uneasy smile, then left.

Sophie glanced again at the clock. She'd lost track of time and was quickly packing up her bag. It was seven o'clock p.m. and she was still in her classroom at school.

Where had the time gone, she wondered, walking to the door. In the hall, darkness enfolded her.

"Creepy," she muttered, hesitantly making her way to the end of the hall. Thankfully, the halls were like streets, with a lamp every once in a while, the light emitting a eerie glow. She turned down the hall toward the Theater when she thought she saw the shadow of someone.

"Phillip? Is someone there," she called nervously.

Without warning, the shadow turned into someone. He growled, "Who's Phillip?"

Like a deer caught in the headlights, she wanted to run, but wasn't sure where to go. Her eyes darted from left to right and her hearing seemed to sharpen, while her heart started racing uncontrollably. Finally, though, her feet sprang into action and she dashed toward the Theater. She remembered they'd been rehearsing for a play and hoped Phillip and his students were still there.

Please be there, she prayed. It was fleeting, though, because the doors were locked.

She shook them and then dreaded comprehension of her predicament settled in. She turned around, facing the man in   the shadows who was there waiting for her, his face covered by a ski mask, making it impossible for her to see it. She thought she recognized the jacket.

With her back against the doors, she slowly inched her way toward the edge of the wall. She didn't think she could outrun him, but she didn't know what else to do. Fighting back her urge to scream, she asked, "What do you want?"

He threw back his head and laughed, before responding, "It's not what I want, lady. I'm just doing what I'm paid to do."

She'd reached the point of the wall where it rounded to the next. Without thinking, she started running. She sensed more than heard him coming up behind her.

"Where do you think you're going?" he asked wickedly, grabbing her by the shoulders.

"Help! Help, please hel--!" she tried yelling, but was unable to finish because he'd covered her mouth and nose with something. It seemed like gauze or a wet washcloth.

She couldn't help but breathe in whatever was on the cloth. Almost immediately, she felt its effects.

He'd drugged her, she realized, most likely with chloroform. *What am I going to do now*, she speculated sleepily, her body slumping heavily into her attacker.

Instinctively, she tried to push him away, but her body wouldn't listen to her internal commands. She couldn't help but smell the sweet stench of cigars clashing with the equally strong smell of stale beer coming from the man who'd captured her.

Ugh, she gagged disgustedly. She tried to yell again.

Before anything would come out of her mouth, he abruptly let go of her and she slumped to the floor. It hurt somewhat, but she still couldn't get her limbs to function.

After a moment she forgot her pain, hearing someone yell, then something sounded like shuffling or fighting. She couldn't tell what was happening, but she wanted to get away. *Please, God*, she pleaded, help me get out of this.

Trying unsuccessfully to roll herself onto her back, she suddenly felt strong hands grip either side of her shoulders.

"No," she tried to scream. A sound must have come out of her mouth because she heard him say gently, "It's Phillip. You're safe now. He can't hurt you anymore. I've got you," he said tenderly, picking her up.

Slowly, he began moving down the hall. All of her fears vanished and peace enveloped her. She allowed him to carry her like a child and had almost given in to sleep when she heard him say, "Sophie, I need you to help me. Can you put your arms around my neck?" With every ounce of her willpower, she flung her arms up, grabbing onto what she thought was his neck.

"Ouch." She heard him groan. The idea of causing him pain awakened her somewhat. Feeling a little better, she tried to open her eyes, to see what she'd done to him, but they wouldn't open. With her head resting against his body, she noticed how good he smelled. Gratitude filled her heart. She tried to speak, to thank him.

"What is it, Sophie?" He asked, his breathing labored from carrying her. His breath felt warm against her lips. She lifted her head slightly toward him, trying to face him, when her lips accidentally brushed his. She hadn't meant to, but didn't move away. She realized she wanted to kiss him. She now knew she had wanted to since the day she met him. He stopped walking.

Surely he was going to push me away, she thought, and couldn't blame him. She was being brazen and he'd just rescued her. Embarrassed, she started to pull away. Before she could, his lips captured hers, returning her kiss.

His lips were soft at first, but abruptly turned passionate. He tightened his grip around her arm and thigh as their kiss turned sensual. Time seemed to freeze, like they were in a dream. She hoped it wouldn't end.

Perhaps it is a dream, she reflected happily.

After a time, he slowly pulled away, groaning a little.

She wondered if it was from the kiss or because he was still holding her. When he started moving again, she heard the sound of sirens in the distance and knew the police were coming.

"They're almost here," he whispered.

f

She tried to open her eyes, an irritating buzz pummeling her ears. After a moment, she realized it was people, several of them talking quickly among themselves. She tried to listen harder, wondering what the problem was.

"Her eyelids just fluttered," she heard a woman say.

"Doctor, her heart rate is up to one hundred beats per minute."

"That's too fast," a male voice responded.

She tried to open her eyes, to tell them she was fine, but she was too tired. *I'll tell them I'm all right in a while*, she promised herself as she dreamily went back to sleep.

Opening her eyes, she looked around, examining her surroundings. It was stark, with nothing but a dry erase board on the wall. *I must be in a hospital*, she thought, lifting a hand to her pounding head.

"Glad you've finally joined us," a woman gushed, walking crisply into the room.

"I'm Glenda. Can I get you anything?"

"W-Water," Sophie stammered hoarsely.

"Of course. I'll be right back."

Glenda left, quickly returning.

"Here you go." Lifting her head, she brought the cup to her lips, allowing her to take a drink. When she'd had enough, Glenda put her head back against the pillows. "I'm going to check your pulse." She did, listened to her heart and checked the bag of fluid hanging from an IV stand. "The doctor will be in to talk to you in a few minutes. Also, there are a couple of detectives here to talk to you."

"Okay," Sophie whispered, then thought of something. "How long have I been here?"

"About twenty-six hours," the nurse answered, walking from the room. That long? She thought, tenderly rubbing her head. She gingerly closed her eyes, trying to remember everything that had happened.

She remembered the man grabbing her. What was it he'd said, she pondered, trying to remember. Before long it came to her. He'd said, 'I'm only doing what I was paid to do.' Her gut told her David was involved; she knew it as sure as she knew she was alive. She also remembered her promise to get far, far away from David, if she made it out of the situation alive.

Still massaging her head, her fingers found a lump. I must've got it when he let go of me. She couldn't believe she'd escaped, but knew it was because of Phillip. She didn't know how he'd done it, but he had. He'd helped her; saved her. To repay his kindness, she'd done what? The memory of their kiss flung itself into her consciousness.

"Oh no," she groaned, her cheeks burning at the memory. *What must he think of me? How am I ever going to be able to face him again?* She was, however, unable to think on it more because a man in a white coat walked in, followed by another man and a woman.

"Hello, Mrs. Berkeley, I'm Doctor Rosen." His eyes were kind and full of sympathy.

"Hello," she replied, shaking his outstretched hand.

"You've had quite an ordeal. How are you feeling?"

"My head is tender," she admitted, trying to sound brave, appear strong.

"I'll have the nurse bring you in something for the pain. It's probably from the traces of chloroform we found in your system and the bump on your forehead."

She nodded in agreement.

"Does it hurt anywhere else?"

"No," she answered.

"Good." He turned to the people behind him, acknowledging them for the first time. "These detectives need to ask you a few questions. I'll leave you to them unless you have any other questions for me?"

She shook her head no.

"Fine. A nurse should be in with pain medication in a few minutes. If you need anything else, just push the button," he said, indicating the buttons on the bed, then was gone.

She was nervous being alone with them. She didn't know what to say. She felt guilty, and didn't know why.

The male strutted forward. His blond hair was short and spiked. He looked to be twenty-six. He had blue eyes and filled out his uniform perfectly.

Big arms, slim waist, thick legs. He introduced himself and the woman.

"I'm Detective Mallory and this is my partner Detective Oborn. We'd like to ask you a few questions, okay."

She nodded.

The female, Detective Oborn, was a lot smaller than her partner. She had blue eyes and blond hair, cut in a bob. She seemed feminine but tough. Although her hair was combed, it looked like she hadn't done much else. She walked toward the bed, expressing her sympathies.

"What a terrible thing to happen. It must've been quite a scary experience for you."

"Yes," Sophie squeaked out.

Detective Mallory came to her bed, standing next to his partner, "Did you know the man who did this to you?" he interrogated intently.

"No," she replied.

"Did you get a look at his face?" he continued.

She tried to sit up, beginning to feel more uncomfortable under his gaze.

"No, he was wearing a ski mask," she answered slowly.

Detective Oborn glared sideways at her partner before asking,

"What can you tell us about him? Was he tall? Fat? Thin?" Sophie focused on Detective Oborn, responding, "He was probably at least six feet tall. He didn't seem overweight, but he had on a jacket and, as I said, a ski mask, so I don't know for sure." She stopped, seeing the disappointment on the detective's face.

"Sorry, there wasn't a lot of light. I know he had on jeans and boots, work boots, I think. When I fell against him, I remember, he smelled like cigars and beer."

"Anything else, Mrs. Berkeley?" Detective Mallory asked, his impatience obvious.

"Did he say anything to you?"

"Only, he was doing what he was paid to do."

Detective Mallory perked up.

"Interesting? Do you know of anyone who would want to hurt you?"

She looked from one face to the other, wondering how much she should tell them. She decided now was the time to tell them all of it. "My husband, David Berkeley," she responded hesitantly.

Detective Mallory looked at her quizzically. "Why would you think your husband wants to hurt you, Mrs. Berkeley?"

She quickly ran through the details of what had been going on over the past two years, finishing with the promiscuous way she'd found her husband, her decision to divorce him and then the strange phone call. She told them about David trying to rape her when she'd gone over to give him divorce papers. She told them about the man she'd seen following her from her hotel to school. Everything except the kiss she'd shared with Phillip.

They'd listened intently, asking a question here or there when appropriate. When she was finished, Detective Oborn declared, "You've been through a lot. I wish you would've reported everything you've told us. We could have protected you."

"Really?" She tried not to sound surprised.

"Of course," Detective Mallory replied fiercely, although the look on his face told her he was lying. Quickly changing the subject, he said, "We're glad Mr. Hansen was there to stop him or this might have had a different outcome."

She sunk back in her pillows.

"I know. I'm thankful he was there, too. He saved my life."

"Absolutely," he concurred absently, entering something into his Blackberry. Looking up, he went on.

"He corroborates the man was wearing a ski mask. He said when he found you, the man was trying to drag you down a hall. When Dr. Hansen yelled out, the man dropped you."

Detective Mallory waited for her to agree.

"I do remember him letting go of me." She shrugged helplessly.

Detective Mallory stared at her a moment, as if waiting for more then went on,

"Dr. Hansen and your assailant fought briefly before the man ran off."

She shrugged again.

"Apparently, this is when Dr. Hansen called the police. We met him at the entrance to the school, where we took his statement. Once the paramedics checked you out, he rode with you in the ambulance to the hospital."

Detective Oborn flashed a congenial smile.

"You're lucky to have a friend like Dr. Hansen around."

"Yes," she responded, trying not to blush as their kiss danced across her mind.

Detective Mallory started to look irritated again asking huffily, "Is there anything else you want to tell us?"

"No, I think I've told you everything."

"Fine. Just a couple more questions and then you can rest," Detective Oborn said kindly.

"Sure."

"Do you want to press charges against your husband for the attempted rape?"

Without thinking about it, Sophie shook her head no.

"I don't want to aggravate the issues between us."

"You know, you can't make this any worse. We're going to go to his work, question him about what happened to you the other night. We're going to tell him we know about the attempted rape, too. You might as well get what happened to you on record."

Nervously, she agreed. Sophie gave them her statement.

Once she was finished, Detective Mallory handed her his card.

Leaving, they promised to be in touch.

Relieved it was over, she closed her eyes, fatigue crushing her. Her head was still pounding terribly. Fumbling for the call button, she was about to push it when Glenda

returned with her pain medicine.

"This won't hurt the baby?" she asked.

"No, dear, it won't. We were wondering if you knew you were pregnant."

"Yes, I've known for a while. Do you know if it's okay? My baby, I mean?"

"While you were still asleep, we did an ultrasound and everything seemed fine."

"That's a relief." Sophie took a deep breath, her concern alleviated.

"You know, physically the doctor says you're well enough to be discharged, although you'll still need a few days of bed rest. What do you think? Would you like to stay another night?"

Just as she was about to answer, Rina walked in.

"Oh, sweetie, I'm glad you're awake. I was worried," she gushed.

"Rina, I'm so happy to see you."

"You can release her. She's coming home with me." She looked from the nurse to Sophie and continued, "No arguments." To the nurse, she promised, "Don't worry, I'll make sure she follows the doctors orders."

Sophie laughed lightly.

"True, she will."

"Excellent. Being with loved ones will be good for you. I'll get the paperwork ready."

An hour later, feeling the wonderful effects of the pain medicine, the doctor released her into Rina's care.

CHAPTER 10

"Have you heard anything from Phillip?" Sophie asked, trying to sound nonchalant. She was staring out the car window, watching the buildings and other cars whiz by, on their way to Rina's house. The sun was setting, making the world around her glow red and orange.

"Yes, he called me when you both arrived at the hospital. He didn't know any of your family. I was his only choice," Rina replied as coolly.

"Did he sound okay?"

"He sounded okay, but as the nurse was taking me back to see you right after it happened, I noticed him in the room next to yours getting stitches over his eyebrow."

"Oh, no. What happened to him?"

"Apparently, sweetie, when he went after the guy, they fought pretty hard. He's also got a black eye and two bruised ribs."

"Oh, no." She gasped again, devastated. A part of her though, had a twinge of joy at knowing he'd protected her.

To Rina, she went on, "I need to apologize to him, tell him how bad I feel."

She couldn't believe Phillip, who barely knew her, would risk his life for her. He'd tried to protect her, and he'd paid dearly for it. "What should I do?"

"Hon, more importantly than Phillip at the moment is what should you do about David? He should pay for what he did to you." She paused, realizing, Sophie guessed, he hadn't physically done this particular incident to her, then continued, "For what he *had* done to you."

"You think it was him, then. I didn't think you thought David . . ." Rina interrupted her, "Without a doubt, I think he's behind this. I just hope the police can tie him to it. Then, when he's in jail, he won't be able to hurt you anymore."

Sophie looked at Rina. She adored her friend. The sun danced against Rina's hair in such a way, she looked like she had a halo.

"You truly are my angel on earth, aren't you, " Sophie asked, touching her arm. "Thanks for being here for me."

"Hon, you know it's my pleasure," Rina returned, smiling.

Sophie sighed deeply, saying out loud what she'd been thinking, "I just wonder if this is worth it? I'm already spent, and I'm sure it's only beginning for David."

"Maybe, but you can't be suggesting you'd rather be in a loveless, not to mention, dangerous marriage the rest of your life, are you?" Rina was obviously concerned.

"No, of course not. I'd love to be with a man who treats me like an equal. Someone who's fun and full of goodness." An image of Phillip sprang into her mind. She pushed it aside almost mournfully and continued, "It's only, I don't know if that kind of life is meant for me. I'm having David's baby; don't I owe him another chance?"

"Sophia Rose Barton Berkeley!" Rina exclaimed. "I cannot believe those words came out of your mouth. What century are you living in? Of course, it's meant for you. You deserve happiness, dear, more than most, and what you owe David, well, I won't say it out loud because it's against the law."

Sophie knew Rina was right. Once again, it occurred to her she could run. She needed to contemplate the idea, but not now. "Thanks for talking some sense into me, Rina."

"I mean it!"

"I know you do; and I don't want my baby growing up in a bad environment either."

"Good." Rina sighed, clearly relieved.

She rested her head against the passenger seat in Rina's car and closed her eyes. The man in the ski mask was there laughing at her, hurting her. Feeling her insides convulse with fear, she tried to think of something else.

Anything else, she thought.

Suddenly Phillip was there, smiling at her, talking softly; telling her she was safe.

She thought of their kiss, accidental but amazing. Sighing inwardly, she knew, even if things didn't go any further with Phillip, she was grateful for their kiss, because now she'd experienced passion and sincerity, and a whole lot of other feelings she'd never had with David. She wanted those kinds of feelings with someone; maybe Phillip, but it seemed too complicated.

She opened her eyes, looking over at Rina, her dearest friend. She wanted to tell her about the kiss, but put it aside almost immediately. It was still too raw, and she wasn't ready.

"When we get to my house, you're going straight to bed. You heard the doctor's orders."

"Sounds good, Rina."

Seemingly pleased, she continued, "You can sleep in my bed and I'll take the couch."

"No, Rina. I can sleep on the couch."

"No arguments."

She didn't have it in her to argue anyway.

"Thank you."

When they arrived, Rina sent her straight to bed. She'd changed into a pair of Rina's pajamas, washed her face and was now trying, unsuccessfully to sleep.

Rina came in with a pill and some water.

"Take this."

"No, I'm fine."

"Look, dear, I'm on doctors orders. You need your rest. Take it, and take it now." She was standing over her, tapping her foot, impatiently.

Giving up, Sophie took the pill with the water, swallowing, then handed the glass back. "Happy?"

"I'll be happier when you're asleep," she replied, sounding miffed. Turning, she left the room and closed the door.

She knew she was hovering over the burning car.

Flames were engulfing it, and there was a woman inside. She could hear her scream, as the flames overtook her body.

"Help! Help her," She yelled, looking around for someone to come and save her. She saw a tall man, with black hair, being held back by four police officers. He was pushing and kicking them. He obviously wanted to get the woman out.

"Why won't you let him save her?" She screamed.

"Sir, you can't go over there. You can't. The car is going to explode."

At that moment, the explosion happened. Pieces of car and burning flesh were everywhere.

"No," the man yelled, running toward the car, finally free of their clutches. They didn't chase him. The man fell to his knees, sobbing uncontrollably.

"Hazel," he screamed, reaching an arm toward the gutted, still burning vehicle.

She could smell gasoline and something else. She realized it was the smell of burning flesh and was disgusted by it.

"Where is the other woman?" The man yelled, on his feet again.

"Where is she? Is she alive?"

She followed the man's gaze, seeing the other car, flipped upside down. There was also an ambulance nearby, with two EMT's loading another body into the back.

The man stood next to them, looking at the woman, shouting, "You bitch! If you live, you'll pay for killing my sister! Do you hear me?"

Two officers ran to him. Putting their hands on either one of his shoulders and pulling him away from the woman.

"Who is she? What's her name? I want to know."

"Calm down, sir," an officer said.

Crumbling, the man fell heavily against one of the officers.

"She was the only family I had left."

"I'm sorry, sir. Come and sit down. We need to get you checked out."

She heard the sirens. Watched the fire truck pull up to the scene of the crash and hose down the burning car. Sophie observed the man watching them. He was kneeling on the ground, rocking back and forth, repeating the words, "You'll pay for this," over, and over.

Poor man, she thought, looking down at herself. It finally dawned on her, she shouldn't be hovering. In horror, she realized she wasn't there, only a grayish-black mist, and she knew if she could see the eyes, they'd be yellow . . .

"No! No! No! It can't be. It can't be me."

"Sophie, wake up. What's wrong?"

Opening her eyes, she saw Rina leaning over her, her face twisted with worry.

"Rina," she cried, "I've killed a woman."

"Sophie, for the hundredth time, dear, you didn't kill anyone. It was a dream, just a dream, sweetie."

"I don't know, it seemed real. I was this grayish-black mist with yellow eyes . . . I see it, in my dreams, all the time."

She knew Rina was trying to comfort her and appreciated it.

The problem was the dream seemed real, as real as this moment, sitting on the couch, sipping herbal tea. She couldn't explain it, but knew, somehow, she was involved in the accident in her dream. Try as she might, though, she couldn't remember how.

"It's okay," Rina said, tenderly. "It was just a dream."

Chapter II

It was a beautiful Thursday evening. Sophie was standing in front of the house she knew would be hers. It was a six thousand square foot two-story made of stone and brick. Way too large, but perfect in many other ways. The land, the house, all of it chanted perfection to her.

The entrance had a huge wood beam on either side, giving it a grand, earthy countenance. More than the house, though, she loved the five acres her house was on. The front was fully landscaped with several different kinds of trees efficiently standing guard all along the driveway, as if they were her personal sentries, there to protect her from all who would try to harm her.

Against the house were plant boxes full of shrubs, a Japanese maple, rose bushes and other perennials. Although David had ruined red roses for her, the Realtor had given her a list of all of the types of flowers in the planter boxes. From it, she read there wasn't a single red rose bush in the bunch. She couldn't help but picture what the front of the house would look like with all of the flowers and rose bushes in bloom. It occurred to her, at this moment, the rose bushes were sleeping or dormant. She sensed the irony, as she realized she, too, had been asleep these past years, like the sleeping roses in front of her.

I must've been to survive my life with David, she thought purposefully.

The porch was the entire length of the front of the house. She knew she'd fasten a wooden swing to one side, put a small table and chairs on the other and fill the rest with pots of flowers and hanging plants. Behind the house was a barn and corral. There was also a chicken coup and a garden area. She put a hand on her abdomen, rubbing it delightfully as she thought of the fun she would share with her child, riding horses, gardening, kindly harassing the chickens for their eggs, and even mucking out the coup.

As a backdrop, the mountains, snow-capped at the moment, prestigiously grand. She imagined herself standing out there in late summer, up to her hips in wheat grass, listening to the chirping of the insects and the gleeful singing of the birds. Behind the large, red barn was a stream, small but still babbling on, even this late in the fall. Taking it all in, she realized the place seemed magical to her, as if she'd dreamed it.

Had she, she marveled, a strange sensation clasping her heart. Holding perfectly still, she willed the feeling to go away.

"I deserve something good," she repeated, several times.

Closing her eyes, she lifted her chin into the crisp evening air and breathed deeply. The sensation washed away and she was left again with peace and excitement.

This is my place, she thought, laughing happily. Opening her eyes, she walked slowly back to Ms. Simms.

"Well, what do you think?" Ms. Simms asked when Sophie stopped in front of her.

She knew her eyes were sparkling. "I love it. It's bigger than I wanted, but, it's beautiful inside, and the outside is perfect."

"Great," Ms. Simms stated, her smile genuine. "Shall we put in an offer or did you want to see the other houses I've found?"

"Let's make an offer on this one.

She asked her to negotiate the price with the sellers, to which Ms. Simms responded she would.

Sophie was thrilled.

Sophie walked out onto the balcony of her thirty-sixth floor hotel suite, shutting the sliding glass door behind her.

Sitting on one of the beautifully crafted chairs, she leaned back. The moon was full and bright. It looked as though she could reach out and touch it. Opening her laptop, she fumbled with the keys.

Even though she was living in the twenty-first
century, David hadn't let her own a computer, and
technology had changed drastically in the past two
years. She knew the basics, though, and was trying to
log onto her bank's web site. She needed to transfer
money into her checking account for the house she
hoped to purchase.

An overwhelming sense of guilt and gratitude
took hold. She knew she had it too easy. She
wondered what she would've done if she didn't have
the money her aunt left her. Rina told her there were
a lot of women going through the same situation she
was, but had no money and no one to turn to.

She'd asked Rina what happened to them and
Rina took her to a women's shelter. She'd been
devastated. The shelter, although clean, looked like
it could use all of the financial support it could get.
Rina told her all of them were the same, clean, but
deficient. She'd decided she was going to donate a
substantial amount of her inheritance to the
women's shelters around Utah and become more
involved. She wanted to do something to help other
women.

Signing off, she leaned back in her chair again
enjoying the chilly night air. There were several
blinking lights in the sky and she realized they were
planes waiting to land.

Her mind jetted back nine years to the night
her parents had been killed on their way to the
airport . . .

It was her senior year in high school. She was excited to have her parents leave her alone for a week, excited with anticipation of the freedoms she would have, staying up late, watching whatever she wanted on television, having friends over, eating whenever she wanted.

Her mother told her, "Take care of the house, Soph. Lock up at night."

"I will, mom," she uttered impatiently.

"I'm sure you will but I'm allowed to worry, you know."

"I know mom and I appreciate it."

"Your dad and I want to see the national monuments, our history," she told her for the hundredth time.

"I'm sure you'll have a great time in Washington D.C.," she returned, handing her mom a carry-on bag she knew was full of half finished knitting projects and crossword puzzles.

Her mother didn't like to be idle. Sophie gave her mom a quick hug and said,

"I'll see you in a week. Have fun."

Her mother blew a kiss as she walked to the car. Her dad was already there, loading the car with endless luggage. She watched through the window at his skill, standing when she saw him coming to the front door.

"Sophie," he said, smiling brightly. "Are you sure you don't want to come? It won't all be sightseeing."

"Yes, it will." She laughed, knowing her dad was teasing her. They'd had a long talk earlier in the day about her week-long liberation and the responsibilities coming with it.

He seemed to choke up a little as he said, "Call us anytime. We want to hear from you." Putting his arms around her, he wrapped her in his warmth and safety. Letting her go, he continued, "We'll call you when we land."

The call from her parents had never come. Instead, she came home from school to find two police officers waiting. They gave her the horrible news that her parents were killed in a car crash five miles from the airport. They'd died instantly. Her happiness turned to devastation, and sorrow permanently planted itself in her soul. It was still there, a dull sprout of pain whose stems had constrained her heart and everything else in her life.

She honored her parents' wishes and went to college right after graduating high school, where she met first Rina, and then David.

Looking back, she didn't regret college. She knew she'd done the right thing. It had helped her grieving process to have something else to focus on. Painting had been especially therapeutic, allowing her pain and anguish to come out onto the canvas. She excelled, her professors raved. The painting she named "Dear Anger" won a National Arts Competition. She felt pride at having such a personal expression of her feelings being validated, but still the peace hadn't come and the pain of losing her parents hadn't wilted.

How I miss them, she lamented anew, wondering what her parents would think of her choices in life, David especially.

"You'd love me anyway," she whispered, knowing they would've been supportive. She wished David would sign the divorce papers and get out of her life. Somehow, though, she knew this battle she'd raged against him was going to change her life forever.

Please help me get through this, she prayed silently, placing a hand gently on her abdomen.

The following morning Sophie awoke with a newfound determination. For one thing, she didn't have any morning sickness. Also, after a lot more thinking the night before, she decided running away wasn't an option. She didn't want to spend the rest of her life worrying about whether or not David was going to find her. She wanted to see this through with him.

She knew it was the best thing for both her and her child. When she walked into her classroom, her newfound resolve evaporated almost as quickly as it had come. Sitting grandly on her desk was a large bouquet of flowers.

Her curiosity was peaked, though, because instead of roses, it looked like some of every kind of wild flower from the mountains: Goldeneye, Sego lilies, Wallflowers, Aster, Bluebells, Cryptantha and Woollybase. The flowers were beautiful but she was skeptical since she'd never received flowers from anyone but David. Past experience taught her receiving flowers didn't mean anything good. There was an envelope with her name on it leaning near the bottom of the vase.

She unconsciously held her breath. Scanning the room, she checked to make sure she was alone and then gingerly walked over to the envelope feeling a sudden need to get whatever David had to say out in the open.

She was pleasantly surprised, however, to find they were from Phillip. She read and re-read the card several times.

Hope you're feeling better. Wondered if you'd have dinner with me tonight.
With deepest regard,
Phillip

Enjoying the feelings she was having, she let out her breath, quivering with delight. *It is good to get flowers, especially from him*, she thought. She put the card back in the envelope, and with the giddiness of a teenager, leaned into the nearest flower, breathing in deeply.

"You had me worried, you know."

She jumped, whipping around. "You scared me!"

"I tend to scare you sometimes, don't I?"

"Yes, you do Phillip," she answered mockingly, walking over to him. "These are beautiful. I love them. Thank you."

"You're welcome."

"I feel bad about your eye and everything. I didn't mean to drag you into my mess." She spoke softly, hoping he understood.

"I'm okay."

She reached up and delicately touched the cut near his eyebrow.

"Well, I'm grateful you were there. I can't even think about what would have happened if you hadn't been."

He reached up and took her hand in both of his. His voice filled with emotion.

"I'm glad I was there, too."

They stood there a moment and then he said, "Will you?"

"Will I what?" Suddenly, it dawned on her that he was talking about his note. Lowering her eyes, she whispered, "Yes, I'd love to."

One thing she'd learned from being with David was how to accentuate the positive. She'd become a professional at getting herself beautiful. Tonight, though, was a different story. From picking out shoes, to buying the dress had been difficult. She couldn't decide what to do with her makeup and she kept messing with her hair. She was skittish, a frightened rabbit, all nervous and jittery.

At eight-fifteen, she finally felt satisfied. She had to admit she looked good. Her long hair was down. She'd put hot rollers in it, so it was full of soft curls.

Applying a little more eye makeup, since it was nighttime, her eyes looked smoky. Over time, she'd come to realize with her fair skin, a little more makeup in the evening enhanced her large eyes and pouty lips.

She'd chosen a black, V-neck wrap around dress. It came to the middle of her kneecaps. Some of her curviness had returned to her body, due to more food and her pregnancy. The dress hugged them tightly. She looked womanly once again. She wore a pearl necklace, earrings and bracelet set which had been her Mothers, hose and a pair of three-inch black pumps to complete her outfit. She walked over to grab her matching cream-black clutch when her hotel phone rang.

"Hello?"

"Hi, it's me, Phillip." He sounded a little nervous. "I'm down in the lobby when you're ready."

"Fine, I'll be right down."

"Oh, great, I'll see you in a minute then."

She hung up, picked up her clutch and went down to meet him. On the way, she couldn't help but wonder why men think women are going to be late. It was a stigma she'd never understood.

When the elevator doors opened, she saw him immediately. He looked amazing. *Cleans up nicely*, she mused.

No jeans on tonight. Instead, he had on charcoal dress pants and a forest green, long sleeved, button up shirt and a charcoal, forest green and black diagonally striped tie. What surprised her most, though, was he'd shaved.

"Wow," she exclaimed.

"Back at you. You look beautiful."

"Thank you," she returned demurely. She liked having him think she looked good.

He took her hand and placed it at the bend of his arm.

"Are you ready to go?"

She nodded, glancing at him sideways.

Once they were in the car, she started to feel nervous again. Luckily Phillip seemed nervous as well. He cleared his throat before he said, "I thought we'd go to this restaurant a friend of mine told me about. I'm sure you've heard of it because it has your name, and is supposed to have amazing food."

She wasn't sure how to respond and she was in shock. Her mind was racing with thoughts about what to say. She didn't want to sound rude, but there was no way she was setting foot inside David's restaurant.

"I'd rather not."

"Why? It's not as good as I've heard?"

"No," she answered cautiously. Her insides were starting to constrict. *Should I tell him,* she debated. "It's my husband I mean, my soon to be ex-husband, owns the restaurant." She could tell it was his turn to be stunned, the response he'd planned frozen on his gorgeous lips. She hurried on, "The food is delicious. Definitely go sometime, but not tonight. Not with me. I can't go in there."

"Right. I completely agree. I guess I should've known," he concurred.

"How could you have known though?" Embarrassed, she shrugged.

He seemed morose momentarily, before he brightened. "Do you want to try something else?"

She'd been thinking of just calling the whole evening off but when he asked her the question, she knew she'd say yes. "I would," she replied, a little of the giddiness returned.

"Okay. Great! How about Spencer's? The food there is really good." When she didn't answer right away, he continued, "He doesn't own Spencer's too, does he?"

"No. I'd be perfectly delighted to try Spencer's. It's supposed to have good steak and seafood, right?"

"Right," he returned, clearly relieved. With care, he pulled out of the hotel parking lot.

CHAPTER 12

"Clive and Janice are your parents' names?"

"Good memory," he concurred, smiling at her. He cut a piece of his rare steak and popped it in his mouth.

Sophie continued, "And your sisters' names are Evelyn and Madeline."

"Wow, you're amazing. Yes, those are their given names, but I call them Eve and Maddy."

She couldn't help but watch him. He reminded her of a child in a man's body, full of energy and enthusiasm. He gushed exuberance and Sophie wondered if she could keep up with him. Admittedly, though, she was enjoying herself. She loved watching him get excited about everything. It was intoxicating.

A memory of herself and David at Sophie's on one of their dates flashed into her mind. She'd enjoyed evenings like this with him, as well, in the beginning, before they married. Sighing, she pushed the thought out of her mind deciding she wouldn't let David turn her into a cynical person.

I want to really know someone. It has to be possible.

She'd been done eating for quite a while, but he didn't seem like he'd be slowing down any time soon. He seemed perfectly content to continue eating until the restaurant closed. She'd learned a lot about him tonight. She found his company gratifying, his manner relaxed. She enjoyed the way he talked too much about everything. Not only did she know the names of his mom, dad and two sisters, but he told her the names and ages of all eight of his nieces and nephews, his grandparents' names and how they'd met.

He told her his family owned a successful import/export business and, even though his father wanted him to take over the family business one day, Phillip had no interest in it. Acting and the theater was, and would always be, where his interests remained. She thought it was great to know someone willing to share himself without holding back. She loved the way he looked, too. Whether vain or not, she didn't care. As an artist, she had to admire the masterpiece God created when He made Phillip.

She knew she was staring at him. It was hard not to, though. His lips were full and soft. She couldn't help remembering their kiss for the millionth time. It must be an oddity to remember our kiss more vividly than the man in the mask.

She let her mind drift a little, thinking about what things could be like with this beautiful man sitting across the table from her. It would be a wonderful life, she was sure.

Abruptly, though, she remembered her situation; she was still married, and was going to

162

have a baby. She didn't need to complicate her life any further by getting involved with someone.

Even if it would be perfect, she mused wistfully. *If only my life were different.*

"Are you going to tell me what you're thinking about?" he questioned softly, gazing at her with his amazing eyes.

"Oh," she responded, flushing. "It's nothing, only I'm having a lot of fun with you tonight and I think it's great we're *friends.*" She'd looked him directly in the eyes, hoping he understood her emphasis on friends.

He understood because his countenance changed. She felt awful, but knew it was the right thing to do.

"I thought we were becoming more than friends," he said intently. He looked as though he wanted to say more but, instead leaned down and brought up the box he'd placed next to his chair at the table. He placed the box in front of her. "This is for you."

"What is it?" she asked curiously, wondering what he could be giving her.

"Open it and find out." He chuckled, all seriousness gone.

Gladly she accepted his offering and opened the box. Inside was what could only be described as a roll of leather. She looked at him, confused.

"You have to pick it up and unroll it," he said.

Cautiously, she did.

Inside were treasures beyond what she could have ever imagined. A trove of paint brushes in all shapes and sizes were wrapped carefully inside the leather pouch. She caressed each brush, unable to hide her excitement at such an amazing gift. Willing herself not to cry, she looked at him and whispered, "Thank you, Phillip. These are perfect. No one, since my parents, has given me such a thoughtful gift. I don't mean to sound ungrateful, but why?"

"Easy. You're in the Art Department but I never see you paint for yourself. I was hoping this would encourage you to start again."

Smiling, she brushed away her tears.

He continued, "The other day I was in Dr. Jensen's office, admiring one of the new paintings he'd hung on his wall. When I asked who the artist was, you can imagine my surprise when he said it was you."

She wanted to say something to help him understand how amazing she thought his gift was, but, before she could begin, he said, "Don't get me wrong. I wasn't surprised by how incredible the painting was. I know you've got talent. I've seen you help your students. What I meant was, it was then I realized I hadn't seen you paint once for yourself since you've been here and that surprised me."

"Oh," she replied, laughing at his long explanation and loving it. "Well, thank you for the explanation. You're right, I haven't painted in a long while and I love it. This is a sweet gift. Thanks again." Carefully, she rolled the brushes back up, tieing the pouch closed.

The drive back to the hotel was somber. The lightness and fun at dinner was gone.

She couldn't help but think her comments about 'just being friends' was what he must be thinking about. Sophie was unsure of what to do. The gift was amazing, she knew she liked him, and she knew she shouldn't get involved right now.

At the hotel entrance, he stopped the car. She quickly got out and started walking toward the entrance. Thinking better of her abrupt exit, she walked back to him, knowing she didn't want the evening to end this way.

When Phillip saw her coming back, he rolled down the window. She stuck her head in.

"I don't know what I was thinking. Thank you for taking me to dinner and for your gift. That you thought of me means a lot."

"You're welcome Sophie. It was my pleasure. I enjoy talking to you, spending time with you, and the gift, well, it seemed natural." He stuck out his hand.

She shook it, feeling weird. Then she set the leather pouch full of the incredible paint brushes on his passenger seat.

"It's too much, though. I can't accept these, but thanks again for dinner." Unable to wait for an answer, she hurriedly walked away.

In the elevator, tears of sorrow and anger fell rapidly onto her face. She tried to wipe them away, but to no avail. "They just keep coming," she mourned aloud.

Unlocking the door to her room, she wondered why she was so emotional. Realization dawned on her almost as soon as she thought it. Placing a hand on her belly, she closed the door.

"It's you, isn't it, little one?" She knew there wouldn't be a reply, and taking off her shoes, she fell exhausted onto the bed.

After spending all weekend fretting about her decision to give him back his gift, she'd decided this morning, Monday morning, she would apologize again and hope he'd understand.

When she got into her classroom, however, the leather pouch of paint brushes was on her desk with a note attached, reading simply:

Keep them.

There was no signature attached; and one wasn't necessary.

She tried several times during the day and throughout the next several weeks to talk to him. At first she'd thought he was just unusually busy, but it didn't take long to realize, except for a brief hello once in a while, when it couldn't be helped, he was avoiding her.

Saddened by the situation, she wished she could say something which would change things back to the way they were but he wasn't giving her the chance. So, she did her best to keep herself busy with everything else going on.

A big part of her life right now was buying her new home. The offer she'd put in had been accepted and she closed within a week. Since the previous owners had moved out of the house, she moved in immediately, well, not exactly moved in.

She had nothing to move in. She needed furniture, a lot of furniture, she thought as she walked into her empty house for the first time.

The furniture store was monstrous, making her first experience inside overwhelming, to say the least. After spending hours deciding what she liked and wanted, she picked out a cottage-style bedroom set with a distressed, antique white finish. At least, that's what the salesman called it. To her, it looked worn but comfortable, new and beautiful.

When she let the men from the furniture store in to drop off her bedroom set, she'd felt more like an adult than ever before. It was frightening, and exciting. It also became evident she needed professional help to decorate the many different rooms in her enormous house.

The realtor advised her to fix up a few things which seemed dated before she moved in to make the process easier. Sophie took Ms. Simms advice and had the entire house repainted, the birch floors sanded and re-stained and all of the countertops replaced in the kitchen, bathrooms and laundry room. Once the renovating was complete, she had the house cleaned and the windows washed.

Her next bit of drama also had to do with her house.

She knew she wanted the furnishings in her house to be warm and comfortable but still feel airy and open, not stuffy like an old library, but something else. She wasn't sure what exactly and after mulling it over for two days, realized she was way out of her league. She made appointments with three different interior design companies.

Her first appointment was with a young woman named Ariel who looked like she was barely out of high school. Sophie was sure she was competent, but knew immediately she wouldn't be able to work with her. She thanked her for coming and waited for her next appointment.

They arrived in style, pulling up in a white stretch limousine. She wasn't sure whether to be flattered or terrified.

Why would they, she wondered. Soon enough, however, Lloyd and Beverly Beasley explained they'd come from an event.

Relaxing at the explanation, they got down to business. While touring her home, they gave her plenty of compliments. Beverly made rough drawings and Lloyd took

notes and measurements. She realized she liked the way they took charge and their overall attitude. They'd said they would get back with her in a couple of days with their ideas.

Her last appointment went about the same as the second, although it was two men, Frank Jackson and Ron Pierce, and they didn't come in a limousine. She liked the energy they exuded. She was excited to see what they'd have to show her.

It was six-thirty in the evening and she was exhausted. Three appointments in one day probably wasn't a good idea, she thought and made herself a peanut butter and jelly sandwich. Locking up her house for the night, she went to her room to eat since it was the only place in the house with any furniture.

She'd finished eating and was about to go to bed when her phone rang.

"Hello?"

"Hello, is this Mrs. Berkeley?"

"Yes, it is. May I ask who this is?" she questioned, trying not to sound bad-mannered.

"Yes, this is Detective Oborn. I wanted to let you know how we're coming along with your case."

"Great." She breathed, relaxing a little, since she knew who it was. She'd called and left a message for Detective Oborn several days ago with her new phone number.

"Well, the news isn't great, I'm afraid."

"Great! What's wrong?"

"We can't find Mr. Berkeley. It seems after you were attacked, he cleared out most of his accounts and left without a word to his contracting partner or anyone at his restaurant."

"You're kidding. You don't know where he is?" Terrified panic washed over her.

"I hate to admit this, Mrs. Berkeley, but no. We were hoping you could give us an idea where he might've gone because we're out of leads." She paused, took a breath then continued, "We'll have to consider the case closed unless we can come up with anything else." She paused again, as if waiting for Sophie to say something. "Any ideas?"

Sophie's mind was spinning. "No; none," she finally blurted.

"Okay, well then, until we receive additional information, we're going to have to stop our investigation. I hope you understand; we've nowhere else to look."

Sophie could hear the sorrow in her voice. She imagined Detective Oborn didn't like to close any case unless it was solved and more importantly, she knew Detective Oborn guessed it wouldn't be the last time she heard from her. The little voice inside her head was whispering something was terribly wrong.

"Mrs. Berkeley? Sophie, are you still there?"

"Yes, I am, detective. I appreciate your call," she intoned, trying to sound calm.

"If I think of anything, I'll call you."

"Excellent. Any questions?"

"No," she answered immediately. "On second thought, yes, I do. Would it be possible to get into the house I shared with David? There's one item in the basement I need."

"It shouldn't be a problem. I'll have an officer in charge over there call you and set up a time."

"Thank you."

"You're welcome. I wish I could've had better news. I'll talk to you soon."

"Thanks for calling." She hung up, feeling numb fear overwhelm her. For the first time since she'd moved into her house, she was afraid. She checked the alarm one last time. Climbing into bed, she hoped the inevitable confrontation with David would never happen.

She dreamt she was being raped over and over, but she was strapped to a hospital bed. There was nothing she could do to stop it. She couldn't tell who her attacker was either because he was the grayish-black mist with yellow eyes.

Chapter 13

"Are you ready to see your baby?" The technician asked, rolling down the top of Sophie's pants.

"I am," she returned quietly, wishing she would've asked Rina to be here with her.

Why didn't I, she wondered, upset with herself, knowing Rina would be upset, too, but hoping she'd forgive her.

"Here we go," the technician began, squirting a cold jelly-like substance onto her slightly raised abdomen.

She sucked in her breath, unprepared for the cold, but forgot all about it once the technician stuck the ultrasound transducer, this was what the technician called it, on her belly and began to move it around.

"There's the head," she started, almost immediately, pointing to the screen.

Sophie strained to see it, squinting, trying to make it out.

The technician continued to point out features, and she continued to struggle to see them. It dawned on her she'd seen one of these once before, in a high school health class. It had been done to discourage pregnancies and make having a baby seem more real. To her, though, it hadn't helped because she couldn't tell what she had been looking at.

Now the technician pointed to something resembling feet. "There are the feet."

Relieved she could finally make out a shape on her baby, she laughed. "Oh yes. I can tell."

The technician looked over at her, smiling sincerely. "Sometimes it takes a while to be able to know what you're looking at, but now I bet you'll be able to see other parts as well." She kindly went back through and pointed out the head, spine, belly, bottom and all the other parts of her baby.

Once she'd finished, she explained she needed to take some of the baby's measurements. When she was finished, she asked, "Would you like to hear the heartbeat?"

She could see the heart beating rapidly on the screen. "Yes, I would."

The technician turned a knob and Sophie was hearing her baby's heartbeat. Tears of happiness sprang into her eyes as she looked at her baby and listened to its heart.

"What a miracle," she whispered.

"Isn't it?" the technician agreed. She did a few other things before saying, "Do you have any questions?"

She tried to get her emotions under control.

The technician handed her a tissue.

Sophie accepted it gratefully. She was trying to think of one of the thousands of questions she'd had before she came into the room, but her mind was blank.

"Before I finish, would you like to know the gender of your baby?"

Sophie gawked at her for a moment, realizing she'd asked one of her questions. Delighted, she answered, "Yes, I would."

"Okay," she said, turning back to the machine. She moved the wand over her belly to where she wanted it. "Look right here. What do you see?"

Sophie looked at it. At first she had no idea what she was looking at, but then it dawned on her. "Is it my baby's bottom?"

"It is. Can you tell what the sex is?"

She tried squinting, but to no avail. "Sort of. No, not really," she answered, a little embarrassed.

The technician smiled sweetly, and pointed at the screen.

"See this and this. It's the . . ."

Sophie interrupted, sitting up on her elbows. "It's a girl. Now I can totally tell."

"Right," the technician returned genially. "And she looks healthy. Would you like a picture of her?"

"I would, thank you." Sighing, happily, she tried to wrap her brain around the notion she was having a daughter.

My sweet Rose, she thought, wiping away fresh tears.

Grabbing a towel from somewhere, the technician wiped off some of the jelly.

"Here, I'm sure you can do a better job finding the goo on your stomach."

"Thank you," she muttered, the tears becoming worse at the technicians thoughtfulness.

"You're welcome."

Sophie was sitting on the edge of an examination table in a hospital gown waiting for Dr. Bowden to talk to her about the ultrasound results. She couldn't help but be excited, as thoughts of her sweet baby kept entering her mind. Finally, Dr. Bowden knocked and came in.

"Hello, Sophie. Everything looks good," she said, getting right to the point.

"Good." She smiled, realizing she hadn't had time to think about the possibilities of something being wrong.

"One thing, though. Some of your hormone levels seem a bit more elevated than they should be. Have you been experiencing a lot of stress lately?"

She opened her mouth to speak. Then closed it, realizing she was unsure where to begin. Frankly, she said, "I have."

"Is it physical or emotional?"

"Mostly emotional," she responded, wondering if she wanted details.

Dr. Bowden looked at her chart, then back at her before she said, "This concerns me a little. Right now is a critical time during your pregnancy and your body is already going through a lot of changes. With your body trying to cope with this new being growing inside, having a lot of stress can negatively affect your baby."

"I understand," Sophie nodded.

"Since this is emotional stress, you should think about talking to a professional therapist. Would you be willing to talk to someone?"

"Absolutely, if you think it'll help."

"It couldn't hurt. Do you know someone?"

Sophie shook her head no.

Dr. Bowden took a card from her pocket, handing it to her. "Helen Hawthorne is a good therapist, and she's my sister. Is it okay we're related?"

Sophie nodded, unable to speak for fear she'd start crying again. It frightened her to think everything going on in her life could hurt her baby. She was willing to do just about anything to make sure her baby stayed healthy.

Dr. Bowden continued, "I think she'd be perfect because she's done some research on the effects a pregnancy and birth of a child can have on the parents." She glanced back down at Sophie's chart. "May I ask, is there a Mr. Berkeley around?"

"N-no," she stammered. "Why?"

"Well, I was hoping he could help alleviate some of your stress. Partners can sometimes be helpful."

"He's not around, nor will he be. We're getting a divorce and he doesn't know about the pregnancy."

Dr. Bowden nodded, as if she'd explained everything as she wrote something on her chart. "I see. Well, then, I definitely think you should give Helen a call. The sooner, the better." She looked up. Noticing the panic on Sophie's face, she walked to her, patting her on the back. "Look, I didn't mean to frighten you. I want you to be careful but overall you look great, and your baby does too."

Then, switching gears, she went on brightly. "I saw in the notes the technician told you you're having a girl. Have you thought of any names or are you still working
on it?"

"I'm going to name her Rose." Thinking she should explain herself, Sophie continued, "My middle name is Rose, and roses were my mothers favorite."

"Rose is a beautiful name." Dr. Bowden went to the door. Opening it, she continued, "Just take it easy. Call my sister and you'll be fine. Rose will be here, happy and healthy, before you know it."

"Alright. Thanks. I'll call her today."

"Great. Now, did you have any questions for me?"

She shook her head.

"Perfect. Go ahead and get dressed. I'll take your chart to the receptionists' desk. Just be sure to stop there and schedule an appointment for next month before you leave."

On her way home, her fear turned into despair. She knew she shouldn't be feeling sorry for herself. Pondering over her situation, she thought she deserved it.

Why should I have to go through this alone? Why did I choose David to be my husband? Why did my mom and dad have to die? She knew these were questions she couldn't answer, but all the same, she wished someone could. *I'm tired of all of this*, she reflected angrily.

All at once, though, she had what felt like a bolt of lightning shoot through her body, and the despair vanished. In its place, the happiness she'd had earlier when she found out she was having a girl. She smiled as she touched her growing abdomen and whispered, "Thank you, Rose. I'm going to be strong for you. We'll get through this, I promise."

Shopping for her baby was exhilarating; exhausting. She'd gone to the mall, instead of going home to her empty, lonely house after her appointment with Dr. Bowden. She wanted to buy some things for her baby.

She'd no idea there was such a plethora to choose from. She knew she needed at least the basics for Rose. Crib. Changing-table. Diapers. Blankets. Clothes. She found some items she liked and bought them. An hour into her shopping spree, though, she decided the rest would have to wait. She was tired and needed to sit down.

Luckily, the Food Court was close by. After buying a drink, she sat at one of the tables. Putting her straw in her drink, she went to take a sip when she noticed a familiar figure.

She couldn't help but admire him. Without a doubt, he was handsome. His chiseled face and bright smile made her heart do a one and a half turn, flip-flop back hand spring, anyway, it was going crazy, even with the distance between them. She had the sudden urge to go say hello and was about to when she noticed *her*.

Probably his date, she growled inwardly. I guess I can't expect him to wait around for me, she thought, feeling . . . What was she feeling? It was an emotion she hadn't experienced in a long time, not since high school. Finally, she recognized it. She was jealous.

I can't believe I'm jealous.

Suddenly, Phillip turned, as if he'd known she was there all along, smiling directly at her. She smiled back, trying to seem unruffled, but inside, she was ruffled.

Ugh, should I get up and leave? Wave? What?

Phillip leaned into the woman, whispering something in her ear. The woman smiled at what he said, before looking Sophie's way. He then started walking over to her.

Raising her hand, she gave a sad, little wave, wishing he'd ignore her. He waved back, which brightened her mood a little. He seems happy to see me, she mused, her heart skipping a beat.

"Hello, Sophie. How are you?"

"Good, and you?" she returned, thinking sometimes pleasantries were ridiculous.

What she wanted to say was, I'm not good; terrible in fact. For starters, I'm sick inside to see you with another woman, my life is a mess and I feel like I've gained fifty pounds in the last two months. What do you think about that, you big jerk? Instead she kept smiling.

"I'm glad to hear it. Where's Rina? Is she with you?" He asked, looking around.

"No, it's only me," she uttered, standing up. "I'm going, but I'll see you at school. Bye."

"Hey, wait a minute, don't go," he said, seemingly frustrated with her.

"Well, your date is trying to get your attention. It looks like it's your turn to order." She pointed dejectedly in the woman's direction.

"Oh, right. Well, uh, then I'll see you at school."
He started to walk away, but seemed to change his
mind because he turned back to her and asked,
"Would you like to meet her?"

"What, meet your date? No, thanks, Phillip,"
she retorted, hoping he'd realize what a stupid
question he'd asked.

"My date?" He returned, looking confused.

Sophie watched his face change from confusion
to realization as it must've dawned on him it was the
only conclusion she could've come to.

"No, no. She's not my date." He turned,
pointing at her, chuckling. "The woman stomping
her foot at me is my sister, Evelyn."

"Sister? Oh," she returned, relief crushing her
green-eyed monster.

"Come on," he stated, gently pulling her by the
arm.

Sophie was enjoying herself immensely. It was
nice seeing Phillip with a family member, watching
how he treated her and vice versa. She certainly had
never experienced a situation like this with David,
nor even with Rina. David didn't have any and Rina
rarely talked to hers. She preferred this. She could tell
Phillip and Evelyn had a great relationship. What
made it more fun was Evelyn liked to talk even more

than Phillip. She looked a lot like Phillip, too. She was shorter and more feminine, of course, but her hair and eye color were the same, and a lot of her mannerisms as well.

"What do you think of my amazing brother?" Evelyn queried, in a matter-of-fact manner.

Taken aback, Sophie responded, "I think he's one of the good guys."

"Nicely put," Evelyn returned. Changing the subject, she asked, "Did Phillip ever tell you about the time my sister Maddy and I dressed him up like a girl?"

"No, he didn't," she answered, a cunning Cheshire grin spreading over her face. *This should be fun,* she thought.

"Eve, please. Don't tell her the story. I'm sure she's not interested," he pleaded.

"Actually, I'm very interested," Sophie chimed in gleefully.

"I've got to tell her. It's one of my favorite memories from our childhood."

"No. I work with her, for one thing, and it's embarrassing. Please don't," he whined, while still trying to keep his dignity.

Obviously not listening or caring, Evelyn began, "Our sister Maddy was given her first makeup kit for her thirteenth birthday and we were both dying to try it out."

Sophie turned to Phillip because he'd groaned and put his head down heavily on the table. Looking back at Eve, they both started laughing hysterically. "This must be good," she cried.

"Oh, it is," Evelyn laughed, nudging her mourning brother. "Come on, help me out."

"Fine, if I'm going to have to be here for this, I'd better make sure it gets told correctly. You tend to exaggerate."

"Do not," Eve charged back.

"Do too."

"Not. Well, maybe a little, which is why I need you to help me tell it, okay?"

Phillip nodded somberly.

"Great. Anyway, where was I? Oh, yeah, we were dying to try the makeup out and Phillip happened to walk into our room. He was young enough so, at the time, he was excited about it."

"Well, I was excited because you guys were paying attention to me. I was ignored as a child, and apparently still am."

"Don't start, Phillip."

He shook his head. "Go on then."

"I would if you'd stop pestering me."

Phillip glared at her, which made Sophie start laughing again. "Phillip, let her tell the story. I really want to hear it."

Eve went on, "We talk him into it and get the makeup on him. I'm talking foundation, eye shadow, eye liner, mascara, blush and lipstick. The whole nine yards."

Phillip made another groan, spurring Eve on.

"Anyhow, he looked so amazing, we decided to take it a step further and put one of my sister's dresses on him." She glanced sideways at her brother and laughing, continued, "Then we got a pair of my mom's nylons."

"Which I got in trouble for, by the way," Phillip quipped.

"Yeah, yeah, my heart's breaking over here," Eve returned.

"Just finish the story. Put me out of my misery."

"I'm trying, bro." Looking at Sophie, she went on, whispering conspiratorially, "Afterward, we had him put on a pair of Maddy's dress shoes and one of my mom's wigs."

"Another thing I got in trouble for," he lashed out.

"For the love of all that is good and glorious, would you let me finish this story?"

"Oh, go ahead, the damage is done. Sophie will never see me the same way again."

"You're right. I'm starting to like you more and more," she jibed wickedly.

"Well, there's *something*, I guess." He laughed, straightening up.

"Anyway, once we got him all decked out, we decided he looked too good to keep him to ourselves. We had to show him off to our whole neighborhood."

"Shut the faculty door. You didn't!" Sophie gasped.

"Oh, yeah, they did." Phillip moaned.

"He looked amazing. At his age, he made a great looking young lady."

"Do you have to go there?"

"You know I do."

"What did the neighbors say?" Sophie asked, extremely curious.

"Well, first you have to understand, he was into it. He had the walk down, and everything."

"I *am* an actor, after all," was all he could come up with, obviously too embarrassed to think more clearly.

Sophie laughed, watching him gleefully.

Eve continued, "Half of them didn't even recognize him. Some asked us who our new friend was, and one little boy went home screaming to his mama."

"As well he should have," Phillip said, obviously glad the story was over.

"What a great story Eve. And, who knows, Phillip? Maybe this experience helped you find your calling in the Theater." Sophie was trying to be earnest, although her face kept smiling on its own.

Remembering she'd promised Dr. Bowden she'd call her sister today and the work day was almost over, she changed the subject. "Listen, I need to leave. I've been having such a good time with both of you, but I just remembered I need to make a personal phone call. I'd better go."

"Oh?" Eve asked, obviously disappointed.

"You have to go, or are you just too embarrassed by my past behaviors to hang out with me anymore?" Phillip questioned, smiling. She could tell by his eyes he was being serious as well.

"No, I do have to go. It was great, though." Turning to Eve, she continued,

"It was nice to meet you. Your brother is lucky to have a sister like you."

"Thank you, Sophie. I agree," she returned, standing, reaching over to hug her. Sophie gingerly hugged her back.

Eve went on, "We'll have to do this again sometime. I'd love to tell you my second favorite childhood memory." Eve looked over at Phillip, who growled helplessly before looking back at Sophie, continuing, "It involves us tying him up and tickling him with a feather."

"Eve! As I recall I still need to get you back for that one." He pretended to lunge forward as if he was going to attack her right there in the mall.

Eve put up her hands, saying in mock severity, "No way, baby brother, don't come near me. We're in public and we're grown. Get over it." Then she relaxed. "Besides, didn't you know the statute of limitations on getting your sibling back for a childhood prank ended two seconds ago?"

He chuckled. "We'll see, Eve. We'll see."

CHAPTER 14

"Don't forget to start a journal. I want at least one entry per day by our next meeting. Agreed?" Dr. Hawethorne stated as Sophie walked to the door.

Sophie turned around and said, "Agreed."

"Also, remember to take it easy. Do at least three pleasant things for *you* as well," Dr. Hawethorne went on more gently.

"I'll remember. Thanks, Dr. Hawethorne."

"You're welcome and please, call me Helen."

"I'll try," she said, walking out of the office. Sophie was glad to be out of there. It had been a long, emotional hour but a good one. It was refreshing to talk about David with someone who had no preconceived notions about him or, more importantly, her.

She knew this was right for her and her baby. Also, she liked having someone tell her to do something nice for herself. She'd already decided what she wanted to do.

She wanted to paint again.

At the paint store, she bought an easel, some oil and water paints and a few other items she needed. Delightfully, she thought of Phillip when she walked past the brushes, knowing she wouldn't need to buy any of those today. She'd been thinking of him a lot since their conversation, with his sister, in the mall.

She knew he was handsome and witty, but seeing him with his sister had allowed her to realize he was generous, sincere and funny as well. *Very funny*, she thought, wishing things were different. She knew having him in her life would be wonderful.

Sophie spent almost the entire weekend in her favorite room in the house—her art studio. The room had a huge bay window which faced the back on the house, giving her an amazing view of the leaves changing colors on the mountains. Presently, Sophie was seated on her work stool in front of an easel finishing her third painting. She'd hardly slept, her trials over the past several months pouring out of her, and onto the canvas. She had peace in this room among all of its smells, and colors. She loved the room because of the view, but also because of the way it had been decorated.

Sophie had decided to go with Frank and Ron to decorate her house. Their color choices found a place in her immediately. They seemed to know her better then she knew herself. They'd tapped into her inner joy. The house looked like a Monet painting, a wash of beautiful color. They filled the house with warm yellows, bright greens, light blue and lavender. The furniture was oversized and comfortable.

In the art studio, though, Frank and Ron had gone the extra mile. It was a large room with a walk-in closet and vaulted ceiling. They had plenty to work with, and they used the space beautifully. The walls were painted sunflower with thick mint green stripes spaced equally throughout, including the closet. On the wall opposite the door, they created a sitting area with an overstuffed couch and chair, a coffee table and two end tables, on each side of the couch.

Behind the chair stood a large poplar tree, and a lily plant sat sweetly atop the coffee table. The end tables had art magazines positioned decoratively on them. The couch was covered in bright yellow and linen checks while the chair was covered in mint green and linen checks.

They'd placed pillows of both colors on both pieces of furniture to tie them together. The coffee table and end tables had glass tops, making it look like the magazines and plant were floating.

Across from the sitting area was a working fireplace and above both the sitting area and the fireplace, directly in the middle of the room, was a large glass chandelier. It looked like something out of an entryway in a mansion, but it somehow fit perfectly in this room. Frank and Ron put all of her supplies in her closet. Different types of easels, in various shapes, were scattered throughout the room. *Exquisite was a good word to describe the room*, she thought. *Or inspiring.*

"Something every artist needs Rose," she whispered to her unborn child.

Frank and Ron hadn't hung anything on the walls, explaining they thought she should put her art work up when she finished them for display. She'd done just as they suggested, hanging one piece above her fireplace and the other above the small desk they'd placed next to her closet. She wasn't quite finished with the third one, but knew where it would go as well--above her couch.

With darkness creeping in through her window, she knew it was time to leave her favored room.

You need to eat or take a shower, she mused catching a whiff of her armpits. Giggling, she walked into her bathroom, turned on the water and undressed. Completely naked, she couldn't help admiring her rounding belly in the full length mirror and was doing so when she thought she heard a strange noise.

The noise sounded like it came from the living room, she thought, trying to stay calm. Still frozen in place, though, she listened.

"Safe and sound," she retorted, walking over to check the temperature of the water. Looking up, she saw a shadow move past her bathroom door. On instinct, she grabbed a towel and yelled, "Who's there?" When no one answered, she quickly ran

into her bedroom and picked up the phone, dialing 911. With her heart beating in her throat, a woman picked up on the other end.

"911, is this an emergency?"

"Yes, I think someone is in my house." She spoke frantically, peeking out her bedroom door. Seeing no one, she closed and locked it. She also locked the door connecting her room to the bathroom.

"Are you hurt?" The woman asked.

"No, I'm just scared. Can you please send someone?"

"Yes, madam. What's your address?"

Instead of an address, the sound of chirping crickets popped into her head. She couldn't remember her address.

"Um, I'm not sure. I just moved in not too long ago. Oh, what is it?" she mumbled, trying to find something in her room which might have her address on it. Finally, her memory returned.

"11815 South 2600 East. In Draper." Sophie noticed her teeth were chattering. Clenching her teeth, she asked, "Are you sending someone?"

"Yes, madam. May I have your name please?"

"My name is Sophie. Sophia Berkeley."

"Thank you, Sophie. My name is Mrs. Capp. I've dispatched a unit to your house. Luckily they were already close by. The unit should be there in five minutes."

"Five minutes," she repeated, walking over to her window, cautiously peeking out. A scream escaped her lips even before she realized it.

"What is it, Sophie?" Mrs. Capp asked.

"There's a man running across my front yard," she muttered, terrified. "Hurry! Please, hurry."

"Sophie, I need you to stay calm. Can you tell me what he looks like?"

"His hair looks longer but it could be red for all I know. It's too dark outside."

"Is he going toward a car?"

"Yes," she answered. "But I can't tell what kind it is. It's too far away." Without warning, a wave of nausea hit her and she ran to the toilet. She could hear the woman on the other end asking if she was okay, but couldn't do anything about it. After a few minutes, though, she flushed the toilet and rinsed out her mouth. Finally she said, "Yes. I'm all right. I'm pregnant. Sometimes I get nauseated."

"Okay, dear, I'm going to dispatch a paramedic as well. Can you hold on for a moment?"

"Sure." She breathed numbly.

"I'll be right back."

She heard the woman speaking to someone about sending a paramedic. She heard her address being read off, then the woman was back on the phone with her.

"Okay, Sophie, the paramedics are on their way. The officer has informed me they're pulling into your driveway. Look out your window and tell me if you can see them."

"Yes, I see the police car," she returned, thinking she couldn't help but notice the neon flashing lights.

"Fine, I'll stay on the line until they get to the door."

"Okay." She heard an abrupt knock on the door.

Leaving her room, she opened the front door. "They're here, Mrs. Capp. Thank you."

"You're welcome, Sophie. Take care."

She realized she'd opened the door too quickly, though. The brisk night air and the stunned look on both of the officers faces reminded her she was wearing only a towel.

"Oh my gosh," she exclaimed, blushing. "I was about to get in the shower when this all happened."

"It's no problem, madam. I'm Officer Larsen and this is

Officer Strong." He introduced them both. "Why don't you let us take a quick look around the house? We'll make sure it's safe first. If everything checks out, you can get dressed."

"Sounds great. Thank you." She smiled, feeling relieved, even if she was barely covered. She sat on one of her newly purchased chairs and waited while they searched the house, including the basement. She could hear them yelling "clear" every once in a while, which would have been hilarious had she not been terrified.

Several minutes later, they walked back in together and the short, round one, with curly hair said, "We checked your house, and there is no one else here. Go ahead and get dressed."

"I'll be right back." She rushed into her room, closing the door. Picking up the clothes she'd been painting in, she put on a pair of jeans, her bra and a T-shirt. Breathing in deeply, she opened the door, walking back into her living room to give the officers her statement.

She gave it as speedily as possible, trying not to leave anything out. They asked questions when necessary, seemingly concerned. After she was finished, the officers looked at each other. The tall one, with bushy eyebrows and gray hair, she noticed, was wearing rubber gloves. He picked up an envelope from off the coffee table.

"Where did you get the envelope?" She asked, the hairs on the back of her neck standing on end.

"First," he started, "We've radioed in your name and address and found a file on you. Is it true you've been having some trouble lately, most likely with your husband?"

She nodded, unable to stop looking at the envelope. Instinctively she knew who it was from and probably what it said.

"Well, I spoke to Detective Oborn about your file and apparently your case was closed due to a lack of leads. Seem about right?"

She nodded again.

"A real shame. I've no doubt this has been a frightening experience, but perhaps it'll help us find your husband.

"I hope it does," she uttered. "The envelope you have in your hands, is it for me?" She asked, needing to move on. They both seemed uncomfortable about it and, she sensed, they were trying to put off the inevitable conversation.

"It is," he replied uneasily, scratching one of his bushy eyebrows.

"We found it in your kitchen. . ."

She finished for him, saying, "Leaning against a dozen red roses."

He looked at her curiously.

"Yes, how did you know?"

"It's something my husband has done since I met him. He thinks I like them," she answered fiercely. "What can I do?"

They obviously could tell she was angry, because Officer Strong finally spoke saying soothingly, "You can relax and let us do our jobs. The dispatcher informed us the paramedics are on their way as well. When they arrive, let them check you out. Okay?"

Shrugging, she agreed. "I guess. Although, I feel fine."

"Let them check you out anyway. We're going out to our vehicle for a moment, but we'll be right back. Will you be all right in here alone?" Officer Larsen asked.

"Sure, I'll be fine."

What followed was a string of flashing lights and mayhem. Four more police cars showed up, along with Defectives Oborn and Mallory, an ambulance, and Rina. She couldn't help but wonder what the neighbors must be thinking.

The paramedics kindly checked her over. When she was given the okay, Detective Oborn came over to talk to her. At eleven o'clock, they finished dusting for fingerprints and everyone but Rina left.

Finally alone, and with Rina's encouragement, they discussed what had been written inside the envelope.

"The note said, 'You belong to me and I'm coming for you'?" Rina asked.

"Yes, exactly."

"What are you going to do?" Rina questioned empathetically.

"Nothing. I've already decided I'm not running from him." She was thinking about the man she saw running from her house. He'd reminded her of Phillip once again, the length of hair and the build.

Surely it can't be him, she thought.

"What are you thinking about?"

"I was thinking about the man I saw leaving my house. He reminded me of someone."

"He did? Who?"

"Well, I'm not sure it was him; only, the man reminded me of him," she answered, not wanting to tell her.

"Who did you think you saw?"

Knowing Rina wasn't going to give up until she told her she reluctantly responded. "He reminded me of Phillip."

"Sophie, that's silly. What would Phillip have to do with all of this? With David?"

"Well, don't you think it's odd his wife may be having an affair with my husband? Don't you think it's odd I saw a man who looked like Phillip following me the other day? And now this, a man who looked a lot like Phillip came into my house. It all seems too coincidental."

"He was the one who rescued you from the man in the school, though, remember? How do you explain away him saving you?"

"I never saw the two of them together. I heard a commotion, but I didn't see the man in the mask and Phillip at the same time."

"Mmmm, all right, it's possible, I guess. Really, though, you can't think it's him."

"My heart tells me it isn't, but I haven't been the best judge of character lately either. I believed in David and look where *that* got me."

"True," Rina agreed simply.

"I want to be wrong, though." She sighed, full of melancholy.

"I want you to be wrong, too. Phillip seems like a genuine guy."

"He does," Sophie added, smiling a little. She couldn't help but think about her personal experiences with him, all of them good.

I've just got to be wrong, she thought, hopefully.

"Why don't you get some rest?" Rina said softly, interrupting her thoughts.

"Yes, I think I will. Night, Rina." She yawned as she walked to her room. "Make yourself comfortable. There are blankets in the linen closet."

"Don't worry about me. I can fend for myself. Night."

CHAPTER 15

You have got to be kidding me, Sophie thought miserably. She couldn't believe it. Sitting on the desk in her classroom was another dozen red roses and an envelope was leaning against the vase. *He's not original*, she thought, picking up the note and throwing it in the trash, unopened. "I hate you!"

"Don't hate me. Whatever I did, I didn't mean it."

She swung around, startled. "Dang, Phillip. Would you stop that?!" She laughed nervously.

"Scared you again, didn't I?" A lopsided smile hung lazily on his mouth.

She chose her words carefully. "You do. I wonder why?"

"I'm not sure," he said, walking over to stand next to her. "Maybe you should tell me why you hate me first."

"I don't hate you, although. . . well, never mind," she huffed, frustrated by her situation. *Why can't I trust him? Why can't I tell him what's going on*, she wondered.

"No, Sophie, I won't 'never mind.' I hope you realize I've come to care about you and I want to help. Tell me what's wrong."

"I'm good. Really." She moved away from him, putting the desk between them. She was able to think clearly when she wasn't close to him.

Phillip sat in one of the students' desks, saying, with resolution in his voice, "I'm not going anywhere until you tell me what's going on."

She walked over to the trash can and pulled out the unopened envelope. Abruptly, she handed it to him.

He took it, still looking at her uncertainly.

"It's a place to start. You said you wanted to know what's going on with me. Open it. The envelope is where we'll begin."

He flipped it over and looked up. "It's not even opened."

"Believe me. I've received many of these. I'm sure I have a pretty sound idea of what it says. Open it."

He took out the note and read it.

She couldn't help but laugh a little when he looked up and seemed frightened for her.

"Sophie, you seem way to calm to know what this says," he exclaimed.

"It says something like: 'You're mine. I'll have you. Watch out'. Am I right? They all say the same thing."

"That man in the school and that man at your house, does it all have to do with your husband?" he asked.

"Yes, Phillip. Apparently, my husband doesn't want a divorce." It suddenly dawned on her he knew about the man at her house. "Hey, how did you know about the man in my house? I didn't tell you."

All of the uncertainties she had about him rushed forward. *He is involved*, she thought and quickly tried to walk past him.

He stood as she moved away from him.

"Rina told me. I was asking about you earlier today and she told me what happened." He seemed to figure out she was frightened, because he continued, "Sophie, what's wrong? You seem scared of me. You don't think I had anything to do with what's been happening to you, do you?"

She shook her head, still moving away.

He gently touched her arm. "Sophie, I didn't have anything to do with what's been going on. Other than the man at the school and this note, I don't know what's going on. Come here," he said, trying to pull her to him.

When she wouldn't budge, he said, "If you don't believe me, you can call either of my sisters. I've been with them almost nonstop for the past week." He dejectedly stuck out his cell phone for her. "Push the green button. I just got off the phone with Eve before I walked into your classroom."

Sophie looked from the cell phone to him and believed what her heart had been telling her. He wasn't involved; at least, not in the way David was.

"Phillip, I shouldn't have doubted you. It's just, I've had a hard time trusting anyone, including myself these past few months."

Hopefully, he stood back up, smiling tenderly at her. "I'm glad you believe me. Will you let me help you now? I want to be a part of your life, if you'll let me."

"You asked for it. Sit back down. It's lengthy." After he sat, she slid in the one next to his.

Sophie started at the beginning, telling him all of it, except for the part where she was having David's baby. She couldn't get it out, although she tried several times.

When she'd finished, he asked, "He started sending you red roses because you told him your mother loved them? I'm just curious, do you love them?"

"I used to think they were pretty and I still do like roses. Although, if I never see another red one as long as I live, it'll be too soon," she admitted.

"Don't hold back. Tell me how you really feel," he said, chuckling heartily.

Laughing along with him, she continued, "Looking back, he never asked what my favorite flower was. He just assumed it was red roses. He's been using them against me our entire relationship." She stood, walking over to the vase.

He stood too, following her over.

"The truth is, I can't stand the sight or smell of them."

"This must be hard on you," he cooed, softly stroking her hair.

She was still lost in her memories. Angrily, she went on. "When I look at them, all I see is him and I hate him . . ." She had to stop, her voice starting to tremble.

Phillip placed his hands on her arms and she crumbled into him. Like a caterpillar cuddling contentedly in its cocoon, she allowed herself to be surrounded by him.

After a moment, he turned her around. She looked into his eyes, as he asked,

"What *is* your favorite flower?"

Unable to help herself, she began laughing and crying at the same time.

Confused and concerned, he asked, "What's wrong? Are you laughing or crying?"

"Both," she replied, wiping the tears.

"It was a stupid question," he stated, worry still evident on his face.

"No, it's a good question, a great question, in fact. It means a lot you asked me."

"Um, are you going to tell me what it is, then?"

She looked away from him, momentarily lacking the ability to handle the love coming from him, the kind of love she hadn't had from anyone, except her parents. She thought the feelings she had for him didn't exist.

"Sophie," he said, gently putting his hand under her chin, lifting her face to him. "What's your favorite flower?"

"Li-lilies," she stammered. "Lilies are my favorite flower."

"Good to know." Leaning down, he kissed her tenderly.

She couldn't help but respond to him, moving her hands over his body, through his thick hair. The kiss ended and she looked shyly into his eyes.

He pulled out his wallet and handed her his card. "You can call me anytime, okay?"

"I will," she responded hesitantly. A business card after a kiss. *Strange*, she mused.

"I'd like to take you out tonight. Is it possible?"

"Yes, very possible. What time?"

"How's eight o'clock?"

She nodded and he continued, "Rina told me you've moved. I'll need your address."

She wrote it down and he left. Still in a daze, she sat at her desk, not hating the roses as much anymore.

Sophie was home. She wanted to go into her house, but couldn't. On her porch were dozens of vases full of hundreds of red roses. More than she'd ever be able to count.

She felt like the bait in a shark tank, a nibble here, a nibble there and now she was in the midst of a feeding frenzy.

"Why is David doing this?" She cried. Picking up her cell phone, dialing his number. Nervously, she closed her phone. His number was no longer in service. *What should I do? What if he's in my house?*

She decided to call Detective Oborn. She pulled out her card and dialed.

"This is Detective Oborn."

"Detective, this is Sophie Berkeley," she began, bravely trying not to cry.

"Sophie, hello. What's going on? Are you okay?"

"Barely." She explained what had happened.

"I'll be right over. Don't get out of your car and don't touch anything. Stay right where you are. Are you safe in your car?"

"For the moment," she responded lamely.

"Good. Stay put and my partner and I will be right over."

She closed her cell phone and waited. Sitting there, she had the distinct impression she was dreaming. *Am I,* she wondered, pinching herself.

"Ouch," she whispered, gingerly rubbing the place where she pinched her thigh.

After twenty minutes, she called Rina but got her voice mail and hung up. *Should I call him?* Her hands had already answered the question for her. Digging around in her purse, she found his card.

"Hello?" he answered kindly, his voice a rich tenor.

"Phillip?" she questioned.

"Yes. Is this Sophie?"

"It is," she responded, laughing nervously. "I hate to call, but I was hoping you'd come over now, instead of later tonight. Something has happened at my house."

"Are you okay?"

"Yes."

"I'll be right over." He hung up.

The police finally arrived and took her statement. Then they began the process of searching the house and fingerprinting.

"I doubt we'll find anything," Detective Mallory stated pessimistically, "But we're going to try, which means we'll be here a while. Is there somewhere you can go for the night?"

"Sophie, is there? You look exhausted," Detective Oborn added, concerned.

"I," she began, as Phillip pulled into her driveway. Relief rushed through her at seeing him. He calmed her and excited her at the same time.

"Do you know him?" Detective Oborn asked, pointing in Phillip's direction.

"I do. I called him," she replied.

He walked over to the three of them. "Sophie, what's going on?"

Detective Oborn stepped in front of him. "I'll let her explain later. Right now I was hoping you could get her out of here; find her a place to get some rest. She looks like she could use some sleep."

Sophie stood there, not sure whether to agree or take offense.

Phillip looked over at her. "Of course." He handed the detective his card. "If you need to get a hold of me, I can be reached at the bottom number anytime."

"Very good," Detective Mallory said. Turning to Sophie, she went on, "We'll let you know when we're done. Go get some rest."

She nodded, walking over to Phillip. Her existence seemed to be taking on a life of its own. She didn't disagree with what was decided, but it would have been nice to be consulted.

Sophie barely noticed when they arrived at his house. Wearily, she let Phillip lead her inside, and into a bedroom. When she was on the bed, Phillip asked, "Do you want your shoes off?"

Numbly, she nodded.

He removed them gently. Gratefully, she lay down.

"Are you cold?" he asked.

"A little."

He took a blanket from the somewhere, covering her. "Get some rest. You're safe now." He soothingly brushed her hair out of her face before turning out the light and closing the door.

Sophie sighed inwardly.

I do feel safe, she thought, closing her eyes, finally succumbing to her weariness.

CHAPTER 16

"Sophie. Sophie, honey, it's your mom. Can you hear me? I want you to come back to us. Please, honey, come back. Your dad and I miss you very much."

"Mom," she called, sitting up with a start. She had a moment of panic as she looked around the room, unable to remember where she was. In the next instant though, she started to remember the whole ordeal.

"I came home to vase after vase of red roses on my front porch." She remembered Phillip coming to her rescue and bringing her to his house. "This must be his bedroom."

Lying back down, she snuggled under the blanket he'd given her. It smelled just like him, earthy, warm, and masculine. As she stretched, she saw the time and sat up again, confused. It said three-thirty. But it can't be in the morning, she thought, because it's light outside. I can't believe I slept so long.

Pulling the blanket back, she stood up. Opening the door and called, "Phillip?"

After a big thump and the sound of shuffling papers, he came around the corner.

"Sophie, you're awake. How are you feeling? Are you hungry?"

She noticed he seemed a little worse for wear. His thick hair was ruffled and his shirt rumpled. It occurred to her he hadn't been able to sleep in his bed last night. By the looks of him, she wondered if he'd slept at all. Finally, she answered, "Yes, I'm starving."

He seemed to have noticed her appraisal of him because he began combing his hair with one hand and trying to tuck in his shirt with the other. "Great. What would you like? I have eggs, bagels, and cantaloupe."

She smiled. "All of it. It all sounds good." She paused, feeling awkward. "But, first, do you mind if I use your bathroom? I'd like to shower and *other* things, if you don't mind."

"Of course. Sure, not at all," he said, obviously understanding her plight. "In fact, let me get you something to change into." He scooted past her, going through the bedroom door and opening a drawer in his dresser. He pulled out a shirt, a pair of sweat pants and a pair of socks. Laying them gingerly on the bed, he said, "You can put these on if you'd like. I'm sure they'll be way to big, but they are clean."

Smiling coyly at him, she asked, "Would you, by chance, have anything for underneath these clothes as well?"

He stared at her, bewildered. She guessed he was trying to figure out what she meant.

Clarifying, she said, "Underwear?"

"Oh, right." He pulled open another drawer, handing her a pair of boxer shorts. "Hopefully these will work."

She grinned. "Thank you. Now if you'll excuse me," she said, gently pushing him toward the door.

"Right. Okay, yes. I'll start breakfast."

She closed the door, laughing quietly. She enjoyed seeing him flustered. Payback, she thought, remembering the day she'd *helped* Phillip in the theater. Although I think I still got the shorter end of the stick. She showered quickly. Dressing was a bit more difficult. Everything was too big, even with the growing bump on her belly. Finally, though, she worked it out, and as she was putting on his socks, the aroma of cooking bacon struck her nose.

Yummy, she thought hungrily.

When she entered the kitchen, Phillip took one look at her and started laughing.

"I told you they wouldn't fit. You look like you're drowning."

"Almost, but I worked it out. See?" she laughed back.

"Come over and sit down. I hope you like your eggs scrambled." He placed a plate full of eggs, bacon, bagels and cantaloupe on the counter in front of her.

She sat on a stool and pulled the plate to her. She ate two big bites before realizing he wasn't eating. "Aren't you going to eat?" she asked, trying to swallow her food.

"I've already eaten. Go ahead."

"I will." She took a bite of toast, then some cantaloupe. "This is delicious," she said, smiling at him.

"I'm glad you like it. I've always thought breakfast should be eaten at night. It tastes better."

She nodded in agreement, her mouth too full to say anything.

After breakfast, they decided to watch Top Gun. The movie was one of her favorites. About half way through it, though, they started talking. She enjoyed being with him, although it puzzled her she could feel comfortable and excited at the same time. It was a concept she was still trying to understand, even though she wasn't complaining.

"Sophie, where did you go?"

"I was just thinking again," she uttered.

"Oh, thinking, huh?" he questioned, leaning in, kissing her.

She hesitated, but only a moment. *This is Phillip, not David.* Need quivered low in her belly. And ignoring all the reasons she shouldn't kiss him, she responded eagerly. Swinging her leg over his lap, she sat, sliding into him. He groaned and pulled her closer, his hands going under the sweatshirt. She let his tongue tease its way into her mouth, grabbing his hair. He moved his lips to her neck. She bit her lip, letting out a moan.

"Sophie," he murmured between kisses.

Their eyes found each other's. She read the question in his eyes: "Did she want to continue?"

And she did, more than anything. But . . . She leaned forward, placing a gentle kiss on his lips. Shyly, she climbed off.

He seemed reluctant to let her go. "Sophie, I think we need to talk."

"As opposed to what we've been doing," she purred lightly.

"What I mean is, and I think you know this, but we need to talk about us," he returned seriously.

"What about us," she asked softly, not really wanting to go there with him right now.

"Sophie," he started, turning his head sideways, looking into her eyes, "You don't seem like the kind of person who'd kiss someone without meaning it, and I could be wrong, but our kiss seemed full of meaning to me. Am I wrong?"

She shook her head no, momentarily lacking the power she needed to open her mouth and speak. *How can I tell him I have feelings for him, when I'm in such a mess with my life right now,* she pondered soberly. She lifted her eyes to meet his and was struck by the love she saw in them. She was paralyzed by her feelings.

"Sophie, I'm falling in love with . . ."

She kissed him, wanting desperately for him to finish the sentence, but feeling equally unprepared for it as well.

Not yet, she thought. Not yet.

Sophie took a taxi from Phillips house to the nearest Mall. She knew teaching in Phillip's sweats was out of the question, and she knew she couldn't go home yet. Quickly finding a casual pant suit, she paid for it, then checked herself into a hotel for the night.

Morning hadn't come soon enough. She'd had a lot of strange dreams, all having to do with her mom and dad, except one. Strangely, it the one she remembered most, she'd dreamt about her baby. She assumed it was her baby, anyway. Her mom was holding the baby on her hip and talking. She wasn't able to understand what her mom was saying, but knew she was talking about the baby because she kept looking from it to

her and back at the baby. She wished she'd been able to understand what her mom was saying.

"Too odd for me to figure out right now," she uttered, a little irritated. She wasn't sure why she was irritated, either. Pushing the dream aside, she quickly hurried to get ready for school.

"Hello," Sophie said, knocking on Rina's already opened door.

"Hi, yourself," Rina replied, looking up from some paperwork. "How have you been?" Sophie asked, trying to sound casual.

"Apparently, not as good as you. You look like you're about to burst. What's going on?"

Sophie told her about the red roses on her desk at school, the hundreds of red roses she found on her porch later that same day and about how Phillip had come to help her.

When she seemed done, Rina questioned, "And this has made you giddy because . . ."

"No, it doesn't make me *giddy* at all. Silly," she retorted, knowing she was being evasive and childish, but enjoying the tortured look on Rina's face. "I'm happy because I spent some time with Phillip this weekend. At his house. In his clothes."

"How did that go?"

"It was nice."

"Sophie, for goodness sake, spill it. What happened?"

She tried to contain a laugh. She could tell Rina was ready to come unglued. Demurely, she answered, "He made me breakfast, we talked and . . ."

"And?" Rina interjected.

"Oh, all right, we kissed," Sophie exclaimed, knowing she probably looked and sounded more immature than most of the students in the high school.

"You kissed? I'm guessing it was good?"

"Seriously, Rina, it was more than good. It was the most amazing experience I've ever had."

"Wow. Okay? Rina inquired slowly.

She could tell Rina didn't seem as excited as she was.

"It was great. Aren't you happy for me? I thought you would be."

"Oh, I'm happy for you, honey. I'm also concerned about you."

Sophie stared at her, waiting for her to continue.

"Look, dear, obviously this is good news. Great news, in fact, but at the same time, it seems trivial compared with the fact that your *husband* doesn't seem to want to let you go. He seems to be getting more demented by the minute, and I think you need to focus on stopping David."

"Trust me, I'm focused on David. He's almost all I can think about. But this weekend, I enjoyed myself. I was happy," she stated, feeling deflated. Without meaning to, Rina had encouraged the waves of reality to come crashing down on her momentary happiness.

"I know, honey, and I want you to be happy. You deserve it."

"But?" she prompted, knowing Rina wasn't done.

"No buts. I'm just wondering if you've told Phillip you're pregnant."

She was about to respond when she heard, "You're pregnant?"

Phillip walked around to face Sophie and continued, "Is it true? Are you pregnant?"

She nodded, the look on his face breaking her heart. She wondered if Rina had known he was there, but hoped she didn't. To Phillip, she said quietly, "Yes, it's true, I'm pregnant." *Why didn't I tell him,* she wondered. She could feel the pieces of her heart falling sharply into the pit of her stomach, because right before her eyes, his face changed from shock to betrayal. She reached out and put a hand on his arm, "I should've told you, Phillip."

He gave her an empty smile as he shoved the bouquet of lilies he was holding into her arms, "Congratulations." Then purposely, he stepped around her and left the office.

As she turned to watch him go, Rina said faintly, "Damn it. I'm sorry, hon."

Sophie looked down at the flowers. "They're beautiful," she declared sadly, willing herself not to cry. She realized, though, two things were certain. She had to make him understand, and she needed him to know she loved him too.

With classes done for the day, Sophie went looking for Phillip. She wanted to apologize one more time. Feeling awful all day, she didn't want to leave things the way they were. Once she arrived at his classroom door, she fumbled with the doorknob, opening it slightly. Poking her head in, she looked around to see if he was there. Sure enough, he was there and he wasn't alone.

She quickly pulled her head back and started walking to her car. The image seared on her brain was Phillip and another woman in each other's arm.

A warm embrace, she thought despondently. He is as corrupt as David!

At her car, Sophie got in, slamming the door shut. She turned the engine on and stopped. She wasn't sure what to do next. Phillip had asked her to come over to his house again tonight.

"After what I just saw, Phillip is out of the question!"

Self-pity was coming on, and she wanted to wallow in it. *Why?* She asked herself over and over. Why do these things happen to me? There was only one place she wanted to go right now. She wanted to go home.

Dialing her cell phone, she called Detective Oborn.

When she answered, Sophie said, "Hello detective, this is Sophie Berkeley."

"Hi Sophie. I was going to call you. What's up?"

Calmly, she asked, "I was wondering if I could go home?"

"Absolutely. We've done all we need to at your house. You can go back anytime."

"I guess you didn't find anything."

"Nothing we didn't expect to find. We are hoping whoever ordered all of those flowers left a paper trail. We're still working on it. When we find out, we'll let you know."

"I appreciate everything you've done to help me. Thanks," Sophie said, feeling her need to wallow increasing.

"You're welcome. For now, though, we're going to have an officer stationed outside your house, to keep you safe."

"Again, thank you," she returned, sensing Detective Oborn was frustrated and feeling the same way. She needed them to find David soon. Hanging up, she drove away, heading toward the only place which had felt like home in a long time.

After spending most of the night wallowing, she came to one conclusion. What she saw must have been a mistake. The intimacy she and Phillip had shared was too real, too genuine. She knew he loved her and those feelings don't disappear overnight, she thought, deciding to give it another shot.

"I've got to fight for him and my love for him. It was a dream, I know it." She concluded, getting dressed for school. *I'll apologize and hope he'll tell me about the beautiful woman he was hugging,* she thought.

Following her classes, she went once again to find him. She checked his classroom, the teacher's lounge and the Theater and unable to find him, assumed he'd gone home early today.

I guess I'll try again tomorrow, she thought questioning herself and her motives.

"Hello, stranger," Rina said, smiling.

"Rina, how are you?" She asked, preoccupied with what she should do next. Then she asked Rina, "Have you seen Phillip?"

"I saw him today, but not recently. I was just about to ask you the same question. I have some paperwork for him. Did you check the Theater?"

"I did, but it was locked," she answered, wondering if she would ever get to tell him she loved him, too.

"Oh, well he usually keeps the front doors locked when they aren't rehearsing. Did you check the side door? It's the one he keeps open when he's in there alone."

Her face brightened a flicker of hope apparent on her face. "Great, I'll try the side door then."

"Good. Would you mind giving him this paperwork while you're at it? I've got a lot to do right now." She was smiling, but she could tell Rina was preoccupied as well.

"Of course. I'll catch up with you later." Determinedly, she headed in the direction of the Theater once again. When she arrived at the side door and tugged, she was happy to discover it was unlocked, opening easily. As soon as she stepped inside, her heart started pounding. She was twitchy, nervous, knowing what she was about to do, tell Phillip she loved him, apologize once again for not telling him she was pregnant and try to explain why she'd done it. Although she'd rather be anywhere but here, she knew their relationship depended on her following through.

She realized she was back on stage. She had no idea where she was going, having never been behind a stage before. It seemed like she'd entered a maze of heavy curtains, abounding in props, lot of ropes and lights. She needed help and was about to call out when she heard voices. She followed the sound, knowing one of the voices was Phillips.

As she rounded a curtain, her feet froze in place when once again she saw Phillip with the beautiful woman he was hugging yesterday.

Long black hair flowing down the woman's back, accentuated by the white, linen shirt she was wearing. The woman also had on a white miniskirt, showing off her long, beautiful legs. She was tall and curvy.

Fury and jealousy engulfed her as she stepped back behind the curtain, trying to listen to their conversation. She knew if she got caught, she'd look like an idiot, but right now she didn't care. She had to know what he was saying to her.

"It's to bad you're going through such a rough time Cynthia, but what more do you want me to do? You divorced me, remember?"

"I know," Cynthia replied sniffling. "But I've made a mistake. I thought he loved me. He told me he did. Now he's disconnected his phone and I have no way of getting in touch with him."

"I'm sorry," he returned kindly. "This actually sounds kind of familiar, if you remember correctly."

"Oh, right, bring *that* up again," she said acidly.

Immediately, her voice softened, "Please help me, Phillip. I'm having his baby and he could care less. I'm alone and I need you."

"You need someone, Cynthia, but it isn't me. Not anymore," he retorted firmly.

Sophie was flabbergasted. Two women and two babies in two days. No wonder he was upset and hurt when he found out about me, she thought. She also understood it was probably because she'd kept the pregnancy from him as well. She knew she should have told him right at the beginning.

"Please, Phillip," Cynthia whined. "What do I do?"

In a somewhat beaten voice, Phillip responded, "Fine, I'll help you in any way I can, but know this. We aren't together anymore. There's someone--"

She cut him off bitterly, "The other woman. Sophie, isn't that her name? You've known her what, three or four months? She's only on the rebound."

Sophie could hardly believe the nerve of this woman.

Phillip had told her what Cynthia did, yet here she was, apparently thinking he was supposed to drop everything and come back to her.

I can't believe this. I should kick her ass, she thought, fanning herself. She knew the heat in her face was rising as her anger increased.

Cynthia was still talking. "You've known me for years. We were married, and besides, I still love you Phillip. I want you back."

It took every ounce of restraint she had to stay behind the curtain. Sophie couldn't remember ever having such mighty emotions of jealousy, hostility, infuriation, and rage.

"You know you want me, too, right baby?" Cynthia asked.

I can't listen to anymore of this, she thought, repulsed.

Not to mention, she was saddened by what she thought was a good point. They had been married and, at the moment, Sophie knew she was nothing but trouble.

She started walking back the way she thought she came in, but somehow got turned around, ending up on the stage, about twelve feet from Phillip and Cynthia. Making matters worse, when she looked over, ready to give an embarrassed wave, she was shocked to see they were kissing. She tried to grab hold of the nearest curtain, feeling suddenly lightheaded, but missed and fell over, making a loud noise.

"Sophie," Phillip called, looking guilty.

She couldn't face him, or her. Quickly, she got up and started running. Having no idea where she was going, she turned left, then right and finally found a door. She stopped for a moment before she opened it, catching her breath. The sound of rapid footsteps confirmed he was following her, and was close by. He called after her. She heard Cynthia call for Phillip.

I'm a foolish idiot, she thought disgustedly, pulling open the door and walking through it.

CHAPTER 17

"You want to do something tonight?" Rina asked lightly, knocking on Sophie's classroom door. "It seems like it's been ages since we've spent any time together."

Looking up at her friend, Sophie could immediately tell something was wrong. Her tone had been easy going. Her demeanor, however, was anything but. "Sure, Rina. Did you want to come over for dinner? I'll make something fabulous and we can watch a movie?"

"Yeah, alright. I'll bring the popcorn and the movie. What time?"

Once again, Rina's words, although calm, were filled with emotion. She knew if Rina had something to say, she'd say it. Letting it go, she asked, "How about seven o'clock?"

"Great! I'll see you then."

She smiled. "Okay." Sophie returned to her work. There were piles of papers to grade and they all needed to be done immediately. Some of these students are brilliant, she acknowledged proudly.

A light noise brought her head up. She saw Rina was still in her doorway and tears were streaming down her cheeks. Frightened, she rushed over to her, grabbing a tissue as she passed the box.

"Rina, what's wrong?"

Rina took the tissue roughly. "Don't you care about me? I mean, we haven't really talked in days, and if I hadn't come to see you now, who knows how many more days it would have been."

Sophie bent her head down, replying quietly, "I know." Remorsefully looking up, she sighed. "You always make the effort and I guess I've grown accustomed to it." She contemplated her friend, recognizing there was more to her tears. "Can you forgive me?"

Blowing her nose, Rina retorted, "I guess."

"Rina, talk to me. Is there anything else?"

Turning her back to Sophie, she answered, "Kind of." Hurriedly, Rina turned back around, cracking a smile. "Let's talk more tonight."

"Alright, if you're sure," Sophie stated, hesitantly.

"Absolutely dear. I know I'm acting a little weird. It must be that time of the month, right?" Rina laughed, but it sounded hollow. "See you tonight," she continued, walking out of the room.

"See ya."

At seven-fifteen her doorbell rang. Walking quickly to the door, Sophie opened it for Rina.

"Hey. Glad you could make it," she said, kissing her cheek.

"Heyourself, sweetie," Rina quipped, coming in. "I've brough licorice ana movie. Whas for dinner? It smells delishussss," she continued, slurring her words.

"Rina, have you been drinking?"

"Maybe alittle hon, bu no biggie. I'm starving." Slipping off her coat and handing it to Sophie, she walked into the kitchen. "Is it garlicbread Ismell?"

"Good nose," she answered, concerned. "Did you drive over here?

"Ocourse. Whynot?"

Trying to keep her rising anger at her friend's stupidity from taking over, she gritted her teeth.

"Because you're drunk, Rina. You could've been hurt or hurt somebody. What were you thinking?"

"Lookgirlie. I'mth emotherly one, notyou. Stop bugginme anlet's eat."

"Fine. I'm glad you made it safe and sound." She went to the kitchen, picking up the pan of garlic chicken and a Caesar salad. She placed them both in front of Rina. Next, she grabbed the loaf of garlic bread and dropped it on the table before slinking into the chair next to her drunken friend. "Can you eat?"

Rina grinned sheepishly replying, "Sure." Setting down the movie and the licorice, she lifted her napkin, placing it roughly in her lap, and picked up her fork.

Trying not to laugh, Sophie said, "Let me get us something to drink, then I'll help you get some food

227

on your plate. Sound good, sweetie?"

"Ar you mockingme?" Rina asked, trying to glare.

Instead, though, she looked like she needed a bathroom break.

Unable to hold in her laughter, she answered, "No, Rina. What would give you such an idea?"

"Isnotfunny."

"Right, sweet . . .," Sophie said, trying to keep a straight face.

Rina accomplished a serious glare.

"Fine. What did you need to talk to me about Rina?"

"Oh it's nothingdear. Everything's worked outnow. Nobiggie."

"First of all, you're drunk, and secondly, it seemed like it was a *biggie* this afternoon." Softening her voice, she continued, "I haven't seen you this upset in a long time, in fact only one other time."

Rina didn't say anything.

Sophie took a deep breath, guessing it had to do with her lack of kindness.

"I should've searched you out sooner. I know. It's no excuse, but I've been dealing with some problems and I've been too wrapped up in myself. I've been an insensitive jerk. Can you forgive me? Please?" She put a hand over Rina's to emphasize her sincerity.

"Oh reallysweetie. It'salright. I'm finenow. I've

beengoing through somstuff myself anI letit get to me." It was Rina's turn to sigh before going on, "Since Iwasalready sadmy feelingssortofexploded when Italked toyou."

She raised an eyebrow, not sure what Rina was talking about, but let her continue.

"Seeing howstrong an independent you'vebecome, Irealized thayou're nota needy lil'girl anymore." She sucked in her breath as she spoke, obviously trying to hold back a sob, "Irealized thayoudon needme anymore. You'rebecoming whoyou weremeantobe. Thewoman I alwaysknew youcouldbe."

"Rina," she said, crying. "You're mistaken. I wish I were stronger, more like you, but I'm not. Thank you for saying it though. It means a lot coming from you." Tears were flowing down her cheeks as she hugged Rina.

How I love her, she thought.

Rina flopped her arms around Sophie.

They continued their embrace for a long while using each other to lean on and gain strength from.

Letting go they both sat back, looking insecurely at each other. As though on cue, they both started laughing.

"We certainly are a pair, aren't we?" Sophie asked, wiping her eyes with her napkin.

"We sur are dear," she answered, struggling to do the same with her napkin.

"Will you tell me what else is bothering you?

I'm listening."

"Why donwe watchthe moviefirst so I can try tosoberup."

"What a fabulous idea."

They finished eating in comfortable silence. After cleaning up the dishes, they watched the movie, the atmosphere calm and relaxing. When it was over, she turned to Rina. "Are you feeling more like yourself, honey?"

Rina shook her head, laughing. "Don't you 'honey' me again. Endearments are my thing. It doesn't sound right coming from you."

"Maybe not." She laughed back. "You do sound better. You aren't slurring your words anymore."

"I'm much better."

"Good, then tell me what's going on."

"Well, I've been seeing someone for the past few weeks. It's been mostly wonderful."

"You have? This is good news. Why didn't you tell me sooner?"

"I was worried. I know you've been going through a lot with David and Phillip. I didn't want to increase your pain by being happy and telling you about my relationship," Rina rambled, slightly embarrassed.

"I appreciate you thinking of me. It's what you always do, but I want to hear when you're happy." She put her hand over Rina's, going on, "I am happy for you."

"Thanks."

"Sure," she returned, smiling. "Is it anyone I know?"

"Kind of. It's Detective Oborn," Rina blurted, her face turning red.

"Shut the freaking faculty door. Serious?" Her voice betraying she was in shock. "I never would have guessed. So, if you don't mind me asking, why were you upset? Did something happen between you?"

"Lana, Detective Oborn and I had a fight. She thought the two of us should break up, which is why I was upset when I came to see you today. After I left your room, though, I called her and we worked everything out," she said breathlessly,

obviously happy.

Sophie sat back quietly, taking it all in. "Why were you drunk when you came over then?"

"I started drinking when I called Lana. While we were talking, I kept on drinking. I'm embarrassed to say it, but when I realized how much I'd had to drink, it was too late."

"Next time, do *not* drink and drive," Sophie scolded.

"I know. A big fucking mistake. I promise it won't happen again."

Nodding her agreement, Sophie said, "I'm delighted for you, Rina. You deserve to be happy. I hope your relationship with Detective Oborn is everything you're looking for."

"Sophie, dear, it is. She's kind, sweet and caring," she responded, giddy.

"I'm surprised. Never would've guessed that about her."

"Oh, I know she has a rough exterior, but it's one of the things I love about her. She's like a present waiting to be unwrapped. I mean, I learn something new about her every time we're together."

"Great. Well again, I'm glad you're happy and knowing something good is coming from everything going on in my life is comforting." She'd said the words but somehow when they came out, they sounded hollow and angry. She knew Rina heard the tension in her voice because her facial expression changed.

"See? This is what I was afraid of," she cried. "I didn't want you to think I was using you or your situation to find myself a relationship. Honestly, it just happened. I'm still worried about you, you know."

"It's fine. Super. I didn't mean to sound rude. It's great you found someone." Even though she tried to sound reassuring, it hadn't worked. She knew it and changed the subject. "What else is going on? I haven't seen Phillip at school in a couple of days. Do you know where he is?"

Rina gave her a wink. "I do know where he is. Been missing him, have you?"

She forced herself not to blush, responding

seriously, "No, not really, well, maybe a little."

Rina continued, "I figured you knew by now or I would've told you sooner. It seems Cynthia, his ex wife, was pregnant. Apparently she had a miscarriage a couple of days ago."

"*No*! How terrible. What happened?" Sophie asked, feeling dumbstruck. *What must Phillip be thinking,* she wondered.

"I don't know. It happened during classes, though, because Phillip ran into my office asking me to cover for him, saying he needed to leave."

She wondered how he told Rina. "How did he tell you what was wrong?"

"He only said his ex was having a miscarriage. Of course I raised my eyes, to which he responded, 'It's not mine, I'll tell you more later. Can you cover me?' I said yes and he left."

Sophie looked at her questioningly, hoping for more.

"I swear, dear, it's all I know."

"Thanks for telling me. I hope she's going to be all right. I can't imagine losing my baby. She must be devastated," Sophie said.

Rina agreed.

Sitting in silence, Sophie wished he would've called her, but couldn't really expect him too. She'd been, if not dishonest, at least distant. She'd given him the impression they were in a relationship, which usually includes sharing pertinent details of ones life. *Honestly, though, what could he expect,* she thought. It was only one weekend they shared quality time together, when they hadn't fought with each other. She'd needed more time, though, and he shouldn't blame her.

"What are you thinking about?" Rina asked, interrupting her thoughts.

She could tell Rina knew, and was teasing her.

"Phillip, I guess, and how I left things with him."

"Are you talking about him not knowing you are pregnant? What could he expect? It's not like you're together or anything."

"Well, I guess we kind of are supposed to be together."

"Get the fuck out. When did *this* happen?" She shook Sophie.

Sophie gave her more details of the time they'd spent together at his house. How he almost told her he loved her, all of it. She also told Rina about walking in on Phillip in his classroom and seeing him hugging Cynthia. And, the most important detail of all, she realized she loved him, too.

Rina listened intently, obviously relishing her role as mentor once again, interjecting comments or questions when necessary. She became concerned with the quickness of Sophie, once again, falling in love with a man she barely knew.

This time Sophie took her friends thoughts on the subject to heart, remembering the last time Rina had questioned her feelings for David, she'd been right. Promising to think seriously about it and talk with her therapist, they moved on.

Finally, at two a.m., they decided to call it a night. After cleaning up, Sophie went to bed. The only dream she remembered again was her mother calling out to her, telling her to wake up and come back to them.

CHAPTER 18

Standing in front of the mirror, Sophie was almost in tears. She'd tried on every pair of pants she owned and none fit. She hadn't bought any maternity clothes and she angrily wondered why as she took off her last pair of pants. Disgustedly, she chucked them on top of the large pile of clothes already on her bed.

I've got to go shopping again, she thought miserably, unable to believe she wasn't more excited about the prospect. She realized, though, that since she found out about Phillip, she hadn't been in a good mood, which made her mad at herself for allowing her moods to be ruled by a man.

"Ugh." She groaned, sinking to the floor in exasperation. Almost at once, though, she wished she hadn't, because her doorbell rang. "Great. Who could that be?" she grumbled, rolling onto her knees and carefully getting up.

She knew she was taking her time, but she had to find something to put on. Finally, she found a pair of sweat pants, *his* sweat pants, and threw them on. When the doorbell rang again, it infuriated her.

"I'm coming," she yelled. Reaching the door, she threw it open, growling, "What?"

Surprised, Phillip chuckled, "Um, I'll come back later." Turning toward the stairs, he stepped down and stopped.

She was surprised as well. He was the last person she'd expected to be on her doorstep. Feeling bad for her manners, and especially since it was him, she stepped onto her porch, saying, "Phillip. I didn't realize it was you."

He looked back at her. His smile was gone, but kindly, he returned, "But if it had been anyone else, it would've been fine, right?"

"No," she replied, trying to choke back her tears. "That's not what I meant. I was rude for anyone." Turning around, she started back to her door.

"Hey, nice outfit, by the way. Those sweats look familiar."

She could tell by the tone of his voice he was trying to make her feel better, but it only made matters worse. "Look, I'm pregnant, okay? And I don't have anything to wear," she shouted, whipping back around to glare at him. The anger wouldn't come though, only tears.

He went to her, putting his arms around her. "Sophie, I didn't mean to upset you," he whispered into her hair.

Trying to get herself under control, she wiped her eyes saying, "Oh, it's not you. I've been trying on clothes for the past hour and not a single pair of pants fit. These are it," she sobbed, grabbing at his sweat pants to show him what she meant.

"I think you look fabulous in those sweat pants," he chortled, pushing her away from him gently, looking her up and down.

"Yeah, right," she huffed, looking down. Feeling a little better, though, she walked toward the door and said, "Did you want to come in?"

"Yes, great." He stepped inside, walking past her.

She shut the door, turning toward him. She was happy to see him, but at the same time wondered what he was doing here since apparently he was back with Cynthia.

"You know, you really do look great," he said tenderly, leaning down to kiss her.

She stuck out her hand, maintaining her distance. "Hold on, mister. I saw you kiss Cynthia, and there's no sharing me. You're either with me or you're not. If you want to kiss someone, go kiss Cynthia." This time the words came out with as much anger as she'd meant them to, although, seeing the pain on his face made the thrill of the delivery less fulfilling. Deflated a little, she continued, "Besides, she needs you right now. How is she anyway?"

Phillip straightened, responding with an odd lift in his voice, "Can we sit down somewhere and talk about it?"

"Okay, sure," she replied, trying to sound casual. She led him into the great room. Once they were seated, she asked, "What is it? Is she all right?"

"She's going to be."

"She had a miscarriage, right? Is there more?"

"Yes, actually. She almost died of a blood clot."

"Oh my gosh, Phillip. How did it happen?"

Phillip explained what had happened to Cynthia, to which Sophie paid attention.

She felt terrible for Cynthia. Losing Rose would be more than she could bear. It must be devastating for Cynthia to lose her baby. Selfishly, she was feeling sorry for herself as well. A lump kept getting caught in her throat. She knew at any second, he was going to tell her he'd decided to go back to Cynthia.

Why wouldn't he, she thought, infuriated. She wants him back and *she* isn't afraid to tell him she needs him. *Oh, just shut up and pay attention*, she fumed inwardly, returning her focus to what he was saying.

"I got into her purse to get her insurance card and her drivers license when I noticed a picture in one of the pockets."

For some reason, the intensity on his face worried her.

What is he talking about, Sophie wondered, frustrated.

She must've had a confused look on her face because he asked, "Is everything all right?"

"Of course. Go on," she blustered, hurrying him on with her hands.

"Right, anyway I took the picture out, curious about who it could be and I was shocked to see . . ." Abruptly he stopped as if questioning himself on whether or not he should finish his sentence.

"Who was it?"

"Well, strangely enough, it was a picture of you."

"Of me?" she blurted, not quite comprehending.

"But how's it possible? I don't know Cynthia."

"True, but . . ." he paused again.

"But what, Phillip. Why did she have a picture of me in her purse? Tell me." Without knowing why, she was scared.

Slowly he continued, "You do know the person in the picture with you."

"I do. Who?"

He shrugged, saying softly, "It was David."

"David? Impossible." She knew her voice was rising and was unable to control it.

"How could you know it was David? You've never met him, unless . . ." She sat back in her chair, comprehension dawning on her. He'd been in on it the whole time. Cynthia,

too. She'd been blind

As if reading her mind, Phillip started shaking his head profusely. "Don't go there again, Sophie. It's nothing sinister. I'm not out to get you, at least not in the way you're thinking."

She sat frozen to her seat, wanting desperately to hear the words which would tell her he had nothing to do with everything awful going on in her life. "Go on. How could you know the person in the picture was David?"

With one hand, Phillip reached into his back pocket and handed something to her.

"What's this?" she asked.

"Just look at it," he answered quietly.

Taking it, she looked down at the picture apprehensively. Immediately, she recognized David and the location where it'd been taken. He was sitting on an old wooden dock, the sun behind him. He had his sunglasses on and he was smiling. She couldn't help but smile back, the memory of the picture surfacing within her. It had been a great time. She'd enjoyed every second of their honeymoon.

All at once, she remembered he hadn't been alone in the picture. They'd asked a local there to take a picture of the two of them. Quickly, but with great emotional difficulty, she unfolded the picture. Sure enough, there she was on the other half, smiling happily as well.

I was naive, she thought sadly, a solitary tear dropping onto the picture.

"Now you understand how I knew it was David. Even if I had a question, though, there's also an inscription on the back," he said tenderly.

She turned the picture over to read what she already knew would be written there. It said: David and Sophie Berkeley. Honeymoon. In addition, a new inscription had been added. Nauseated, she read: Cynthia, my darling, Here is the picture you asked for. Love, David.

What an egotistical jerk he is, she thought. To Phillip, she said, "I can't believe he didn't, at least, rip me out of the picture." She wanted to rip the picture and every thought and thing which had ever had anything to do with David to shreds. Instead, she deliberately handed the picture back to Phillip saying, "You had no idea Cynthia was pregnant with David's baby as well?"

"No." he returned. "She's completely broken up about losing the baby. She wanted it, even though David wants nothing to do with her."

She understood because those were the feelings she had for her baby. "Did she say why he didn't want anything to do with her or the baby?"

"No, but I'm guessing it's because of everything he's been doing to you. He had to run so they wouldn't catch him, right?"

"True." She nodded.

"Also, she told him she was having a girl and after that he quit answering her calls and refused to talk to her."

Sophie remembered David saying he only wanted a boy.

Phillip went on, "It was probably just a coincidence because the police are after him."

"Probably," she agreed and wished things could be different with her and Phillip. Now she was sure he was going back to Cynthia. She'd heard enough and was certain Phillip had come over to tell her their small but significant relationship was over. She didn't want to hear the words from him.

Curtly, she stood and said, "Well, thank you for telling me all of this. It puts a lot of things into perspective. Cynthia is lucky to have you in her life. If you don't mind, though, I'm tired and I'd like you to go."

"Wait. Why?" he asked, shocked.

She turned away. She didn't want him to see her crying again.

In an instant, he had his arms around her. "What's wrong?"

"Would you stop being nice to me? Just go to Cynthia. I know she needs you and loves you."

He turned her around. "Sophie, you've got it all wrong. Cynthia doesn't have me for anything more than a friend. I stayed with her until her parents flew in from New York because I thought I should, but the whole time I was thinking about you. All sorts of crazy ideas." His breathing had become more rapid as he continued, shaking her a little, "Don't you know how I feel about you?" He bent down and kissed her, his soft lips crushing hers, begging her to understand.

After a long while, they broke apart. Caressing her cheek with the back of his hand, he said, "I've fallen for you. No, that's not totally true. I've fallen *in love* with you Sophie."

Pulling his head down to her, she opened her mouth and kissed him, feeling love and longing course through her body. *I really do love him*, she realized happily. In the back of her mind was a nagging question, though. Letting go of him, she asked, "Phillip, what about the kiss in the theater? I *saw* you kissing her.

Softly, he answered, "No, *she* was kissing *me*. It was completely unexpected."

He tried to kiss her again, however, she wasn't finished.

"Do you mean it? Because I'm not asking for anything. If you want to be with Cynthia, now is the time to tell me. I can take it. Believe me, I've endured worse."

"Sweet, Sophie. You are the only one for me. I've known it since you helped me in the theater. I only want you."

"What about my baby? I'm pregnant with David's baby, the same man your ex-wife was having a baby with. You'd have to be a father to a baby whose biological father stole your wife. Can you live with all of the history this child will carry?"

Tears of fear, and sadness rolled down her cheeks. This was hard, because of what she her feelings for him, but her child was more important than anything else. She wanted Rose to have unconditional love, by both parents. Barely getting out the last, but most important question on her mind, she asked, "Can you love this child?"

"Honestly," he started slowly, obviously realizing how important this moment was, "You're pregnancy threw me, and finding out your husband

and my wife were together . . . really threw me. The fact remains, though, I love you. I've thought a lot about it, and, it doesn't matter who the biological father is. The baby is a part of you, which means I'm already in love with this baby and she had better get ready for me because I'm going to be an overprotective dad."

Sophie carefully considered the lines and furrows in his face, trying to determine whether or not he was lying. He seemed genuine. Nothing in his demeanor suggested otherwise. Relaxing the tension she'd been holding inside, she leaned into him, saying,

"Good. Although we might have to work on the overprotective part. Trust me, it has the opposite effect."

Once again, their lips found each other and, after a moment, once again, he let her go, saying, "Sophie, there is one more thing I need to tell you."

"What is it?" she asked, opening her eyes.

His demeanor had changed.

"Tell me," she prodded.

"I've got to go to New York for a few days."

"Why? Cynthia," she choked out, feeling ice form around her heart.

"No. I don't ever plan on seeing Cynthia again. This has to do with my father and the family business."

"You're sure?" she asked, trying not to sound like a child.

"I promise. I'll be gone a few days, then I'll be all yours.

She nodded as he leaned down and gently kissed her again.

After they said their good-byes, she closed the door, leaning heavily against it. She realized she was crying again; only this time, she didn't care.

Please be telling the truth, Phillip, she thought, trying to ignore the foreboding in her soul.

CHAPTER 19

For the first time since she'd started teaching, school seemed like a chore to Sophie, as if she were carrying a burden which couldn't be lifted. Classes seemed to move in slow motion. Looking at the clock, she wondered if the day would ever be over.

Part of her problem was Phillip was gone. He'd told her he loved her, then he left, but it was much more. She sensed something wasn't right. It was a feeling in the deepest part of her being telling her to be careful. If only my intuition could tell me what to watch out for, she thought, guessing, though, she already knew.

Finally at three forty-five, she finished up her paperwork for the day and went to find Rina. Sitting heavily in a chair opposite Rina's desk, she began gloomily, "Rina, I'm tired."

Rina looked up vaguely amused, obviously preoccupied. "I'm not surprised, dear. You're carrying a baby, working full-time and dealing with emotional issues. I'd be exhausted, too, if I were you."

"Any suggestions?" she questioned, knowing there wasn't a good answer.

"Hon, you've got to take it easy," Rina retaliated softly.

"Take it easy, huh? Sounds simple enough, except my life is happening right before my eyes. As it is, I'm still trying to catch up."

Rina smiled indulgently. "You're right, dear."

"He left, you know," Sophie said, sulking.

"I know, but he'll be back. He isn't gone for good. Phillip is a good man, and I've no doubt he cares about you. Hang in there. Things can only get better from here."

"You think?" She started anxiously. "I feel like something bad is going to happen."

"Like what?" Rina asked, tolerantly.

"Well, for example, last night I dreamt I was trapped inside something, like a box, only it was transparent. I could see out, but I couldn't get out. I looked everywhere for a door, only there wasn't one."

"Strange dream, hon," Rina interjected.

"It was. All of these people were walking past me. I kept screaming for someone to let me out, but it was as if I wasn't even there. Finally, you walked up to me, stopped and smiled. You had such a sad look on your face, and you kept trying to say something to me, only I couldn't hear you."

"I'll say it again. Strange dream, hon, but that's all it was, a dream."

"Maybe, but there's more. Do you mind if I tell you the rest? It's got me kind of freaked out."

"Oh, of course. Go on," Rina replied.

"After a while, you walked away and Phillip came up to me. He was saying something to me over and over again. I tried with all my might, but I couldn't understand him. I kept yelling, 'Let me out! Please, help me.' He smiled sadly, walking away."

"Dreams can be crazy sometimes," Rina said, trying to keep her voice light.

Sophie could tell Rina was starting to think it was weird as well. Quietly, she continued, "Finally, my mom and dad came over to me. I was sobbing. My clothes were wet from my tears at seeing them and not being able to touch them. I screamed, 'Help me! Help me!' My mom smiled, and I was momentarily comforted. I thought they were going to get me out, only before they could do anything, they began to disappear. I started banging on the glass, yelling, 'No! Wait!' When they were almost gone, I heard my Mom say, '*Wake up Sophie.*'" She didn't tell Rina about the grayish-black mist with yellow eyes which had been there with her, inside the glass cage. It seemed to freaky, and she didn't want Rina to think she was losing it. The last time she tried to tell Rina about it, she'd ignored the comment completely. Repeating her dream out loud made it seem less frightening; however, her instincts told her there was something wrong and her dream was trying to give her clues.

What they were, though, she could only guess.

Rina tried to smile. Instead she grimaced. Finally, she said, "You know, I've heard of women having crazy dreams when they're pregnant. It's obviously bothering you. Why don't you call your doctor, see what she thinks?"

"Good idea. I will," Sophie responded, sensing she already knew what the doctor would say.

"I'm sure it's just your stress coming out in your dreams. They say they're healthy. Besides, look how far you've come. At this time last year, you were living a lie with a creep for a husband and nowhere to go. You've come a long way since then. I'm proud of you."

Sophie appreciated all of her encouragement, but her words didn't decrease her feeling she was in danger. Still, there wasn't anything more she could do about it here. Standing, she walked to the door, said good-bye to Rina and left.

Maybe a drive will do me some good, she thought. When she was young and had been upset, her dad had always taken her for a drive. It worked then and she hoped it worked now.

When she'd almost reached her destination, she knew she was going to do more than just drive by. She wanted to go for a hike. She wanted to be up, once again, in the mountains which always made her mom and dad seem closer to her.

Parking, she stepped out of her car, closing the door. A thought came to her that perhaps she should've let someone know where she was, but she pushed it away, starting excitedly up the trail.

The air was crisp, yet inviting. And although most of the trees were bare, there were still several different types of pine trees holding onto their greenery. Breathing in deeply, she continued up, enjoying the firmness of the earth beneath her feet and the smell of the mountains. It didn't matter the time of year, she loved being in the mountains, loved the peacefulness abounding there.

Maybe it's the higher elevation, she thought vaguely.

She decided to take an easier trail because of her condition and was glad she had. Half way up, she was breathing heavily and needed to rest. On her right, she noticed an opening in the trees, with a large rock situated close by.

Veering off, she walked over and sat down. As her breathing became normal again, peace enfolded her.

"Oh, mom, how did I let myself get like this?" She closed her eyes, hoping for an answer, gently rubbing her increasing abdomen. Thoughts poured out of her. She wondered if her mother had met her baby's spirit, if she knew her grandchild.

What's she going to be like, she marveled, hoping she'd like her and the feeling was mutual.

I *hope I'm half the mom you were to me,* she thought. *I want to give her a life full of love and joy, a place where she feels safe.*

"I've thought of a name, too, mom," she confided. "I'm going to name her . . ." She stopped, hearing someone near her. Whipping around, she saw him, the man who'd come to represent the opposite of everything good and kind in the world.

It was David.

"Hello, Sophie," he said casually, taking a step toward her. Standing quickly, she looked around, trying to plan an escape in her mind.

If I can just get to my car, she thought.

"David, what are you doing here?" she yelled, trying not to sound panicked. She wanted to kick herself for coming up here alone, for ignoring her instincts and especially for underestimating David.

Simply, he said, "I've been following you." With fortuitous ease, he bent down and picked up a rock, flipped it over, looking intently at it, like he was on a nature walk and he'd just discovered his treasure. After a couple of seconds, though, he chucked it away, walking toward her again. "I'm sure you had to know I've been keeping track of you. It's what I did while you and I were living together; you can't believe I'd stopped. I'll always need to know where you are."

He stopped about three feet in front of her, smiling maniacally. "You're my wife, Sophie, which means you're mine." His words sounded forced, as though it was taking all of his effort to maintain his composure.

Full of fear, she tried to take a step backward, but he caught hold of her wrist, holding it fast.

"Where do you think you're going? Stay and talk. It's been a long time since we've had a good talk," he cooed venomously. He reached into his back pocket and pulled out a rope, resting it on top of her wrist.

"What're you going to do with the rope?" She cried, trying to wiggle her wrist free. "I've got to go. Let me go, please," she pleaded, trying to use her other hand to pry his off. Instead, he grabbed her other wrist, twisting it behind her back. Crying out in pain, she instinctively turned her back toward him, hoping to ease some of the pressure. It did momentarily, when he let go of the first one he'd been holding. She realized too late, though, she'd done exactly what he wanted her to do.

"Ouch, David, you're hurting me," she yelped, dropping her head. She noticed the rope had fallen to the ground during the scuffle and quickly put a foot over it.

"Nice try, Sophie," he growled, sliding his hand down her leg menacingly.

She tried in vain to crush his hand with her foot. All it did was allow him to get to the rope easier.

"Perfect," he stated waspishly, snatching her other hand and proceeding to tie them both tightly behind her back. Once he was finished, he grabbed her by the arm and turned her around to face him.

"Why are you doing this?" she sobbed, looking up at him through her tears.

He roughly wiped them away.

"Sophie, Sophie, Sophie. I'm afraid you've driven me to this. I can't have my wife telling people I'm a bad man, now can I?"

"But I wouldn't tell anyone David, really I--"

He slapped her hard across the face.

"Don't lie to me. You've already told plenty of people. Rina, the police, a lawyer, your new boyfriend and your psychiatrist. It's been decided. I'm going to have to get rid of you."

"Get rid of me?" she repeated, with a catch in her throat. She peered into his eyes again, noticing this time the insanity within them. The kindness and gentleness which had once been there were gone, replaced, without a doubt with evil.

She thought how absurd it was to say people don't change, when she realized in this moment, based on choices a person makes, everyone can change, either for good or bad. It plain boiled down to choices.

"I've tried to win you back," he continued. "I've sent red roses, explaining my love for you. I've given you more than enough chances to come to me and apologize for your mistakes. Well, Sophie, time's up and now I'll have you my way. Dead."

He'd been talking to her while he was pulling her along, like a dog, unsure how to use its leash.

"David, no," she yelled. "Let me go."

254

"I won't. Now shut up or I'll use tape," he yelled back, pulling a roll of duct tape out of his jacket pocket for emphasis.

Choices, she thought, finally understanding what she had to do. Without question, she was tired of being bullied by him and she knew she didn't want to die, nor would she let anyone hurt her baby without using every bit of fight in her.

Stopping abruptly, she forced him to stop.

"Knock it off, Sophie, get moving.

Owww!!" he groaned, letting her go, falling to the earth. "Son-of-a-bitch!" He screamed, grabbing his knee.

She'd back kicked him in his right knee as hard as she could. Not sticking around to access the damage, she took off, running as fast as she could down the mountain. Several branches hit her in the face, but she barely noticed, the adrenaline flowing through her, keeping the pain at bay. She knew she had to be near the bottom.

"Almost there," she whispered to her baby and herself.

While she'd been running, she'd also been trying to get her hands out of the rope. She knew once she got to the bottom, she'd need them to get into her car.

"Yes," she cheered out loud. Her car was still there and her hands were almost free. She stopped about twenty feet from her car to pull the rope the rest of the way off. Breathing hard, she turned around to see if he was coming when everything went black.

"Where am I?" Sophie whispered, slowly opening her eyes. Darkness surrounded her, but she could tell from the smell beneath her she was on a wood floor. Her throbbing head felt wet and sticky. She guessed it was probably blood from where David must've hit her.

Gingerly, she raised it, trying to look around. A soft moan escaped her lips as she rolled onto her hands. They were tied behind her back and the pressure of her body was crushing them. Quickly, she rolled onto her other side. Breathing heavily, she noticed a slit of light coming in near the floor. As she looked up, it became evident the light

was coming from under a door. The doorknob looked familiar and she recognized the smell, too. She realized where she was.

"He's got me in our coat closet," she spat out angrily. It was the main floor, hall closet, to be exact. Overflowing with coats, it smelt strongly of David's cologne.

She tried to sit up, hoping she could reach the knob and open it, but her pregnant belly had other ideas.

"What am I going to do?"

She wept nervously, even as she began to loosen the ropes from her wrists. She needed a plan, a way to escape or change Davids mind. While she discarded different ideas, she continued to loosen the ropes. It was a painful process, though. The rope, as well as the wood floor, was starting to burn her wrists and rub them raw. It didn't matter. Her efforts were paying off. I've got to hurry, she thought, ignoring the pain and focusing instead on what David had said he was going to do to her.

Kill me. Death isn't an option, she reasoned, concentrating instead on her daughter. She wouldn't allow anything to happen to her.

The sudden thump-thumping of someone coming down the stairs sent a shiver of terror through her body. She knew it was David.

"No," she trembled, pulling on the ropes with even more furor.

The door opened, letting in a bright stream of light.

Squinting, she tried to see who it was, although she'd already guessed.

"I'm glad to see you're awake," he drawled slowly, smiling brightly. His smile quickly disappeared, though, and she wondered why. Following the direction of his gaze, she realized her efforts to get the rope off her wrists had caused her shirt to ride up and her ever more protruding belly was fully exposed.

"What's this?" He questioned, touching her lightly, his voice changing from sardonic evil to a startled wonder. Without waiting for a response, he tenderly asked the obvious, "Are you pregnant?"

"Yes, David, I am," she hissed, trying to sit up.

Still staring at her pregnant mound, he absently helped her. "How far along are you?"

"I'm five months along," she responded, trying to stay calm even though she was repulsed by his touch.

"It's mine, right? You haven't been with Phillip yet, which means it must be mine." He looked over at her, his face accusing. "Right?"

"It's yours," she stated blandly, wishing with all her heart it wasn't.

Quickly, he asked, "Is it a boy?"

"It's a girl, David, and I'm going to name her—"

"A girl?" he interrupted, obviously disappointed. "Well, isn't that nice," he continued, his voice steely and hard once again.

Startled by the change, she replied, "Yes, David, it's a girl. Your baby girl."

"I want a boy, not a girl. You know I want a boy, Sophie," he said. His momentary tenderness completely vanished.

Astounded, she glared up at him. "I didn't have a choice, David. A girl is what you and I created. A girl is what's inside of me. Our girl. I can't change it, nor would I want to."

"It should've been a boy. If it were a boy, things might be different. I've got to go. I'll be back in a while," he said numbly as he stood and walked away.

Out of sheer human necessity, she yelled after him, "David, wait!"

He reappeared, saying gruffly, "What is it?"

"I -I need to go to the bathroom and I could use a drink of water. Please." She didn't want to push him, but she couldn't help herself. She knew if she was going to keep her strength, she needed water.

He looked down at her as if he hadn't heard her or he'd forgotten she was a living, breathing being.

Carefully, she tried again. "David, please. At least let me go to the bathroom."

"I guess I don't want you stinking up the place." He harshly lifted her off the floor and pushed her into the guest bathroom. "Hurry up."

"Um, David, I can't get my pants down."

He rapidly undid her pants, pulled them down, her underwear as well and stood back.

"Thank you, David," she continued, sitting down.

Once she finished, he helped her get her pants back up, then put her roughly back in the closet.

"Don't even think about trying to escape. I'll be back in a minute," he sneered.

True to his word, he quickly came back, and to her great relief, was holding a glass of water with a straw in it. He set the water down on the floor next to her. "This'll have to do. I've got to leave now." He slammed the door.

Listening to him walk away, she got on her knees to take a drink of water. After she drank it all, she started working again on removing the ropes. David hadn't checked them, obviously shocked by the pregnancy.

It seemed to have slowed him down momentarily, but somehow she knew in her heart it wasn't going to stop him.

Maybe if I were having a boy, she thought wistfully, slipping back into her old mentality. Swiftly, though, she brushed those thoughts aside, she needed to escape and do it fast.

After what seemed like a lifetime, the ropes still didn't seem any looser and her wrists were hurting worse and worse. She kept at it, though. There wasn't anything else she could do.

CHAPTER 20

Sophie was surprised when she woke up. She hadn't realized she'd fallen asleep. For a brief moment, she thought she'd died because of the bright light pouring in on her.

Quickly, though, she realized the door to the closet was gone, removed completely from its hinges.

Is he letting me go, she wondered, momentarily excited.

The feeling speedily disappeared when David stepped in front of her.

"Glad you finally woke up. I don't want you to miss any of this," he stated, smiling brightly.

Squinting up at him, she noticed in one hand he was holding a brick and in the other a trowel.

"Miss any of what? David, what're you doing?" she questioned nervously.

"Just a second. I'll be right back," he replied lightly, walking away.

This is it, she thought. He's completely lost it and now I'm going to die. She heard a sloshing noise, some tapping before he was standing in front of her again. Her eyes were adjusted to the light now. Seeing what he had in his hands this time sent a shiver down her spine.

"What are you going to do with those?" she asked, nodding toward the hammer and nails in his hands.

"First things first," he squawked, setting them down.

She noticed he seemed almost robotic, unreal. His face, although cheerful, seemed empty. She couldn't see or feel any emotion coming from him. It was as if he'd turned himself off to any feeling. He stood her up, turning her around, untying her wrists. With relief, she rubbed them, glad for the freedom he'd given her.

He picked up a wrist casually. "It looks like you've given yourself some sores. To bad, because this is going to hurt."

Before she could react, he grabbed both of her wrists in one hand and proceeded to tie them up again, this time in front of her.

"Wait, David! Please! Don't do this," she cried. Helplessly, she watched him tie her up as tears streamed down her cheeks. She'd actually thought he was going to let her go.

"We've been over this, Sophie. You didn't think I changed my mind, did you?" he asked, laughing mirthlessly.

Ashamed, she lowered her head, unable to believe he knew her as well as he did and hating him for treating her this way. She wanted to tear his eyes out, twist a knife deep into his heart, bash his head to bits with a large bat. It sounded sick, but she couldn't help it. Her hate for him boiled her blood.

Roughly, he pulled her face up, making her look at him.

Surprised, he chuckled. "Hey, I guess it's a good thing I tied you up. You look ready to kill me. I had no idea you had such fire in you."

She stood there, steaming.

There's got to be something I can do, she thought.

David continued, "I'll tell you, the pregnancy threw me. I had no idea." He stopped a moment, pushing her back farther into the closet, whispering with a tenderness which would've sounded sincere if she hadn't been able to see his cruel, twisted face.

"Now, I want you to lie on your back for me."

"No, David, I won't," she yelled, allowing some of her anger to escape.

"Either you do it of I'll make you do it," he replied coldly.

Full of fury, she spit in his face.

His mouth opened in shock, as if he couldn't believe she'd had the gall.

"Bitch," he yelled.

She regretted what she'd done immediately. He grabbed her by the neck, slamming her down on her back. She literally saw stars from the force of the blow. Her throat throbbed where he'd grabbed her neck.

"I can't breathe." She gasped.

"Like I care," he responded calmly, once again in control of his emotions. "Now hold still or one of these nails could be hammered into your body."

Ferociously, he nailed her shirt into the wood floor. When he was finished, he looked directly into her frightened eyes and whispered, "These are because I don't want you getting away."

"If you're going to kill me, get it over with." She sobbed hysterically, her voice coming back a little, but still raspy.

"Absolutely not. You've made me suffer these past several months and I intend to return the favor," he declared, chuckling, before he went on, the cold, unfeeling stare back in his eyes. "You see, I have a plan for you."

"A plan?" She gasped.

"Of course," he replied, sitting in front of her. Crossing his legs, he rested an elbow on his leg and his chin on a fist. "Want to hear about it?" he asked, gushing like a child ready to tell an amazing story. When she didn't answer, he went on, "You know, I've thought a lot about what I want to do to you." He halted a moment, as if waiting for a response.

When she didn't say anything, he continued, "Torturing you was my first idea. I thought it seemed fitting, with all of the pain you've caused me." He leaned his head and an arm out of sight for a minute. When they were back in her view, she was horrified to behold a large butcher knife in his hand. "As you know, I have a knack for one of these."

He held it up in the light for her to see. "I can cut through almost anything with it. Chicken, lamb, or even you." Lingering over his words, he regarded her a moment, gauging her reaction. He touched the blade to her leg.

She yelped. "No."

He smiled. "I was thinking I'd start with your ears and eyes, followed by your scalp." As he spoke, he touched the knife to each area, causing Sophie's limbs to quake. "Then, I'd slowly work my way down and up, cutting off your hands, your arms. Your feet and thighs." He touched the sharp edge to her cheek. "Get the point." He laughed, like he'd told a cruel, dirty joke; full of emptiness, but forced and loud. When he noticed she wasn't laughing with him, he stopped, looking intently at her. "Are you still with me?"

The scream came out of its own accord. She hadn't meant to do it. Inside, though, she was seething, a combination of terror and rage boiling up inside of her. Her heart was racing rapidly. Her pulse quickened. It seemed her hearing became sharper. Her eyes clearer, and even her pain more excruciating.

He responded swiftly, pulling duct tape out of nowhere, ripping off a piece and placing it firmly over her mouth. He didn't even seem bothered by her outbreak. He looked, in fact, like he was relishing it. "Can't have the neighbors hearing us, now can we?" He smacked off. Then he sat back down again. "Now where was I? Oh, right," he answered for himself, picking the butcher knife back up, spinning it deftly on his pointer finger.

"I had it all planned out, but you surprised me with the bump on your belly." He'd stopped twirling the knife on his finger and was pointing it at her instead, like a father scolding his child. "I have no desire to torture our baby, even if I don't want her. Instead, I've come up with another plan. One, I think, which is even more fitting." Pausing, he looked away, as though he were deciding how much he wanted to tell her.

After a few moments, he looked back at her.

"Did I ever tell you I had a sister?"

She could only stare.

It seemed he wasn't expecting a response because he went on, "I did. Her name was Hazel and she was beautiful. She was three years younger than I and had such spirit, such joy. Even with all of the evil and hate which prevailed in our house, she never let it get her down for long. She kept me from going insane." He stopped again, seemingly lost in childhood memories.

Her mind caught hold of the name, Hazel. Where'd she heard the name before? It wouldn't come to her. She couldn't help but think his sister hadn't kept him from insanity or premeditated murder. She also realized this was the first time he'd shared a memory of his family with her and wondered, absently, why he was telling her now.

"She was only here six months when she died in a car crash."

Sophie couldn't help but be startled by what he was telling her.

How awful for her, she thought. Her head was still spinning, trying to put together the pieces. *Hazel, and a car accident*, she thought. *This seems familiar.*

"The thing is, she didn't die immediately. You see, I'd just bought her a new car and she wanted me to go for a drive with her. I was apprehensive because it had been raining hard all day, but she talked me into it. When the other car struck us, I was thrown from the vehicle. My sister, however, was caught behind the wheel. While the paramedics and the police were waiting for the Jaws of Life to get on the scene, the car exploded and she was burned alive inside." He stopped again, obviously experiencing the pain of the memory, before he went on, "Sophie, she was trapped inside the car. Understand?"

She would've shrugged she had no idea, but couldn't. She sensed he was blaming her for his sister's death. Was she to blame? She would've questioned him further; she had a feeling she should know what he was talking about, but realized it wouldn't have done any good. He was gone, lost in his own thoughts.

Rather than saying anything, she stared at him through her tears, watching his sick, twisted face contort with pain or pleasure at whatever feelings were going on inside his head.

"Well, let me show you," he gushed excitedly, getting up and walking away. When he came back, he no longer had the knife, but was holding a brick. "What I'm going to do instead is brick you into this little closet. Trap you inside, like my sister was trapped." He hunched down close to her, letting her get a good look at the brick before he continued, "As you know, the way this wall is situated under the stairs, I can easily do it and no one will ever know."

She tried to shrink away from him, the evil emanating from him cutting into her.

"After a while, I'm sure the stink of you might offend someone, but since no one knows I'm here and no one knows you're here, it'll be a good long while."

The horror of his words engulfed her. She would be left here to die. It wouldn't be a quick death, but a long, slow death over many days. And the thought of her baby suffering, starving to death inside of her, it was almost too much for her to bear. She had to get out of there.

If I try to escape, maybe he'll kill me quickly.

Without preamble, she started to kick her feet, shake her head and body. Her shirt ripped in several different places, giving her the encouragement she needed to continue.

"Stop it now, Sophie, or I'll crush her," he hollered, placing a booted foot on her pregnant belly, pressing down.

Immediately, she stopped. She couldn't allow him to hurt her unborn child.

She shook her head no. She was starting to feel a little lightheaded.

In his revoltingly calm voice, he asked, pulling the knife out of his back pocket, "You don't want to be tortured with this, do you?"

She shook her head no again.

"All right then," he continued, taking his foot off her belly. "Hold still and keep your whoring mouth shut. I'll get to work making your tomb so I can get on with my life." He paused, tenderly looking into her eyes. "You know, it'll be nice to know you're here, safe and sound, in our house with our baby. This way, you'll always be mine."

He wasn't waiting for an answer, obviously back in his own demented, little world. He bent down, brushed the hair out of her face, and kissed her softly on the forehead. She tried to plead with him with her eyes but he only smiled.

"Good-bye Sophie."

He got up and walked away. Guessing from the sounds she could hear, he was doing what he said he would. She could hear him mixing the cement, sloshing it onto the brick, wiping it with the trowel, and placing it on top of another.

It's really over, she thought, wondering what

death would be like. It can't hurt worse than this, can it?

He slapped her with such force, she cried out, through the tape, "Stop it!"

"What's wrong with you?" he asked angrily, ripping the tape off her mouth. "There's blood all over the floor."

"Afraid I might not survive long enough to see myself bricked in?" she whispered fiercely, although weakly.

"Yes, as a matter a fact, I am. Now, tell me what's wrong."

She had no idea what was wrong, nor had she realized she was bleeding. Her body was numb, as though she were detached from it. She couldn't feel any pain.

I'm going to die, she thought.

She realized she should be angry, devastated, or worse. Instead only peace. Almost reverently, she whispered, "It's too late, David. You've already killed me and our baby. I hope you . . ."

She realized she'd stopped talking to him and wondered if she died or was unconscious again. Strangely, this time, though, she knew she was unconscious. She could hear David slapping her face again and again. She knew he walked away and came back again, this time shaking her body, but she couldn't or wouldn't allow herself to wake up. She knew these were her thoughts, knew somehow inside her body, her mind was awake and alert.

This must be the end, she thought, almost happily. Still, though, for her daughter's sake, she wasn't ready to give up.

She tried to open her eyes, but they didn't respond. She tried to scream, but nothing came out.

Calm down, she told herself. *Maybe this is meant to be.*

She decided, instead, to focus on her baby.

"Dear, sweet baby girl," she cried, in her mind. "Please forgive me. Somehow I hope you know I've loved you from the moment I knew you were a part of me. I wish I could've met you."

CHAPTER 21

"Charge to three hundred! Hurry, we can't lose her."

"Charged to three-hundred, doctor!"

"Clear!"

"Clear."

Her body shook from the jolt of electricity hitting her body. She knew it should've hurt, but it didn't. She could hear all of the activity happening around her and wondered what was going on.

"Okay, doctor, she has a pulse."

"Good, let's keep it strong. I want to know what happened. She's been catatonic for such a long time. I want to know what's changed. See if she's got an infection."

"Yes, doctor."

"Hope," he continued, "I want blood work done on her. Let's go. You all know what to do."

Sophie listened intently to him bark out his orders. She could tell her body was being touched, poked and prodded because she could feel the pressure, but not the touch.

It doesn't make sense, she thought.

"Has someone called her parents? They ought to know what's happened," she heard a woman say kindly.

After several more minutes, she sensed more than heard them all leave the room. Slowly she tried to open her eyes, but couldn't. She tried to sit up. Nothing happened.

She tried to yell, with all her might, "Help! Please help me!" To her, it seemed like she had, but no one came. She felt like a prisoner trapped inside her own body.

What's wrong with me? She wondered helplessly.

She decided, finally, to relax her mind, letting herself begin to drift off to sleep, when she remembered what David had been trying to do to her.

"My baby," she yelled, and this time she heard it with every fiber of her being. Now, she knew, she was awake. Immediately, she realized her body seemed strange, heavy.

David must've really hurt me, she pondered nervously, slowly opening her eyes. She noticed, squinting in an effort to see, her eyes were blurry. After a few tries, however, her eyes began to clear up. She could tell what she was looking at.

She was lying flat on her back with a perfect view of the shabby ceiling. It was one of those cork board ceilings, covered with tiny holes which, at one time, had been painted white. Moving her eyes to the left, she saw a sink. Next to it, awkwardly sat several huge machines, with a surplus of switches.

What's it all for, she wondered, continuing the inspection of her surroundings.

Directly across from her was a wall covered in windows which were open, letting in a slight breeze. With the curtains drawn, the natural light consumed the room, warming her at once. Like the craving some people have for chocolate, she ached for the beauty outside.

Majestically, the mountains stood before her. An overwhelming feeling of joy, at being alive, pressed on her. The mountains were full of color, greens, yellows, oranges and reds, singing out in unity, fall had arrived.

He may have hurt me, she thought, but somehow I survived. Somehow, I got out of there before he was able to finish what he started.

"We're safe baby-girl," she cried happily, reaching down to put her hand on her ever growing belly.

Undeniable pain swept over her, for she realized her stomach was flat. Then it dawned on her, when David had taken her there'd been no leaves on the trees. They'd all fallen, leaving the trees bare, in preparation for a long, cold winter. She looked out the window again.

It's definitely Fall, she thought.

"How long have I been here?" she whispered, wondering what'd become of her baby. She needed to talk to someone, now, before her heart literally broke with the pain she was having at not knowing where her baby was. She moved her head again, looking in vain for the button which usually comes with a hospital bed, but she couldn't find it.

Finally, with tears of frustration streaming down her cheeks and into her ears, she cried, "Someone, please help me!" She'd meant for it to be loud. Instead, though, she sounded hoarse. Clearing it, she tried again, "Help me, please!" It was better, she thought, but still no one came.

"I need help," she shouted.

As a woman walked in, she took a deep breath, saying, "Thank goodness you heard me. I'm having a hard time moving, so I know something is wrong, but first and foremost I need to know what's happened to my baby. Is she . . ." Sophie stopped because of the look on the woman's face.

If she didn't know any better, she'd think the woman had seen a ghost. Her eyes looked shocked and amazed, but the strangest and probably most frustrating thing was the woman was smiling.

Anxiously, Sophie asked, "Why are you smiling? Is my baby okay?"

The woman walked over, took her pulse, turned and looked at the machine standing menacingly next to the bed. Once she'd fiddled with it, she took her temperature, all without saying a word.

Sophie was trying to be patient, understanding the woman was doing her job, but she'd asked an important question and needed an answer. "Did you hear me? Where . . ."

"Yes, dear, I heard you," she began, her voice shaking slightly. "Can you give me just a minute? I need to get the doctor."

She was at the door when she stopped suddenly, seeming to regret her decision. She stood there a moment, as if frozen in place, before she turned to Sophie, uttering,

"Don't worry. Everything is going to be all right."

Without another word, she was gone.

"Okay," she replied to the empty room.

When he entered the room, Sophie unwittingly gasped. It wasn't necessarily because of his looks, although he was exceedingly handsome, but it was the presence he brought with him, as though she knew him.

Ridiculous, she thought. *I've never seen this man before.* Still, the sensation was undeniable.

Behind him was a plethora of people. All of them looked like they belonged in the medical field, and she wondered what they were doing in her room.

He walked purposefully over to her, saying, "Sophie, I'm Dr. Hansen. Sorry about the flock behind me, it's only . . ." He paused, obviously trying to carefully choose his words. "I . . . *We're* all excited you're awake and alert. We hoped this day would come. At the same time, however, we're surprised." He paused again, as though hoping she understood what he was talking about, then shook his head and went on.

"You see Sophie, you're what some, well, no, *most* of the medical profession would call a miracle." He turned and pointed toward the throng behind him.

"These men and women are here to see you for themselves, to document this amazing day."

She could tell he was begging her with his eyes to understand, but she didn't. *Obviously something terrible has happened to me,* she thought, *but I need to find out what's happened to my daughter.* Speaking clearly, she began, "I need to know what's happened to my baby. I was . . ." She stopped, flabbergasted. Dr. Hansen had turned away from her, whispering to the mass of people behind him. Frustrated, she decided to try a different approach. "I can barely move. What's wrong with me?"

Dr. Hansen turned around, responding with a chuckle. "I'm surprised you can move at all." He put his hand in hers, asking, "Can you squeeze my hand?"

She did her best, watching his kind eyes.

In response, he nodded, turning back to the others, talking again to them.

Rude, she thought, feeling peeved.

"Hey, is someone going to tell me what's going on?" She was trying her best to sound upset, but her voice wouldn't cooperate. It still sounded weak. She continued, however, "Where's my baby? Has anyone found David? You know he tried to kill me. Why aren't the police here?"

Dr. Hansen whipped his head back around, asking, "What did you say? You know about David?"

Anger flashed through her, giving strength to her voice.

"Of course I do. I was married to the man for two years." She noticed the bewilderment on his face as well as the others and wondered why they were all looking at her as if she'd spoken something prohibited. "What? What did I say? What's wrong?"

Quickly, he came to her, putting a hand to her forehead, checking her pulse.

"She's feverish," he said, speaking to a woman who stood next to him. She was the nurse who'd come in when she'd yelled. "Hope, take her temperature and give her something to keep her calm. We don't want to lose her again."

"Lose me? What do you mean? Tell me what's going on." She was near tears, anger giving way to defeat.

Why is no one talking to me, she wondered.

"Sophie, I'll explain everything. I promise. I understand you have a lot of questions. First, we need to run some tests," Dr. Hansen said, tenderly brushing some hair out of her face. "This must be hard. Please be patient. In due time, all of your questions will be answered."

His touch was calming, although his I'm-a-doctor-and-I know-what's-best attitude wasn't.

"All right," she conceded, "I'll try to be patient for a while." Then something dawned on her and she had to ask, "Are you related to a Phillip Hansen? He's a teacher over at Sacred Heart."

Dr. Hansen's face revealed shock, and surprise, but he immediately concealed his emotions, answering, "We'll talk again later, after we've run our tests."

Turning, he walked away, followed by the multitude which had come in with him.

While they were all leaving, and slapping each other on the back, talking excitedly, the rage of before resettled.

I'm not a lab rat, she thought. *I'm the patient. They should be giving me the answers I want. What have they got to be happy about?*

"Why can't I get my answers now?" she asked angrily, slamming her hand down on the bed.

"Wow, what a great sign," the nurse said, walking back into her room, a big smile on her face. She came over and stood next to Sophie, putting a needle full of something clear into one of her IV bags. When she was finished, she took a thermometer from her pocket and stuck it in Sophie's ear. "I've just given you a little Demerol to help you relax."

Barely able to contain her emotions, she uttered, "I don't want to relax. I want to know what's going on."

The woman smiled patiently, "Absolutely, dear. Give me just a few more minutes.

My name is Hope, by the way, and I'll be taking care of you."

She nodded her understanding, the Demerol beginning to take its effect on her body. She fought against it, trying to keep her eyes open, but couldn't. Before she fell asleep, she whispered, "Please be all right, little one."

When she woke, she was inside what looked like a stark, white column. For a brief moment, she thought David had found her and buried her alive. Before she could really start to panic, though, she heard through the humming in her ears.

"Sophie, I need you to hold very still. We're almost done."

"Phillip?" she whispered.

"It's Dr. Hansen. Just a few more minutes and we'll have you out of there."

"Okay," she responded quietly.

After what seemed like much longer than a few minutes, she was exhumed. The light in the room was too bright for her eyes. Instinctively she lifted both hands to shield them.

"It's incredible how quickly your body is recovering now you're fully awake."

"It is?" She questioned, not understanding what he was talking about.

"Absolutely."

Two men came to either side of her, each grabbing a side of the sheet she was on. The first one said, "On the count of three." Together they counted, "One. Two. Three." In unity, they lifted her onto a gurney.

Dr. Hansen said, "I'm going to let these two capable young men wheel you to your room." She must've allowed her nervousness to show, because he continued in a more gentle tone, "Don't worry, I'll be in later."

Before she could respond, he was gone and she was left alone with the two young men. She looked from one to the other. They were gawking at her as though she were an exotic creature they'd never seen before. Unable to take it, she closed her eyes, feigning fatigue.

Once they'd lifted her onto her bed, she waited several minutes to make sure they were gone, then gingerly opened her eyes.

Immediately, she realized she was in a different room. It was smaller; private. The room she'd been in before had been white. White walls, white ceiling and white floors. In this room, the walls were painted a light warm shade of green. Where her other room had been stark, this room was overflowing with furniture.

Under the big, picture frame window, was a couch. Next to it, a dark green chair and a side table. A cupboard and a storage unit sat against the adjacent wall. The storage unit looked like it held a television. The curtains were drawn and once again she had a great view, this time of the city.

It was dark outside, making the city lights twinkle more brightly. The scene was mesmerizing. She was almost asleep when her nose suddenly caught the aroma of something sweet. It smelled amazing. Lifting her head, she turned her gaze toward the smell.

She hadn't noticed before because of where they were located, but sitting on another side table, next to her bed was an enormous bouquet of lilies.

How beautiful, she thought, smiling happily. I wonder if Phillip sent me those or if he even knows I'm here. *Probably not*, she speculated, the chill of loneliness creeping in on her. In some ways, David did win. *My baby's gone and I haven't heard from Rina or Phillip.*

Her thoughts were tumbling in circles, like a dryer. They were constantly turning from her daughter, to David, to Phillip, to Rina and then back again.

I need answers, she thought, for what seemed like the hundredth time.

Even their lack of chatter seemed strange. Why weren't Dr. Hansen and Hope telling her anything? *Usually it's the first thing they do,* she reflected. She was still contemplating her circumstances when she dozed off.

She was once again in the closet David had placed her in, bleeding everywhere, knowing she was losing her baby, seeing him sneer at her in glee. He'd betrayed her, violated her, and she was angry. "

"No!" she yelled, sitting up in bed. She looked wildly around the room, not knowing where she was. Her covers were damp, probably from sweat. Absently, she wiped the tears from her face, lying back down, allowing her body to shake from the cold and her sobs. The sadness of loss and loneliness her only companions.

At once, there was a quick knock at the door. Hope entered, followed by two more women. They looked like nurses as well, but were wearing different smocks.

"Sophie, honey, it's all right," she cooed calmly. "I'm going to give you something to calm you down, and then these girls will change your sheets and your gown. We need to keep you warm." She injected something into her IV bag, then whispered something to the other women. To Sophie, she said, "What happened? Did you have a bad dream?"

Sophie nodded, unable to speak, the apparent dream still too real and her sadness still too raw. She allowed the girls to roll her from side to side as they changed her bed linens and her gown while she was still in the bed. When they were done, and had left the room, Hope asked, "Is there something I can get you?" She looked briefly at her watch, then back at Sophie. "If you'd like a drink, I'd be glad to get you one. It's been long enough."

The thought of a drink of ice water sounded incredible, like it'd been years since she'd had one.

"Yes, thank you Hope, I'd love a glass of water."

"Be right back," she bubbled, an instant smile appearing on her face.

When Hope was gone, her mind immediately went back to what she'd been dreaming. The Demerol had begun to relax her mind and body once again. This time, however, she was more awake and more able to fight its effects.

David, why did you have to be crazy, she wondered, allowing herself to think back over their time together. She'd never met his parents. At first, it bothered her.

She'd tried to explain this to him, telling him it was okay if they were different, but he always said no.

After a while she quit asking because it was obvious the subject upset him. She'd actually learned about his dad by accident. He'd come home drunk and let it slip his father was in jail. When she asked him why, he glared at her, before rolling over in their bed, going to sleep. She doubted he even remembered telling her, and by then she had no desire to bring it up with him again.

She accidentally discovered more a few months later when she'd been in the basement going through some boxes. In one, she found a journal. She didn't want to pry, but couldn't help herself. She wanted to know who'd written in it, if anyone. As she thumbed through the pages, she could see it was David's because he signed his name at the end of each entry. Knowing they were his words, she read through each page with the fervor of someone feasting on a meal after fasting for days. She couldn't get enough, as though she was finally getting a glimpse of the man she'd married. In those three hours spent reading his journal, she learned more about him than he ever told her.

She read his father had physically abused his mother. When David was old enough to realize what was going on, he'd asked his mom to leave his dad, had begged her, but he wrote, she'd been angry with him for suggesting "such a horrible thing."

He'd also written in a lot of ways he felt more betrayed by his mom than his dad because she'd chosen to take the abuse. It was after he'd written those words a new quote started to appear at the end of each entry, before he signed his name. He'd written it so many times she'd it memorized quickly. It said: "If you tell a woman what to do, in the end, she'll love you."

With that quote had come an instant change in the way he wrote, the texture of his words. He seemed to have taken the quote to heart. She'd been frightened by some of the things he'd written, understanding a little why he was the way he was.

When she read his last entry, she'd been shocked by it. He'd written his dad killed his mom. She still remembered the words on the page vividly. "She'd taken her last beating out of love for the bastard, and it killed her. Serves her right for staying. Maybe she's the lucky one."

She'd cried for him, thinking she better understood him and wanted to be the one to heal his wounded heart. She thought by loving him enough she could change him; help him to love her the way she desperately needed to be loved.

Obviously she'd been wrong, and had nearly paid for her choices with her life and possibly the life of her child.

"How I wish I'd never met him," she whispered fiercely, then immediately regretted her words. She'd become stronger than she ever thought possible because of her need to leave David, and stand on her own. Just as importantly, though, she'd been given the blessing of being pregnant. She'd felt more womanly than ever before, and had such an intense love for the little baby growing inside her. Absently, she rubbed her belly, longing for the roundness which had been there. A profound sorrow welled up inside. Her heart was breaking.

Where's my daughter, she wondered, hoping against hope she was safe.

"Here you go, dear." Hope said, walking to her, gently putting the straw in Sophie's mouth.

Despite her breaking heart, the water tasted better than she ever remembered.

"Thank you," Sophie muttered.

"Sure. Would you like some more?"

"Please."

"I'm actually surprised you're still awake. Didn't the Demerol help?"

"A little," she lied.

"Well, try to get some rest."

"Thank you," Sophie replied. She had a lot of questions. "Hope, can you tell me anything about what's going on? Is my baby all right?" She noticed the shocked look on Hope's face, but didn't care. "Please, Hope. I'm going crazy not knowing."

Hope looked down at Sophie, a sad smile on her face. "Dr. Hansen has asked us not to tell you anything yet. He thinks he needs to be the one to do it."

"Hope, ple . . ."

She interrupted, saying, "I'll only say you needn't worry, dear." Then she quickly walked away.

She tried not to worry as she watched the sun begin to come up, falling asleep at around six o'clock the next morning.

CHAPTER 22

"Hello, Sophie," he offered kindly, giving her arm a slight shake.

"Phillip, I had the weirdest dream," she began, opening her eyes. At once, she realized it was Dr. Hansen, and she must've been dreaming. "Oh, Dr. Hansen, hello," she said, her face reddening a couple of shades.

He smiled, apparently a little embarrassed himself as he sat on a stool next to her bed. Hope walked over, taking a place behind him as he began, "Sophie, I have some serious, important matters to talk to you about." He stopped to rub a hand over his face before he continued. "It's actually incredible, fantastic news, but at the same time, because of some of the questions you've asked, I'm a little concerned as well.

Fully awake, she tried to sit up. Hope came to her rescue, sticking pillows behind her back and head.

"Thank you, Hope," she nodded to the nurse, then looked directly at Dr. Hansen, letting everything she'd been feeling come out in a big rush. "I've been patient long enough, and I get the feeling no one really understands what happened to me."

"Sophie, trust . . ."

"Hear me out, please. Let me tell you what's happened to me."

He sat back, a mixture of intrigue and confusion visible on his face.

Sophie took a deep breath and began, "I was taken by my husband and locked up in a closet like an animal, forced to listen to him describe exactly what he was going to do to me and my baby. Then, as he began to brick me into the closet of the home we shared together, I started to bleed profusely, and lost consciousness." She paused, fighting back the tears. "My baby. Can you please tell me what's happened to her?"

Hope and Dr. Hansen exchanged a curious look before he looked back at her and said, "Let's start at the beginning. First of all, do you know what year this is?"

She took another deep breath,

"Yes, it's two thousand and six."

Once again, both doctor and nurse exchanged strange looks. "It's amazing you know the year."

Frustrated, but trying to contain it, she asked, "Why is it amazing? Am I not supposed to know what year this is?"

"Frankly no. In most cases like yours, the patient has no idea what year it is, and that's if they come out of it at all."

"I don't understand. Come out of what?"

"In a minute," he said, shaking his head and putting up a hand to stop her interruption. "What do you remember about June sixth, 1996?"

"I don't know. Why does it matter?"

289

"It matters, trust me. Can you answer the question?"

She laid her head against the pillows, closing her eyes, the events of June 6th, 1996 all to clear in her mind.

Why was he asking her about it, though, she wondered.

Finally, she opened her eyes, and said softly, "It's the day my parents died."

Dr. Hansen sucked in his breath, as if she'd slapped him.

"You remember your parents dying? Where were you when you got the news?"

She looked at him, trying mightily to figure out where he could possibly be going with this. He seemed sincere, though, and he did promise to tell her what was going on.

Didn't he, she thought, trying to remember.

"I was getting out of my car to go in my house. Can you tell me what this has to do with what happened to me?" She asked, trying to remain calm.

"I can. I promise you'll understand in a minute. Do you know what happened to them? How they died?"

"Yes, Dr. Hansen, I do. A kind police officer told me my parents died in a car accident, on their way to Washington D.C." She was angry with him for making her repeat such a painful memory.

"Your *parents* were in a car accident," he repeated.

Unable to contain her emotions any longer, she started, "Listen, they were *my* parents. I think I'd know what happened to them. Why are you being like this? Stop treating me like a child and tell me what's going on." When she finished, she was breathing heavily.

Hope came over to her, taking the cup, allowing her to take a sip of water.

"Hang in there Sophie, dear. You'll get your answers."

"You're right. A lot has happened since you've been with us and I feel like I know you. I want you to know both Hope and I have great affection for you. You mean a great deal to us."

She was more confused than ever. Both Hope and Dr. Hansen seemed to be holding back tears of their own. Slowly, she responded, "Thank you. I appreciate your concern."

Dr. Hansen looked at Hope and Hope nodded.

"Okay, Sophie. I'm going to tell you, but I need you to let me say it all, without any interruptions. You are going to have questions, but I need you to wait until I'm finished. Okay?"

She nodded.

"You see, Sophie, you came to us a little over ten years ago."

Her mouth dropped open, but kept her promise and didn't say anything.

"*You* were in a car accident on June sixth, 1996. The paramedics rushed you to Jordan Valley

Hospital, where your serious injuries were treated. We weren't there . . ." he said this as he pointed to himself and Hope. "But we were told you died for several minutes. They were about to call your death when you came back." He stopped for a minute, as if collecting his thoughts before going on. "Even after all of your physical injuries healed and you were stabilized, you never woke up. After several months, you were moved here, to this facility, where we care for long-term coma patients. You've been here the longest, as I said, for ten years."

Sophie was furious. "Is this some kind of joke? Did David put you up to this? I haven't been in a coma. You're lying," she yelled. "I went to college, graduated from the University of Utah with a Masters degree. I got married. I was pregnant," she cried, exhaustion leaning heavily on her body. "Don't do this to me, please. Let me go."

Hope rushed over to her, putting a hand on either side of her face.

"Sophie, David didn't put us up to this. We're here to help you, sweetie."

"Stop it, just stop it." She sobbed. "You're lying. No! No! Please let me go! Where's my baby?"

Dr. Hansen stood.

"Hope, go ahead and give her ten of morphine. This was too much. I won't lose her again."

"Yes Dr. Hansen," Hope responded, letting go of Sophie's face, walking over to her IV bag.

"Please, no more. Just let me go. I don't want to be here. Let me be." She wept uncontrollably. A part of her knew she was being irrational, knew not even David was this clever, but it was even more painful to know she hadn't been pregnant.

Her baby wasn't real.

"I'm sorry," Dr. Hansen began, "Rest a while, we'll come back later."

The morphine hit quickly. She was slipping back, and suddenly Rina was there; Phillip, too. They were standing over her. She wanted to reach out to them, ask them to help her, but she couldn't get her mouth open. She didn't have the energy. Still, though, their presence comforting her.

Sophie was sitting on a blanket watching a little girl with long blonde hair playing on the monkey bars. She looked around, seeing her mom and dad sitting on a park bench a little way off. Phillip was there, too. She was happy, at peace. Her mother was watching the little girl, but suddenly turned to her and said, "Wake up. Wake up, Sophie. It's me. It's your mom."

She opened her eyes, at least she thought she did, but realized she must still be dreaming because standing before her was her mother.

Maybe I'm in heaven, she thought, reaching out to touch her. Her face permeated warmth. *This can't be*, she thought. "Mom, is it you?" Sophie cried weakly. "Are you
real?"

Her mom grabbed her hand in both of hers, kissing it softly. She touched the tears on her mother's face and knew without a doubt she was real, she wasn't dreaming.

"Oh mom, I can't believe it's you," she cried happily, still barely able to believe it.

"Yes, it's me. Your dad's here, too."

"Dad?" she called.

He seemed to appear out of nowhere. "Hey, Sophie. I'm here."

Still crying, she stammered, "I-I thought I'd l-lost you both. I-I can't believe th-this is real."

Her dad stepped closer, leaned down and kissed her on the cheek. She put her arms around him, holding him tightly.

"Dad, it is you. You still smell like you."

"And what's that supposed to mean?" he asked in mock severity. "It means you're here. You're *both* here. I have my mom and dad back."

They hugged, cried and talked for the better part of the rest of the day. Hope came in and checked on her occasionally, changing her fluids, taking her temperature and checking her blood pressure. Otherwise, though, it was just the three of them. She still had the gnawing sadness in her heart for her daughter, but tried her best to set it aside, letting the joy of seeing her parents again, after all this time, flood through her.

As the day began winding down, she couldn't help but bring up her joy at seeing them again.

"All this time, the time I've been in the coma, I thought I was alive; living. Without a doubt, I thought you both died. I've mourned your deaths for such a long time, a part of me still can't believe I'm not dreaming now, which I guess is what I've been doing for the last ten years." She leaned back on her pillows, trying to stop the throbbing which had begun in her head. Admittedly, she was having a hard time adjusting to this reality.

Her mother said, "We understand your mourning. Even though you weren't dead, you weren't really with us either. We've missed you Soph, very much."

She watched her mother's eyes fill up with tears, her own do the same.

"We always knew you'd come back to us, though," her mother continued, gently stroking her hair. "Several doctors, even friends, told us we should let you go. It was something we pondered and prayed about several times over the years, but each time we knew you'd come back to us."

"I'm glad you waited for me. In a way it's strange, though. I guess because everything I've been dreaming about these past ten years seems real. I mean, I went to college, got married. I'm an artist, and a teacher. I can't believe those things didn't happen." She stopped, looking at her parents, realizing, though, she was glad to have them back or to be back with them.

"You know, I'm sure a big part of the reason it seemed real was because of Dr. Hansen," her mom began. "We knew from the beginning he was different."

"Really?" Sophie interjected, interested to learn more about him.

"Absolutely," her dad answered. "His theories on coma patients are cutting edge. He told us from the beginning we should talk to you, tell you about our lives. Read, sing, whatever we could think of. He had all of the nurses, orderlies and whom-ever else came to visit you do the same. 'Talk to her as often as possible,' he told all of us. You also went to physical therapy four times a week. He wanted to keep your body, and mind active. Some of his colleagues even think he's a quack. We heard from several of them over the years, telling us Dr. Hansen was giving us false hope, and we should let you go. Hopefully, now they'll change their tune because of you. We think he's a wonderful man."

"He sounds like it," Sophie said, trying to stifle a yawn.

"You must be exhausted, dear. We'll let you get some rest and come back tomorrow."

"I don't want you to go. I've missed you both, and I still have a lot of questions."

"I'm sure you do. We'll be back first thing tomorrow."

They kissed and hugged for several more minutes, no one really having the heart to let the other go. Finally, amid their tears, her mom uttered, "C'mon, Bill, we need to let her rest."

She never saw her dad this upset, and although Sophie was sad to see them go, she was tired, falling asleep before they reached the elevator.

During the night, she was awakened several times by a nurse or night orderly checking her pulse and blood pressure, changing her fluids, and taking her temperature. Each time, she relished the knowledge she was actually awake, that this time she wasn't dreaming. Twice she pinched herself to make sure, but realized pinching wasn't a guarantee, either, because during her time in her coma, she experienced pain as well.

By dawn, she couldn't sleep. The thought of her parents returning and everything else full recovery meant exciting her beyond belief. She knew she had specific questions she needed answered, having remembered a class she'd taken her last semester in high school. It had been a college preparation class in Psychology. There'd been an interesting chapter on dreams, and how they relate to what is going on in reality.

She couldn't help but wonder what had happened around her to allow her to dream such dreams, namely David, Rina, Phillip, and her baby. It all seemed too vivid to be for nothing. She had to have her questions answered, the sooner the better.

CHAPTER 23

"I'm twenty-eight, right?"

"Yes," her mom answered.

"I thought I was."

"Honestly, it's amazing," Dr. Hansen interjected. "Even with all I've thought, and believed about coma patients, I never would've hoped it would be possible for you to know your age."

Her mom, dad and Dr. Hansen were sitting around her bed, patiently trying to answer her questions. She was overjoyed at seeing her parents again. Under Dr. Hansen's gaze, though, she still imagined herself a science an experiment. She hadn't been trying to be a miracle, hadn't even realized she was doing something amazing. She just thought she was living her life. To her, it seemed a miracle to be sitting next to her parents, that they were alive. This thinking led to her next question.

Instead of responding to Dr. Hansen's comments, she said, "Thankfully, my parents didn't die, but what happened? How did I end up in a coma?"

"Your car and another one hit each other going around sixty miles an hour," her mom responded.

"Whoa." Sophie closed her eyes, trying desperately to remember the experience. She could sense a memory sitting on the edge of her consciousness, waiting to burst free, but nothing came.

"It's not unusual for the mind to block out a horrifying experience," Dr. Hansen interjected helpfully. "Sometimes the brain does it to protect itself from the pain or grief the situation may cause."

She opened her eyes, nodding her understanding, although, it didn't alleviate her sense of inadequacy. It seemed strange; the last ten years of her life seemed real, but she couldn't remember her own car accident.

"I remember finishing my painting in the art room at school. My teacher and I talked about it before I left. She'd been complimentary, telling me I should consider pursuing Art as a major in college. I was excited about it, my painting, I mean; happy it'd turned out better than I expected. I remember being excited about graduating, and going to college." She stopped a moment, soaking in the last "real" memory she'd had in ten years, then shrugged and continued, "Beyond talking to my teacher in class, I guess everything else I remember is a dream."

Her mom lovingly reached over, taking Sophie's hand in hers. "I'm not surprised you don't remember the accident, honey."

"Nor am I," Dr. Hansen added. "When you were first brought to us, I read your charts. Honestly, all of us were amazed you lived through the crash."

"Why? Was I really in such bad shape?" She questioned, surprised even Dr. Hansen seemed genuinely shocked.

Dr. Hansen cautiously looked from her mom to her dad, then back at her before continuing, "For starters, both of your knees were broken. One of your lungs was punctured, and four of your ribs were broken." He stopped a moment, allowing what he'd said to sink in.

She was stunned. "A punctured lung does sound serious, as does broken knees." She absently rubbed them, continuing, "But those injuries don't sound like they would cause me to go into a coma."

"True, although any kind of trauma can cause a coma." He smiled lightly, running his fingers through his thick hair, as though trying to comprehend how she survived. "We think your coma was caused by serious head trauma. You see, your head hit the steering wheel during the crash. When they x-rayed you, they found almost every bone in your face had been fractured."

She shook her head, trying to remember something about such a terrifying experience. Still, nothing came to her. As far as she could remember, it was the day her parents died. At the thought, she reached out and grabbed her mother's hand, squeezing it tightly.

Lovingly, her mom and dad smiled at her.

How thankful I am they didn't really die, she thought for the hundredth time. She also noticed all three of them seemed to be holding something back. She shrugged it off, knowing there was a lot of information they had for her, recognizing she needed to be patient. At least, for now, she thought. Her dad discreetly wiped his eyes.

"While you were in your coma, you had three facial reconstruction surgeries. We had to give the plastic surgeons some of the pictures we'd taken for your graduation. The surgeons did a great job. You look like you, even awake."

"Thanks, dad." She laughed. Then asked her next question. "What happened to the other driver? Is he all right?"

She watched Dr. Hansen look down nervously, watched as her mom and dad looked at each other, obviously having a conversation most couples can have after they've been together a long time, without saying a word. Her dad nodded while he and her mom traded places, allowing him to be next to her. He sat on her bed, picking up her hand, and putting it in his.

"No, Sophie, she wasn't all right. The police say she . . ."

"She what dad?" Then a memory of something David said to her right before he started bricking her in prompted her to ask, "Was she trapped in the car somehow?"

Surprised, he answered gently, "Yes. She was trapped behind the steering wheel. While they were waiting for the Jaws of Life to be brought in, a fire started in the car."

"A fire?" She interrupted, terrified by the thought.

"Yes, they smelled the spilt gasoline, but there wasn't anything they could do about it. What they didn't realize is the young woman behind the wheel had been smoking when the crash happened."

"No," was all she could express.

Nodding, he continued, "Clearly, the butt of the cigarette was still burning, and it lit the gasoline."

"What did they do? Please tell me they got her out in time?"

Shaking his head sadly, he answered, "No, I'm afraid they weren't able to. The car exploded while she was still inside."

"Oh no! It was my fault." Sophie cried.

"Sophie, it wasn't anyone's fault," her dad growled defensively, obviously trying to protect her. "It'd been raining, and the two cars collided head on. The officer who spoke to us said it looked like you tried to brake, but your car hydroplaned into the other car. There was nothing you could do."

Sophie started to cry. The thought of the young woman dying was almost more than she could bear. She felt her mother stroking her hair, her dad saying consoling words to her, but she couldn't brake free of the pain.

"Okay. Enough for today. I'm going to give her some morphine, and keep a close eye on her," Dr. Hansen broke in, concerned.

"I don't mean to interrupt," Hope called from

the doorway. "It's time for Sophie's physical therapy."

"Oh," Dr. Hansen started, a little embarrassed. "I hadn't even mentioned she would be starting today."

Hope walked in and parked the wheelchair, turning to Sophie's mom and dad.

"I know it's still relatively early, but her physical therapy should last two hours. Afterward, we're going to try getting some real sustenance into her body. I've no doubt by then she'll be exhausted, and in need of rest."

Dr. Hansen concurred. "The first day of this type of rigorous physical therapy is tough for anybody, but will most likely be even more intense for you. You will be very fatigued by the time you're done with the therapy."

"We understand," her mom said. "We'll be back tomorrow." She kissed her quickly on the cheek followed by a kiss on the forehead from her dad. Then they were gone.

Sophie couldn't help the tears. She was miserable.

Hope patted her on the leg.

"It'll be all right. You want to get your body completely working again, right, dear?"

She nodded, wiping tears from her eyes.

"I do. I've just found them again, and I'm sad to see them go."

"I understand."

Sophie heard her take a deep breath before she gently changed the subject.

"I've been here since the day your parents checked you in. We've had a lot of one-sided conversations, you and I. You're a good listener."

"Oh, really?" Sophie laughed, her body tingle with the knowledge she somehow already knew this.

"Yes, really. Now let me help you into the wheelchair."

Sophie gingerly tried to sit up. Although she could sense her body, it was stiff, awkward.

"Sweetie, I still can't believe how well you can move." She helped her get situated in the chair, putting the feet of the wheelchair in position to rest hers on. "You know, I've never seen such resolve in two people."

"What do you mean?" She asked, hoping she was talking once again about her parents.

"I could tell your mom and dad knew without a doubt you'd wake up. At times, I was so overwhelmed for them, wondering if they'd made the right choice, keeping you alive such a long time."

"Ten years is a long time to wait. I'm glad they did."

"I am, too." She smiled, pushing Sophie's wheelchair out of the room.

Sophie rode in silence, realizing there was still a lot more she wanted to know. As she was trying to decide which of her questions to ask first, Hope said, "The doctor thinks it would be all right for you to eat something after your physical therapy."

"Some toast sounds great."

"Well, more specifically, he thinks you can try some bouillon. Then in a few hours, if everything goes well, maybe some Jello." Hope laughed.

"Oh." She laughed back, enjoying the feel of it, "I guess bouillon would be great, too."

Hope took her into the physical therapy room, situating her next to her first station. She locked the wheelchair in place. "They should be here in a minute." She turned to leave, but swung back around. "You know dear, if you need anything, someone to talk to, or a shoulder to cry on, I'm here for you."

A little surprised by her familiar mannerisms, she nodded, "Thank you Hope." Their eyes locked a moment. Sophie asked, "Do you know someone by the name of Rina? You remind me a lot of her."

Now it was Hope's turn to be surprised, "I do. My daughter's name is Rina."

Her mind began swirling with a myriad of questions, none of which she was able to contemplate because the Physical Therapist walked in.

"Hello, I'm Bob. Are you ready to begin?"

Taking her eyes from Hope's, she looked over at Bob. "Sure, ready as I'll ever be." She watched Hope leave the room, recognizing the tingle within her again. She definitely wanted to talk to Hope again soon.

Physical therapy was difficult, seeming to last forever. Finally, though, she'd finished and Bob wheeled her back to her room. After he helped her back into bed, and covered her, he left, saying he'd be back again tomorrow. Sophie sighed wearily, closing her eyes, ready for a nap, when she heard a knock on her door.

"Do you mind if I come in for a minute?" Dr. Hansen asked.

She shook her head no.

"Great." He pulled up a chair next to her bed. "How was Physical Therapy?"

"Good," she answered sleepily.

"I can tell Bob gave you a tough workout. I won't keep you long."

"Thanks, Dr. Hansen."

He went on, "I talked to Nurse Hope right before I came in. She said she was bringing in your bouillon."

Sophie nodded, trying to be more alert, as obviously he had something to discuss with her.

"Fine. Now there is something I need to talk to you about."

She kept her eyes closed but smiled. "Okay, but you told my parents I needed to rest."

Dr. Hansen chuckled as well. "You're right, we can talk tomorrow." He stood to leave.

She opened her eyes, making her face serious again. "It's fine Dr. Hansen. What did you need to talk to me about?"

Sitting back down, he questioned, "Are you sure?"

She could tell he had something important to talk to her about. Nodding once again, she answered, "I'm sure."

"Good, I'll get right to it, then. As I've said before, you're a miracle. There aren't many patients in the world who have been in a coma for ten years, and come out of it. Much less, come out of it able to walk and talk."

She moved up a little, wondering where this was heading. She knew she didn't want to be a trophy is his case to show off to the world. She wouldn't have it.

"What's even more incredible, though," he said, absently tucking a pillow firmly behind her back, "is, while in your coma, you were dreaming as if your life continued to go on."

"Yes. Right. I'm still having a hard time believing this is what's real." Sophie offered.

"Exactly," he replied, slapping a hand on his knee excitedly. "I've often wondered if dreaming occurs in coma patients, but have had little opportunity to see if I was right.

Most of the time, the patient dies of a complication or is let go by their loved ones. When a rare case does wake up, they've had such serious brain damage; there's been little or no way to communicate." He paused, looking intently at her, "You're rare, Sophie. Very special. Do you understand?"

"I'm beginning to," she returned. "To me, I don't seem any different than I did a week ago, or even a few days ago, except I'm alive."

Dr. Hansen eagerly scooted closer to her. "What do you mean?"

In response, she pushed herself farther into the pillows, uncomfortable by the force of his question.

He must've noticed because he sat back a little. "I don't mean to frighten you. It's only right before you woke up, you almost died. Your heart stopped beating. For nine years your body didn't do anything strange, then we almost lost you twice in the last eleven months."

"Twice?" She questioned.

"Yes. One minute your body was functioning normally, the next we were trying to make sure you didn't die."

"Wow. That explains a lot though. I noticed everyone seemed weird. I guess I would've been, too." She remembered the night the man in the mask had tried to take her. She remembered hearing people talking, mentioning her parents. She wondered if that was the first time.

Interrupting her thoughts, Dr. Hansen asked, "Are you all right? Did you think of something?"

"Perhaps," she responded lightly. She wasn't

ready to go into too many details with him right now.

"Look. I understand I'm probably being overbearing and I apologize. When most patients bodies react the way yours did before you almost died, they actually do. Die."

Bewildered, she said, "I didn't know."

"It's true. I've always wondered why, and now you might have some of the answers. Now you can tell us what you remember right before you came out of your coma."

She stared at him, guessing why he would be interested, but embarrassed he thought she had the answers. "Look, Dr. Hansen, I think I understand why you would

be interested . . ." she broke off, laughing nervously before she continued, "But right before I woke up I was having a nightmare. A nightmare I thought was as real as you and I are talking right now."

"A nightmare." Dr. Hansen started inquisitively, pulling a pad of paper from his jacket pocket and a pen from the pocket on his breast. "Sophie, this could be important. Would you be willing to tell me what it was about?" He questioned, raising an eyebrow.

"Oh, I don't think you want to know. It's silly." She stopped, unable to continue, the thought of her unborn child causing such agonizing pain, tears welled up in her eyes.

"It wasn't silly, actually," she started again in a whisper. "I don't see how what I was dreaming

310

would be important. I think somehow my dreams are unimportant, knowing I killed another person."

Dr. Hansen tenderly touched her arm. "I understand, Sophie. It's a difficult situation. Remember, though, it wasn't your fault alone. Sometimes things happen, usually for a reason."

She nodded, closing her eyes. She didn't want him to see her crying.

"Realize it's normal to be sad. The best thing a person can do, I believe, in traumatic situations, is try to make something good come from it. From my point of view, what you were dreaming may be the key to why you woke up. This is exactly what I wanted to talk to you about. I was hoping you'd be willing to tell me the whole story. From what you thought happened to your parents up until two days ago when you woke up."

"But why?" She wondered aloud, unsure she wanted to share her dreams with other people.

"You see, I'd like to write a book about you. More a manual, I guess, to let other doctors and other people with a loved one in a coma know there's hope . . ." He stopped because she was shaking her head. He leaned forward again, going on, "It would include my theories, and beliefs about coma patients. The therapy I used on you, my notes and such."

She watched him run a hand through his thick, dark hair and thought for a moment he reminded her of someone. "Is your first name, by chance, Phillip?"

He stood up, a look of shocked amazement on his face. "How would you know my name?"

Blushing, she answered, "You don't look exactly like him, but you remind me a lot of my, this man from my dreams."

"You're kidding?" He sat back down, writing something on his notepad. "Who was I to you? Was I your doctor?"

Her face turning even more crimson, she answered, "Well you were a doctor."

"I was. What kind?" he asked curiously, his notepad forgotten.

"You had a doctorate in Theater. You were the Theater Director in a private school."

"Fascinating. While you were in a coma, I did tell you my name, but you remembering it and incorporating me into your dreams. Well, as I said before, fascinating. Did you and I . . ." He didn't finish because Hope walked in, setting a tray on a table next to her bed.

Her blush deepened even further, wondering how much Hope had heard.

"Oh, nurse Hope. I didn't hear you come in," Dr. Hansen quipped uneasily. He was obviously unfamiliar with being caught off-guard.

She noticed Hope smile slightly. "Would you like to take a break, and have some bouillon?"

"Yes." She sighed in relief.

"Um, yes, we can finish this later. Would it be all right if we do this, the book, uh, manual, I mean?

Your information could be the key to helping other coma patients have a full recovery."

"I'd like to think about it."

"Sure. We'll discuss it again tomorrow," he said, waving awkwardly before walking out.

"From the blush on your face, I'm guessing he was a special someone in your dreams," Hope said with a straight face, although she thought she heard the shaking of laughter in her voice.

"Maybe, but I'm not telling." Sophie crossed her arms trying not to laugh as well.

"Uh-huh, well I'd love to help with the book. Record you and such, if you decide to do it. In fact, maybe Dr. Hansen wouldn't mind if your mom and dad helped out as well. Then, if there were parts you'd rather not reveal directly to Dr. Hansen, you could tell your parents or me."

"I'll think about it," she said again, taking a sip of her bullion.

"Sounds good. I've got to go but I'll be back later. Enjoy your bouillon."

CHAPTER 24

"This manual would help others?" Sophie questioned, already knowing she was going to do it, but wanting to hear it once again from Dr. Hansen.

"Absolutely. I've already had several hospitals call me asking if I would come out and give a lecture. I've put them off, reassuring them I'd have them something as soon as possible. I'm hoping it'll be your dreams, as well as my notes and theories. We should be able to provide these doctors with a lot of helpful information."

"But why do they need my dreams, my story? It seems like your theories and notes would be enough."

"See, this is where you're wrong, as well as all of the doctors I've been talking to. They're thinking the exact same way as you. But I want them to be able to start viewing each coma patient as an individual once again. I want them to understand the patients haven't checked out, but are in a dream state so deep we have to do all we can to wake them, not forget about them. It'll be good for all of these doctors to hear what's been going on from the perspective of the patient. In my opinion, your dreams are even more important than my notes, or anything else I could tell them."

She was shaking her head again, the prospect of tons of people hearing the intimate details of her dreams over the past ten years making her turn green with nausea.

"Listen, Sophie, I know this sounds scary. It's a lot to ask of you. I promise you, though, this book is going to revolutionize the way coma patients are viewed and treated. In my professional opinion, its contents will be as important to them as residency is to new doctors."

Sophie stared at him for a long moment before she spoke. "All right. If you honestly think my dreams are important, then I'll do it. On one condition, though."

"What?" he asked apprehensively, running his fingers through his thick hair.

"I can tell my dreams, my story, to my mom, dad and Hope."

He seemed a little hurt he wasn't mentioned. Quickly, she added, "And you, of course."

"Agreed," he confirmed with a smile.

"We'll start first thing tomorrow. Your mother asked to be the first to record for you. She said she'd see you at nine o'clock sharp." He tapped once sharply on his notepad as if to emphasize his words before walking out.

She couldn't help but smile as well. Obviously everyone else knew she was going to say yes even before she did. She wasn't sure whether she should be angry or admire the people who'd surrounded her the past ten years. She chose the latter, of course.

Her mother was sitting patiently opposite her. Sophie couldn't help but stare. She'd aged, but still had the same beautiful twinkle in her brown eyes. Her hair wasn't quite as brown, having hints of gray cascading throughout. Her bangs, though, were mostly gray, cut just above her eyelashes. She had them parted down the same side as the rest of her hair. Thick and shiny, it flowed down, a little past her shoulders.

Her makeup was light and fresh, with a light tint of cocoa lipstick. Her clothes, as always, were simple, yet elegant. White button-down, long sleeve shirt, and simple, black pants. She was wearing her favorite jewelry, the pearl earrings, necklace, and bracelet her dad gave her mom as a birthday present one year. Her mom was sitting in what looked like a comfortable high back leather chair. It was dark chocolate, except in the center, where it looked worn. Dr. Hansen brought it in himself right after she came back from physical therapy. She wondered if it was his office chair.

"Sophie, let's begin right after the accident," her mom said finally, pressing the record button.

"I will, mom, only I'm a little nervous, worried."

"About what. You're safe now."

"I know, and I'm glad. I'm just afraid once I've vocalized my dreams, they won't seem as real."

Tears spilled from her mothers eyes.

"Mom . . ." she stopped, realizing what she'd said, and immediately tried to correct it. "I didn't mean the part about you and dad. With all of my heart, I'm happy you and dad didn't die." She paused, trying to collect her thoughts.

She needed to explain that even though, in her dreams, the last ten years had been difficult without her parents, trying to live her life without them, it was all she had. She was afraid if her dreams faded, somehow she would too.

When she thought about how she'd been lying in a bed of some sort, her body rarely moving the past decade, it was almost more than she could stand. Thinking about her dreams made reality seem more bearable. Sophie tried again, "Mom, what I was trying to say is the thought of me being in this bed, doing nothing, not living for the past ten years, scares me." She shook her head, trying to clear it. "No. It more than scares me, but I'm not sure how to describe what I mean. Knowing my last real memory was right before I graduated from high school. In my mind, it seems like I've accomplished a lot, experienced so much, and to realize those accomplishments aren't real . . . It's difficult for me beyond what I can describe. Am I making sense?"

She prayed she was because, at the moment, she had no other way of describing it.

Her mom smiled. "Soph, I'd like to understand what you mean. All this time, I've hurt for you, wondering if there was something more I could or should've done. Wishing I was the one in a coma instead of you. I would've done anything to have allowed you to experience your life. In a way, I'm relieved. I'm glad, at least, in your dreams, you've been living. Which is why I'm excited to hear about your dreams." She shrugged, the twinkle coming back. "I want to know what you've been up to the past ten years."

Sophie laughed with her, reaching out to grab her mom's hand. "How I've missed you, mom."

Wiping her eyes and clearing her throat, her mom sat up straight.

"Let's try this again. Why don't you start with our, er, deaths."

Eying her mother nervously, she began. She talked about the funeral and about her decision to go to college. They talked at length about her hikes into the mountains

and how she'd been close to her parents there.

At one point her mother interjected, "I talked to you every day. Told you about current events, about what your dad and I had been doing. Without fail, though, before we left I would whisper in your ear, 'Wake up Sophie. I love you and want you to wake up.'"

Sophie was stunned.

"I heard you say those words several times, mom. I heard you."

There was another surprise when she told her mom about her best friend, Rina.

Her mother said, "You know Nurse Hope's daughter's name is Rina."

"I know," she returned. "She told me yesterday. Do you know her daughter? Is she nice?"

"She sounds nice. I've only met her a few times. Mostly, though, I know of her from the conversations Hope and I have had over the years. It seems like you know her better than I do."

"It's strange. I'll have to ask Hope more about it tomorrow."

About noon, Hope came in with lunch. She'd graduated from bullion to jello, and was excited for something different. After lunch, she and her mom continued. She talked about how she'd met a man named David. They'd fallen in love, and married quickly. She told her mom about her wedding, where they went on their honeymoon, and about the life she'd lived under his roof. It was difficult describing the way he treated her, and how she'd allowed it.

Sophie couldn't help but notice, the more she talked about David, the more agitated her mother became. When she told her mom about David trying to rape her, her mother's face went white as a sheet.

"Mom, what's wrong?" She finally asked, concerned she'd shared too much information, even if it were a dream.

"Oh, honey, there're some things I have to tell you. Important things you need to know. I'm just not sure where to begin."

"What is it? You can tell me; I'll be fine." Sophie tried to sound reassuring, but inside, she had a sense of dread, and something else.

"Maybe I should wait and let your dad tell you."

"Mom, please, you're scaring me. What is it? Tell me."

"Okay, but before I begin . . ." She trailed off, a sob escaping her throat, tears streaming down her face once again. "Please know how much your father, and I love you."

"I know," she whispered softly.

Her mom reached down, picking up her purse, grabbing a tissue from within, and wiping her eyes. "Well, there was a young man; a night orderly here in the coma unit who . . . We found out later he was . . ."

Without a doubt, Sophie knew what her mom was trying to say, and finished the sentence for her. "He raped me, didn't he?"

"Yes," her mother muttered, relief she hadn't had to say the word visible on her face. "We didn't find out until it'd been going on for more than six years. Apparently, he'd been . . ." she paused, and with her hands tried to say the word without saying it.

"Raping," she helped.

"Yes, doing that to the girl in the bed next to yours as well."

Sophie watched her mother struggling over what was obviously a serious act, but realized she didn't feel as though her mom was talking about her. She had no real recollection of the experiences, other than the one time. Calmly, she waited for her mom to continue.

"Sophie, as soon as we found out, we had him arrested. He's serving fifteen-to-twenty years in prison for what he did to you, and the other girl."

"Do you know why he did it?" She asked frankly.

Her mom seemed ready to bolt from her chair. She started fumbling with the tissue in her hands. Then wiped an invisible piece of lint off her shirt before she stopped and stared at the floor.

"Mom, even if it's hard or painful, it's part of my life I missed, and I need to know what happened while I was in a coma. Please tell me."

"Oh, it's awful, I don't know if I can tell you. He was so calculating."

"Mom, go on. It's okay."

As if suddenly understanding how important it was to her, she dove in. "He started working here about seven years ago. Your dad and I didn't know him because he worked nights."

"Uh-huh," Sophie said.

"Well, the reason he started working here is because . . . the woman who died in the car accident . . ."

"He was her brother, wasn't he?" Sophie finished for her.

"Yes," she replied quietly. "He started working here to have his revenge. He told

the police he wanted to make you suffer for killing his sister. He said every night he worked, he would talk to you about his life, cursing you for taking away the only good person he'd ever known and, after a while, raping you as punishment."

Sophie tried to nod her understanding. She tried. But, the *something else* which had been bothering her for the last few days suddenly smashed in on her consciousness and her mind wouldn't allow her to focus on anything else.

She was once again in her horrible nightmare, hovering over David, watching the events of the car crash unfold. Watching as the car exploded with Hazel burning inside.

Watching David running to save her. She remembered the anguish she had for David. And, she remembered her own pain, the pain of knowing she'd been the cause of Hazel's death. The intensity of her guilt flooded through her. Wave after wave of shameful agony crashed down on her, threatening to drown her, once again, into a coma. It seemed as though she was drifting beneath the water, waiting benevolently for what should've happened in the first place. . .

Sophie was standing in the middle of her favorite park. There were large trees all around her, as though hiding her from her shame, and keeping her safe. She noticed Rina sitting against one of the trees. She waved, and walked over to her, happy to see her again. Rina, on the other hand, didn't seem as happy.

After she sat down, Rina asked sourly, "Sophie, hon, what're you doing? This isn't where you belong."

"Rina, I'm glad you're here. I've missed you."

"You realize we aren't anywhere. You're dreaming again. Do you really want to be back? In a coma, you're not living, you know?"

"I know," she conceded softly.

"What's wrong?" Rina asked huffily.

"I killed David's sister. I think it should've been me? How can I live knowing I killed her? How can I live my life when I took hers?"

"It's hard, sweetie, but there's only one way to find out. You've got to try. You've got to put on your big-girl thong, wake up, and accept everything you've done. Make peace with yourself, and move on. Wake the fuck up, Sophie!"

When Sophie finally opened her eyes, she saw her mom, dad, Hope and Dr. Hansen standing over her. The first one to speak was Dr. Hansen.

"Sophie, are you all right? You gave us all quite a scare."

She tried to speak, but realized she had an oxygen mask covering her mouth. Lifting it, she answered, "Yes. I think I am."

She watched as her mom fell into her dad's outstretched arms and realized what this must've meant to them.

"Sorry mom and dad."

Her mom came to her side. "Don't be, Soph. I'm the one who should be sorry. I told you to much too soon. Can you forgive me?"

"Mom, no, it wasn't you. I remembered my car accident is all." Unable to look into the loving faces of her parents any longer, she wiped her watering eyes. "It must've been painful for him to watch his sister die in such a horrible way."

CHAPTER 25

The next couple of weeks were agonizing for Sophie. Dr. Hansen had decided to allow her to heal more fully before they recorded or talked about her dreams again. The days were spent in therapy as she worked to get her physical body back in shape. The nights were the worst, after everyone had left, and she was alone to contemplate what she'd done, and what she still needed to do.

The healing did happen, though. When she faced the reality of the car crash, she knew it'd been an accident. By allowing herself to grieve for what she'd done, to grieve for what she'd done to David, even if it wasn't on purpose, helped strengthen her immensely.

She also thought she was beginning to understand why she'd dreamed of a marriage to David. She knew what he'd done was cowardly, and she needed to talk about it. She was tired of being treated like a broken eggshell. She was as healed emotionally as she was going to get until she had more answers.

Dr. Hansen came in to check on her. She sensed he was conflicted by something, but didn't have the first clue what was troubling him.

"Dr. Hansen, I'm ready to start talking about my dreams again. I need to."

"I don't know Sophie. Maybe we should give it another week."

"I don't need another week. I don't need another minute." She was frustrated, and letting it show. "I'm not broken inside anymore, and if I'm going to continue to get better, I've got to talk about it."

She noticed he was looking at her with a mixture of amusement and, she couldn't believe it, but desire. Embarrassed, she pulled her covers around her. It suddenly dawned on her she hadn't looked into a real mirror in over ten years.

Holy crap, she thought, *what must I look like?*

He seemed to notice her discomfort, because he cleared his throat, as he walked to the door. "Fine, you can start in the morning. I'll tell your mom and dad."

"Thanks," she said, still unable to believe she hadn't even thought about what she looked like since she'd come out of her coma. She'd been showered, and had had her hair washed several times, but hadn't ever thought about her appearance.

"I need to get to a mirror," she whispered, when he was gone.

Since a mirror wasn't possible at the moment, she sat up, letting her covers fall away. First, she touched her eyes. She still had eyelashes. There weren't any wrinkles at the corners.

A good beginning, she thought, shrugging. Next, her fingers moved to her eyebrows. She touched the left one, noticing some hair was missing. In its place was soft, thick skin. "A scar," she guessed. Next she touched her hair. It was long, although slightly tangled. I need a mirror and a brush, she thought, doing a mental checklist.

Nervous, and feeling a little vain, she pulled at the collar of her gown to reveal her breasts, and look at the rest of her body.

Not bad, she thought, shrugging again, laughing self-consciously. She wondered if Dr. Hansen had seen her naked over the years since she'd been in his care, guessing he probably had. Remembering someone could walk in at anytime, she quickly covered herself back up before continuing her checklist.

Mirror.

Brush.

Underwear.

Her mom was first again, which Sophie was grateful for. She quickly repeated what they'd discussed during the first recording, then tried to explain her thoughts to her mom.

"Mom," she started. "Maybe that's why I married David, while I was in my coma. It was my subconscious dealing with what was happening to my body." Then she thought of a question. "How did you find out he'd been doing this?"

"He confessed," her mother responded frankly.

"Really?" She asked, stunned.

"Yes, it was almost like he'd started doing it expecting to get caught. He was full of anger, and grief. When he didn't get caught, he told the police he couldn't handle the guilt anymore, and confessed."

"In a way I feel sympathy for him."

"I understand," her mom responded tearfully. "He did seem remorseful, but your dad and I decided he needed to be prosecuted to the full extent of the law."

Sophie listened quietly while her mother told her about the trial, how David's lawyer tried to use temporary insanity to get him off.

"In the end, though, the judge didn't buy it. David took a deal offered by the district attorney."

It was amazing how her dreams were starting to make more sense. "But, if he was raping me to get revenge, why did he rape the other girl as well?"

"It's a good question. One that not even David could answer properly. 'She was available,' was all he ever said."

"No wonder," she said out loud.

"No wonder what, Soph?" Her mom asked, blowing her nose.

"It explains a lot about my dreams. Why I married him, why I got . . ." She trailed off, something dawning on her.

Could it be possible, she wondered hopeful.

"What is it, dear?" Her mother asked, obviously concerned she'd said too much again.

"In my dreams I was pregnant. It was David's baby." She saw her mom lean forward as she stumbled over how to ask, "Did I, could I have been pregnant?" Her insides spun with dread, and excitement.

"Yes, dear. But, by the time we found out what had been happening, you were seven months pregnant. The girl in the other bed was pregnant as well."

"Shut the faculty door!" Sophie sat higher in her bed. She knew she should be revolted by the thought, but after all the love she had for her baby in her dreams, all she could focus on was love. "What happened," she asked, afraid of the answer.

"Once we had the results, Dr. Hansen asked us what we wanted to do. He felt terrible, by the way. He had such guilt, but we assured him there was nothing he could've done. We wanted to know what our options were." She stopped a moment, as though contemplating what to tell her. "He explained it was possible to terminate the pregnancy, but because of how far along you were and the coma you were in, it would be dangerous. He also explained you could carry the baby to term. Stating in his professional opinion, it was the safest route to take. He said we could put the baby up for adoption once it was born, if we decided to make that choice." Her mother stopped once again, blatant pain coursing through her.

"Mom, its okay, whatever your decision," she assured her.

"Oh, Sophie, it was one of the toughest decisions your father and I have ever had to make. You've no idea the discussions and prayers we offered, wanting to do what was best for you. Dr. Hansen didn't give us much time because he said if we decided to terminate the pregnancy, it would be best to do it sooner rather than later."

"Sure," she mumbled, trying not to get her hopes up.

"We finally decided to do what would be safest for you, and had you keep the pregnancy. Soph we've . . ."

"You gave her up for adoption," she finished, her hope deflating.

"No, Sophie, actually what I was going to say is even though it was probably selfish on our part . . ."

"What, Mom? Tell me?" She cried, unable to contain herself.

"Hon, she's part of our family. She came from you, and we couldn't give her up. We kept her."

Sophie stopped crying, not sure she heard her mother correctly, "You kept her?"

"Yes, Sophie, you have a daughter. I hope you're not too upset."

"Mom, no, I'm not upset. Quite the opposite, I'm glad you both decided to keep her."

"Are you sure?"

"Mom, I know I was raped, and it's awful. But the baby, she isn't. She had nothing to do with his perverse decisions."

"Oh, I'm glad you're not upset because, Sophie, she's the most amazing child. Your dad and I couldn't imagine life without her. She's been such a blessing in our lives."

"Where is she?" Sophie asked, an overwhelming burst of happiness growing inside her. "Where's my baby?" All she could think about was that her baby wasn't dead. She's alive.

"Sophie, she's not a baby anymore. She's five years old."

"She's five?" Sophie repeated, shocked. "Right before I woke up I was pregnant with a girl. I guess I expected her to be a newborn."

"I'm sorry you had to miss her being born. She's been such a joy."

Something dawned on her. She'd dreamt one time she was having her baby, and wondered if she that was when she'd really delivered the baby. She also remembered a dream she'd had about a little girl. "What did you name her?"

"We named her Rose. We thought it was appropriate, since your middle name is Rose."

In her dreams, Sophie had grown to hate red roses because of David, but realized in real life, his sending red roses hadn't happened.

"Rose is the perfect name, mom. It's the one I chose for her in my dreams, as well. Does she know about me?" She questioned tentatively, wondering what her daughter would think of her.

"Not only does she know about you, but she knows you. She knows you're her mommy," her mom said, brushing fresh tears from her eyes. "We've been bringing her to see you since she was a baby."

"What does she think about me?"

"We've told her you've been sleeping like Sleeping Beauty and it would take something special for you to wake up, and when you were ready, you would."

"Really?" Sophie asked, sobbing. "She's seen me. She knows I'm her mommy?"

"Yes, and she knows you love her very much."

"Mom, she *is* the something special. I woke up because of her, because I thought I was losing her," she said, crying happily. "And mom," she continued, "I do love her, with all my heart."

"What a relief. We, your father and I, and Dr. Hansen were worried about how you'd take learning everything. Knowing she's here because you were, you know."

"It doesn't matter. I mean, don't get me wrong. Being raped *does* matter, and I'm glad he's paying for what he did, but I wouldn't have come out of my coma without her. When can I see her?" She hoped her mother understood. She wasn't making light of what David did. Only because of it, Rose had been born, and she was what had finally allowed her to wake up. As Rose got older, she'd make sure her daughter understood as well.

Dr. Hansen walked in, interrupting her thoughts. "How is our miracle patient?"

His presence reminded her of her checklist.

Mirror.

Brush.

Underwear.

Unable to help it, her face began to burn red with embarrassment. Trying to act like nothing was wrong, she answered, "Excellent, Dr. Hansen. My mother has told me I have a daughter."

"Oh, you're already there, are you?" He asked, looking at her curiously.

She saw her mom looking at her curiously, too.

Promising herself to discuss her checklist with her mom, she answered, "Yes, and I'm happy." She wanted him to know she was happy with her parents' decision. Still trying to contain her mortifying thoughts of him seeing her naked, she continued, "I can already tell what I was dreaming while in my coma was a kind of reflection of what was going on around me."

"Incredible. Now I need you to lean forward and take a deep breath."

Startled, she leaned forward, realizing her back was bare, as he touched her with his cold stethoscope. The heat of her embarrassment went down her back to where he was touching her.

"Now blow it out."

She obeyed, her heart beating rapidly.

"Good. Another one."

Again she complied.

"Excellent." He took a seat next to her mother, saying with a sly grin, "Do I play a part in your dreams?"

Sophie's blush grew even deeper. "Oh my gosh, please go," she said, pulling the covers over her face.

"Are you all right, Sophie?" She heard Dr. Hansen ask, a note of worry in his voice.

"I'm fine, but I need a minute alone with my mom," she answered quietly.

"Hmmmm. Okay, if you're sure." He seemed like he wanted to say more, but instead said, "I think you've done enough for today. It's getting late, and you need your rest."

When he was gone, her mom pulled the covers off her and asked, "Would you please tell me what's going on?"

Nervously, she told her mom about the Dr. Hansen in her dreams, about the feelings she couldn't help but have for him now. Explaining it wasn't necessarily love, but because of what they'd had in her dreams, she was embarrassed about what he must think of her now.

"I completely understand."

"Tomorrow, when you come, you'll bring me some underwear, and some *real* pajamas?"

"Of course, Soph." Her mom laughed. "You're absolutely right."

"Are you going to bring Rose tomorrow too?"

"Yes, I will. Promise."

With the help of her mom, and Hope, Sophie was able to get to a mirror. She couldn't help but cry when she looked at herself. The plastic surgeons had done a great job of patching up her face.

There was only the one scar above her left eye. She looked older, though. She looked different. Her mom and Hope cried too, as they hugged her, and told her how beautiful she was.

It was one of those girlie moments which might've been uncomfortable to guys, but to her, it was wonderful. Her mom brushed her long, blond hair and Hope helped her put on a little makeup. They all worked together to get the blue cotton pajamas on her. Once they'd finished, they helped her back into bed.

Kissing her on the cheek, her mom said, "I'll get Rose, and be back. Okay?"

Hope left too. Once again, all alone, nervousness at meeting her daughter for the first time settled in. *What if she doesn't like me?* She had no time to ponder the question because the door opened, and a beautiful little girl walked in.

CHAPTER 26

Rose came shyly into the room while her grandma waited at the door. Sophie later found out she'd told her grandma she wanted to go in alone. She looked like an angel, in

a light blue dress with a white collar and white trim around the bottom. She had long blond, curly hair and bright blue eyes which matched her dress. She walked over to the bed slowly, looking back at her grandma once or twice.

Sophie tried to reassure her. "It's all right, Rose. I'm okay. You can come to me."

Rose seemed unsure, although she continued to walk slowly to her mother's bed. Finally, when she was standing right in front of her mother, she stopped and stared with unabashed innocence.

"Hello, Rose," she said quietly. "It's nice to finally meet you."

Rose smiled timidly. "It's nice to meet you, too, mommy."

Sophie looked over at her mom still standing in the doorway and gave her a nod, hoping she understood she wanted some time alone with her daughter. Her mom seemed to understand because she stepped out, closing the door.

Sophie looked back at her daughter. "Do you want to know a secret?"

"Yes," Rose answered calmly.

"Even though I was asleep, I was still thinking about you. Did you know that?"

Rose nodded, climbing into the chair next to the bed.

"How did you know? Did grandma tell you?"

"Yes, but mostly I knew because of the dreams I had about you."

"You had dreams about me?" She asked, trying to hold back her tears, not wanting to frighten her child. This was too new, and she didn't want to ruin it.

"What were they about?"

Rose looked down at her hands. "Mostly they were about you and me and grandma."

"What were we doing?" Sophie asked, encouraging her daughter.

"I was swinging on a swing, and you and grandma were watching me. You blew me a kiss and made this sign." She held up her hand, making the sign.

Sophie recognized it was the sign for *I love you* in sign language. Sophie made the sign with her hand, too, reaching out to touch her daughters' hand.

"Rose," she began, blinking back tears, "I had the same dream."

"You did?" Rose asked, as a wide smile spread over her face.

"I sure did."

Suddenly Rose stood on the chair, climbing into the bed with her mom. Sophie helped her, not wanting her to fall. Then Rose said, "Mommy, I love you. Thanks for waking up." She put her arms around Sophie's neck, hugging her tightly.

"Oh, my Rose, I love you, too."

Nurse Hope sat down in the large leather chair, her plump body filling most of its volume. She had kind, brown eyes and short, straight brown hair. Her face was soft, and round. Leaning over, she pressed a button on the recorder and said,

"Where do you want to start today?"

"Actually, before we begin, can you tell me something about Rose being born? Were there any problems with my pregnancy?"

"No. You had her by C-section at thirty-eight weeks. I'll tell you, sweetie, she seemed ready."

"Did she cry when she came out?"

"Oh, you have no idea. Her screaming was deafening," Hope answered, laughing. "She was definitely ready to come into this world, and had no qualms about letting everyone know it."

"Crying is a good thing, right?"

"Absolutely. After we checked her, I wrapped her in a blanket and laid her on your chest. We wanted her to know your touch, recognize your smell." Hope paused, pulling a picture out of her light purple jacket pocket. "We took this picture of the two of you together. You can have it." She handed the picture to Sophie.

"She's beautiful. Thank you for taking this picture. It means a lot."

"You're welcome, Sophie, dear."

She looked up because she heard Hope clearing her throat. Tears were streaming down her face. "Hope, what's wrong?"

Shaking her head, Hope said, "Nothing's wrong. It's only, over the years, you've become like a second daughter to me. It's wonderful to see you awake. Truthfully, I'm sad as well, because it means you'll be leaving here soon, and I won't get to see you every day." She wiped her eyes, smiling. "Never mind, though, I'm sure we'll work something out."

Nodding, she said, "Thank you, Hope, for everything."

"No thanks needed, dear. It was a pleasure."

"You know, you do talk a lot like my best friend Rina, from my dream life," Sophie began tentatively.

"I'm glad you brought her up. I've wanted to talk with you more about your friend Rina."

"My mom said she never came into my room, but I seem to know a lot about her, although you sound just like her."

"Well, dear, with everything we've discovered about your dreams already, it doesn't surprise me." Hope paused a moment to readjust herself before continuing. "When I worked the evening shift, I would sit here, next to you, and talk to you for hours about my daughter. She's my only family, you see, which means my life seems to revolve

around her and work. Dr. Hansen encouraged us to talk to our patients. It was weird at first, but I got used to it. I'm guessing my chatting up a storm is where you got her name."

"Makes sense." Sophie nodded.

"Will you tell me about the Rina in your dreams?"

Sophie proceeded to tell her all about Rina. How they'd met in college, and the part Rina played in her dreams, while in a coma. When she told Hope how Rina had become a Vice Principal at a private school,

Hope interrupted her. "You know, Rina really is a Vice Principal, but at a public school here in the valley."

"Wow, it's amazing I seemed to pick up on quite a lot of what was going on around me."

"You really did, Sophie." Hope agreed in amazement.

She told her how she met David and the subsequent pain involved. Explained Rina's part in helping her. She also told her about Phillip. When she first mentioned his name, Hope gasped and chuckled.

Sophie laughed in return, saying, "I know. Dr. Hansen's first name is Phillip. He was obviously talking to me as well."

She described how she met him, and how their lives came together, even discussing his ex-wife Cynthia.

"I can't believe her name was Cynthia," Hope interjected.

"Why?"

"Because the young woman in the bed next to yours was named Cynthia."

"Nothing is surprising me at this point. What's her story? My mother told me she'd been pregnant like I was, but nothing more. In my dreams, she was pregnant with Davids' baby as well, but ended up losing it. Am I close?"

"Exactly. Although not quite in the way you've described. She wasn't as far along in her pregnancy as you were, and she had no family. Dr. Hansen decided it would be better for her to terminate it." Hope wiped her eyes, clearing her throat. "Before he could, however, she suffered a blood clot to her heart and died."

"Oh, how sad. The poor girl."

"It was a sad time in our little coma unit. We all felt like we'd lost a child."

Sophie thought of something awful and had to ask, "But, if she had no family, what happened to her body? Did she have a funeral?"

"Dr. Hansen took care of everything. He arranged the funeral, bought the flowers, the casket and everything else. Only the staff from this unit attended her funeral. It was simple and sad, but would've been much worse if Dr. Hansen hadn't taken care of her."

"He seems like such a caring doctor. I'm glad he took care of her." Sophie couldn't help but think of the Phillip from her dream life. He seemed to be similar to the one in real life, although they did look a little different.

Not much, though, she marveled, wondering if this was real or if David really had killed her.

"Sophie, are you okay? Where did you go?"

"Oh. Oops, I drifted. I was thinking Dr. Hansen seems a lot like the one in my dreams and I'm wondering if this is real or if I'm dreaming now." She spoke lightly, but it was seriously weighing on her mind.

"I can understand. Let me reassure you, this isn't a dream. You're awake after a long time being in a coma."

Sophie nodded.

"Hi, mommy," Rose called, bouncing into the room. "Look who I found."

"Hi, Rose," Sophie returned, sitting up straighter in bed. She'd put on a white pair of pajamas this morning and Hope had helped her do her hair. She'd put it in hot rollers, making her blond hair, soft and wavy. Sophie applied the mascara herself, as well as some clear lip gloss. Nervously running a hand over her hair, she nodded for Rose to come closer.

"This is my friend, Dr. Hansen. He's nice. He gives me piggy rides." Rose was looking up at Dr. Hansen like he was her hero.

Sophie had to smile. "He gives you piggy ride? Sounds fun." She laughed.

"It is. He's a great doctor, too, mommy. You're lucky."

"I know," she responded shyly, looking from her daughter to her doctor.

He smiled. Squatting next to Rose, he said, "I'm going to let you read the book you're holding to your mommy."

"Okay, Dr. Phillip, I mean Dr. Hansen." Rose giggled.

Turning to Sophie, he uttered with a wink, "I'll be back in a while. It's my turn to sit with you while you talk about your dreams."

After he left, Rose climbed onto her mother's bed.

Sophie kissed her, hugged her and snuggled her under the nook in her arm. When they were settled, Rose read the story to her. It was obvious she was bright. Her mom and dad must've read to her often, as they did with her when she was little. By the third time through the book, both mother and daughter fell asleep.

"Hello, sleepy head. Did you actually read the book or nap the whole time?" Dr. Hansen asked in mock severity.

"Both," Sophie said sleepily, stretching her arms. Rose was still sleeping. Behind him were her mom and dad. They came over after a moment, and took the sleeping Rose from her mother's reluctant grasp.

"We'll bring her back later, after your time with Dr. Hansen," her mother whispered, winking.

What's up with the winking, she thought, wondering if they were all in on something she wasn't aware of?

They left quickly, and before she knew it, his large, masculine frame was seated on the big leather chair. He looked over.

"Ready when you are."

"Why do I get the feeling you're excited about this?" Sophie pulled the sheets up a little higher around her legs and smoothed her hair again.

He gave her a Cheshire grin. "I've listened to all of your previous tapes, and it turns out I do play a part in your dreams."

Blushing slightly, she looked down. "Well, now you know."

"Don't be embarrassed," he said tenderly. "I'm honored you thought enough of me to allow me to be your boyfriend."

"You weren't. I mean, he wasn't my boyfriend, per say. We were friends, more or less."

345

"Technically, though, I am a boy and if we were friends, then boyfriend does apply."

"Why are you teasing me?" She laughed, throwing one of her pillows at him. "Can't you see this is uncomfortable for me, and you're making it worse on purpose."

"You're right, let's get started. When did you first know you were in love with me?"

"You're awful, and mean," she playfully growled, getting out of bed in a flash, punching him in the arm.

"Hey, I need my arm," he countered.

Sophie stood there flushed, breathing heavily, wondering how exactly her body had responded with such quickness to the voice inside her head.

"You realize you've just proven you're almost ready to get out of here."

Feeling a wave of nausea, she answered, "I know, I'm a miracle . . ." The room started spinning, before everything turned black.

"Sophie. Sophie, wake up. You fainted, which means you're not quite as ready as we both thought," Dr. Hansen said seriously.

She nodded.

"Mommy, are you okay?" Rose asked, tears rolling down her chubby cheeks.

"Rose, mommy's fine," Sophie uttered, trying to sit up. "Don't cry, Rose. I got up too fast, and it made me dizzy. Don't worry."

Rose came over to her, climbing on her bed.

"Good," she said, snuggling next to her mother.

"Listen, I'm going to run a few tests, make sure everything in there is doing what it's supposed to," he said as he pointed to her head. "I'll need to ask all of you to leave. The tests will take a few hours. Afterward, she'll need to rest."

Her mom and dad came over, each kissing her lightly on the forehead.

"You sure you're all right?" her mom asked.

"Yes, mom, I am. It sounds like Dr. Hansen is going to find out for sure but, I feel fine."

"Good. We'll see you tomorrow," her dad said gruffly, his voice full of emotion. He picked Rose up. "Let's give your mommy some rest, okay?"

"Okay," Rose responded, hugging him tightly. Then she touched Dr. Hansen on the shoulder, saying, "Take good care of mommy for me. She's special."

"I know she is, Rose, and I will. Promise," he returned, stroking her jubilant blond curls.

"Bye, mommy. See you tomorrow."

"Bye, Rose. I love you."

She and Dr. Hansen watched them leave. When they were gone, he turned to her, his face serious. "Sophie, can you forgive me? As a professional, I shouldn't have baited you. I should've known better."

"It's fine, doc. For the tenth time, I'm fine."

"I'm going to run some tests to be sure, though."

For the next several weeks, Sophie and the people around her fell into a routine. She would go to physical therapy, spend quiet time with Rose, reading to her, talking to her or napping. Next she would talk about her dreams to her mom, dad, Hope or Dr. Hansen, while they recorded her dreams. By the end of the four weeks, she was sick of talking about her dreams, and much more interested in the reality around her.

David weighed heavily on her mind. She thought a lot about contacting him. He'd raped her countless times, which disgusted her, but she also realized she'd caused him incredible pain as well. Sophie knew if she ever wanted to completely forgive herself, she needed to apologize to him for killing his sister. It wouldn't be enough, but she wanted to do it anyway.

Sophie explained her thoughts to her mom and dad.

Grudgingly they agreed, and found the address for her. She'd started a letter to him at least ten times already, but nothing seemed right. She couldn't figure out how to tell the man who'd done such awful things to her, she was sorry. It was a process, she realized, and it was going to take time.

Her bond with her mom and dad continued to grow. She thanked God every day they were alive, and able to be here with her. She loved them and treasured every moment they spent together.

She also realized Hope was her dear friend, even though, in her dreams, she'd been named Rina, and looked a lot younger. Talking to her was the same as talking to her dear friend. She had the same foul mouth, sarcastic lingo, and mannerisms Rina had in her dreams.

Rose was her precious flower, tender and innocent. Seeing life through her eyes, her bravery, and her courage only encouraged Sophie on in her recovery. When she was down or sick of therapy, she would remember Rose, which strengthened her resolve, filling her with joy.

And, Dr. Hansen. She felt something for him too. She found him to be charming, witty, smart and kind. She loved watching him with Rose. He never teased her again about her dreams after the first time, and their conversations had become one of the highlights of her day. She loved watching him talk, loved the way his hazel eyes would light up when he was discussing something he was passionate about. Everything about him was perfect, right down to his crooked nose.

Although it was never spoken of by either of them, she knew he reciprocated her feelings. She also knew they couldn't be anything more than friends, not while she was his patient, and maybe not ever.

Still, though, she enjoyed each moment with all of her loved ones, experiencing happiness as she'd never known it before. The only thing ever bringing her down was the topic of her leaving. She knew she would be released soon, and this happy haven they'd created would come to an end. It frightened her. Truth be told, it excited her as well. There was a whole world out there waiting to be experienced for real.

Finally, the day she'd been dreading came. Dr. Hansen came in and took her pulse, listened to her heart and had her walk around the room.

"Doc, you know I'm healthy," she teased sadly.

"Look, I'm out of my pajamas and everything." Her mom had brought her a pair of jeans and a gray sweater. They seemed weird after spending over a month in comfortable two-piece pajamas.

"I noticed," he said, smiling. "Although it's still my job to make sure. Do as you're told."

"What?" she growled, until she saw the Cheshire grin on his face. "Nice, Dr. Hansen. Are you always this bossy with your patients?"

"Well, no, but then most of my patients are in a coma. You're the first one I've had talk back to me." He laughed, writing something in his notebook. Still looking down, he said, "You do realize we're still going to be spending a lot of time together, don't you?"

"No, I didn't. Why?" She asked, perking up a little.

He was still writing, and she wondered if he was going to answer her. Finally, he dotted the page with gusto and looked up.

"Finished," he said, handing her his pen, his face grim. "I need your signature, here, and here." He pointed with his finger.

She signed her name, then handed him back his pen.

"Excellent. You are no longer my patient and I'm no longer your doctor. If you get sick, contact your family physician." He ripped out her copy of the paperwork, handing it to her.

Shocked, her mouth fell open. She looked at him intently, trying to see if he was serious. "Okay, but . . . then . . . how . . ." she began, until he cut her off.

"How will we be spending time together?" Phillip finished, returning her gaze with a smile in his eyes. "There are a couple of ways."

"There are?" She whispered, unable to look away.

"Yes. The first is, once our book is published, I'll need you to go to conferences with me. Everyone is going to want to meet *the* Sleeping Rose."

She scrunched her face, confused.

He continued, "Do you like it? I was thinking Sleeping Roses would make a great title to our book."

"Sure," she began. She wanted to spend time with him, of course, but not if it meant spending less time with her daughter.

As if reading her mind, he interrupted, "Rose is going to come with us. I've already talked to her about it. And, if it's okay with you, then it's okay with her. Her words, not mine. You know, she means so much to me."

"Okay. Then, I love the idea." She was brimming over with happiness at the thought of getting to be with him.

It's childish, I know, she thought, *but I'm still excited.*

Remembering what he'd said, she asked, "What's the other way we're going to be spending time together?" She tried to sound nonchalant, but knew the question had come out sounding the opposite.

Clearing his throat, he answered, "Oh. Yes, well, the other way is I was hoping, wondering . . ." He stopped, running a hand through his thick, sandy brown hair, before continuing, "This is awkward. I don't want you to think I always do this or this is how I find dates or anything."

"Dates? Dr. Hansen, are you trying to ask me out?" She knew she was tormenting him, making the situation more awkward, but she couldn't resist.

He deserved it, she thought.

Perceptively, he laughed. "Well, yes, it's exactly what I was trying to do. How's it going so far? Am I being as smooth as I was in your dreams?"

Trying not to double over with laughter, she choked out, "Smoother."

"Everything okay in here?" Hope asked, her voice dripping with skepticism.

Both suddenly serious, Dr. Hansen answered, "Great, Nurse Hope. Thanks for asking."

"All right," she continued, obviously still not sure they were telling the truth. "Your mom and dad have the car waiting for you outside."

"Wonderful." She smiled, walking over to Hope, glancing sideways at Phillip.

Their embrace was tearful, but full of joy. When Hope pulled her away, she said, "I'm going to see you next week for lunch, right?"

"Absolutely."

Dr. Hansen stood next to Hope, holding out his arms. "I'd like one of those, if you're passing them out."

Shyly, she went to him, wrapping her arms around him tightly. They stayed in each other's arms for several minutes. She couldn't help hoping there would be many more. Sophie knew, though, as soon as she thought it, there would be.

EPILOGUE

It has been a year since Sophie awoke from her coma. A lot has changed. She celebrated a birthday with her daughter, as well as one of her own. She's been painting, and she recently became engaged to the love of her life, Dr. Phillip Hansen.

Phillip, Sophie and Rose have traveled the country, sharing Sophie's story and Phillips theories on treatments for coma patients. They've already seen changes.

As a final thought, it's a common belief throughout the medical community that the brain can't tell the difference between a dream and reality. It's a belief Sophie agrees with because although physically she wasn't awake those ten years she was in a coma, emotionally she lived. She lived while she was dreaming.

SECRET ROSES
(#2 Dead Roses series):

"Why the hell do some killers think they have to be creative?" Rose asked, bending over the dead girl. The key she wore on a chain around her neck escaped her white button-up blouse and dangled in front of her. Quickly, she tucked it in before her partner, Jack, joined her next to the body.

"So we'll give them a name—make them famous. So we'll recognize their work." Jack slid on his rubber gloves before gently pulling the Mars bar, which had been placed just as the other candy bars found with the other dead girls, out of the girl's mouth. "This psycho has already been dubbed The Candybar Killer by a lot of guys at the Agency. Even the national papers have picked up on it."

"Seriously! Don't they know they're giving this jerk exactly what he wants?" Rose brushed the girls' dark hair off her face, revealing brown eyes. Opened. Frozen in fear.

"Holy mother of fuck, she looks just like you," Jack shouted.

ACKNOWLEDGEMENTS

A lot goes into writing a book. Time. Sacrifice. And there are many, many people who helped make this novel possible. I'd like to thank them. My sweet husband, James. My amazing, best supporters— Emily, Kaylee, and Jacob. Mom and dad. Jeremy, Chandi, Jason, and Alicia. All of my extended family. My dear friends. You know who you are. Also, I have to thank my amazing critique partners. Thank you. Thank you. Thank you. For reading and re-reading my manuscript. And a special thanks to Steven Novak for designing another beautiful cover. You're a genius, Steven.

About the Author

As well as being a toffee-maker extraordinaire, a cupcake baker, and Mom Of The Year (it's true, ask her kids), RaShelle writes YA sci-fi romance and adult romantic suspense. She's also the wife to a math-genius-of-a-husband. Together they share their home with three children and three dogs. When she gets a quiet moment alone, she loves to read about far away places.

Made in the USA
Lexington, KY
28 October 2012